THE MARRIAGE

BETHANY-KRIS

Published by Bethany-Kris

www.bethanykris.com

ISBN 13: 978-1-989658-48-2

Editor: Elizabeth Peters

Cover Design © Mignon Mykel

For all those Russian Guns fans … you've waited long
enough. XO.

CONTENTS

ONE

Roman wanted to touch Karine while she stood across from him—tuck the stray strands of wavy hair that had fallen out from behind her ear—feel the shivers race over her shoulder blade when his fingertips glided down the column of her throat. But he made do with her palms tucked inside his larger hands as the officiant stood at their sides at the little makeshift church. The inside looked even less like an actual church than the outside—signage and proper placement could really do a lot for things.

The man in his robe was reading from a book, smiling at his own words and putting on quite a show. At least, the guy did seem to enjoy his job and some people might enjoy this kind of thing. Although, Roman didn't care about the words, or much for the man speaking them—it was all a means to an end.

And a very beautiful beginning.

He just wanted to be married to this girl—he wanted to be bound to Karine for life. Even if the fraudulent paperwork

1

made the marriage illegal, it was the act itself that couldn't be undone. A bell that would *never* unring.

Besides, it wasn't like following the law had ever made much of a difference to men like him before—it certainly wouldn't matter to Dima to learn Karine had married Roman in a ceremony. Legal or not, that didn't change what it was.

Or what it meant.

If she belonged to Roman, like he was tying himself to her, then nobody, not even Dima would take her away from him. He would die to make it true. There was no cost he would not pay.

The woman who stood close by was also the official witness to the wedding—the officiant's wife wore a bright smile throughout her husband's theatrics. No doubt, it was something she had seen a hundred times.

He was just more interested in Karine than the finer details of the happenings around him. He was fine pretending nobody else existed but him and her. Her in that red jumper, with her silky dark hair laying in messy waves over her shoulders. *Her* with her eyes so bright, and a sweet mouth stretched into the prettiest smile.

Could she feel his racing heartbeats through his fingertips?

Was she as excited as he was?

As *eager*?

They would walk out of there as man and wife—till death did they part. And he still wasn't even entirely sure they were going to make it out of everything else alive, let alone *this*.

But she didn't stop staring back.

And *that* smile ...

Those nerves that he was too proud of a man to show quieted with her in front of him, hands still steady in his. At one point, he had to repeat words after the officiant. Nothing religious, Roman had been quick to specify, not even a single verse. It was the basic, legal wording the officiant technically had to use. Karine repeated the same.

Roman hadn't attended many weddings in his lifetime— the one's he'd been forced to suffer through had been worsened by hangovers and stolen drug-fogged memories. So, he wasn't completely aware of the proceedings. He

^{THE}MARRIAGE

simply did what he was told until finally the moment came that he'd been waiting for.

The *only* part that really mattered.

"You may kiss your bride."

He lunged at a laughing Karine who had already pulled her hands from his to reach back for him. Engulfing her in his arms, he pulled her to his broad chest, crushing her there in the hard wall of his hold. Staring up at him, he realized—not for the first time, but certainly in the most significant way— how much smaller she appeared against him, barely toppling five-foot-three without a pair of heels. But she liked it—he saw that in her stare when those hungry eyes of hers locked on his mouth.

She liked being swallowed by him, inside his embrace, close to his heart. Always watching up at him through thick, lowered lashes. There, he thought she felt safe. He hoped it was always that way.

"Well," Karine whispered the moment their lips started to graze, "*kiss me.*"

He made it good, too.

Bruising and breathless.

Undoubtedly uncomfortable for the other two people in the room watching, although he gave them credit for the fact they didn't stop clapping until he finally pulled away from his grinning, new wife.

Karine weaved her fingers in his hair, her lips grazing the side of his stubbly cheek as she said, "This is not how I pictured my wedding day."

"Someday, we'll do it again—exactly how you want it."

He took her hand in his, and brought it to his mouth to give her fingertips the gentlest of kisses.

She shook her head, tugging her fingers out of his to run them over his mouth and chin. "That's not what I meant, Roman."

She, too, had seemed to have forgotten about the others in the room. Or maybe they were just more important.

"What I pictured as my wedding day was going to be the end of my life. What *little* of it that I had. This is not what I was told it would be, and this was perfect."

3

Well, then ...

Never one to be at a loss for words, he framed her delicate face with both palms, and said the only thing that really felt appropriate after her admission. "I love you."

"I love you, too, Roman."

Karine kissed him that time—leaning up to her tiptoes to press her lips to his before nipping at his tongue when he dared to taste her.

His hands travelled down the deep cut in the back of her jumper, the pads of his fingers dancing dangerously low on her silken skin. Enough to make him hard. Just to know he was touching his *wife*. This was his wife. The baser part of his nature reveled in the idea that she was his to adore, spoil, enjoy however he wanted to, and there wasn't anything anyone could do about it.

The rational side of Roman reminded him there were still people watching, and he didn't care to let them see what came next.

"Come on, let's get outta here," he said, groaning the words against Karine's teasing kiss.

With the very last of his control ...

She at least took mercy on his soul.

• • •

Roman carried Karine over the threshold of the room he'd booked for their honeymoon—it only seemed fair to keep *some* traditions. Even if they were being silly, it made her smile and laugh. That's all he wanted.

Karine was beyond fascinated with Las Vegas, and as things were going well—there were no apparent dangers— Roman felt like they could do anything. Within reason. If anything, maybe for a few days, the two could live like nobody was watching.

Wouldn't that be something?

He had booked them one of the best suites at The Venetian Resort with a view some people would have killed for. More than anything, he just wanted to give Karine everything her heart could possibly desire while they still had the chance to enjoy it.

She kept her arms locked around his neck when he carried her in. Tipping her head back to look up at the intricately engraved ceiling of their suite, she marveled at the many details covered in gold leaf.

"I don't think I have ever seen anything as beautiful as this," Karine remarked.

"No, I haven't, either."

When she met his stare again, he'd not once looked at anything but her.

Karine's smile bloomed instantly, her next words bubbling out with a laugh. "You keep saying you don't know anything about weddings, and yet you know exactly what to do to make it all perfect."

Roman spun a slow circle in the middle of the large room with her still cradled in his arms. "I don't know much about weddings—that doesn't mean I don't know anything about loving you the right way. I've had some great examples of love in my family."

He put her down, but Karine clung to him sinking into his body. Never too far away, he knew. She didn't like that at all. His hands traveled down her back until he cupped her ass.

"Your mother and father, you mean?"

"My grandparents, too," he added. "Not that I ever really understood it before you. That's okay, though. I'm not sure I was supposed to."

She nuzzled her face in his chest, breathing deeply like she was sucking in the very scent of him directly to her lungs. He stroked her hair, staring out through the glass wall that overlooked the view of the Las Vegas strip. God knew he had better things to consider, but he couldn't ignore the sinking of his stomach.

Karine wouldn't know he dared to do it.

That he let his mind go *there*.

For a few moments, he allowed himself to think about the fact that this was not forever. This feeling, no matter how good and wanted—like they were invincible and their journey together would be easy just because they had each other—none of it was permanent.

Or even real.

Their current circumstance was not forever. The truth was harsh, and too concerning for him to put the weight on Karine's shoulders when he was sure she already had enough to handle. Roman didn't know what the future held for them. Everything could go tits up tomorrow, and that alone stayed like a heavy lump of cement deep in his gut.

Never far from his mind.

Not that he wanted it there.

Not now.

So, he took Karine's face in his hands and gave her another deep kiss, letting the seconds tick by them in silence as the taste of her on the tip of his tongue chased away those bad thoughts he shouldn't have let ruin their moment.

Ending with a kiss on the tip of her nose, Roman winked, saying, "Time for an important decision. You have to decide whether you want me to fuck you right now, or go shopping."

Karine's laughter really was infectious. There was never a time when he wasn't amazed at how happy she was. The way her whole face beamed was truly a sight to behold, and for some reason, he was the person who could make her do this.

How had that happened?

Love was *crazy.*

"That's probably the hardest choice a girl has to make," she replied through a wide grin.

Roman only shrugged.

It really *was* up to her, though he had a side he was leaning toward if he was being honest. Who could blame him?

The very tease that was Karine in her sexy, red jumper-dress, the low dips in the back and front showing off just enough to make his mouth water, hadn't been far from his mind all damn day.

It was a good thing his wife—he still couldn't believe that she was his *wife*—seemed to be able to read his mind as she let her fingers graze the red straps and lower down the deep dip along her chest. Her breasts heaved. When she slowly parted her lips, he knew what her answer was going to be.

"Fuck me," she said.

• • •

"I can't decide which is the better view," he said, smirking at her.

Karine stood with her back to the glass wall of windows facing the bright lights and a city that never slept. She had stripped down to nothing but her bright red thong. A good choice, even if it did tempt his control, for their wedding night.

Roman couldn't take his eyes off her, so his statement had been a false one nonetheless. Nothing in the world was more beautiful than her.

"Tell me how to make it a better one," she told him, dragging her teeth over her lower lip. "The view, I mean."

"It's already perfect, but I still want you to touch yourself, Karine," he said, a cigarette burning between his fingers. The smoke rose up to the ceiling, clouding his vision as it passed his face, but he didn't look away from the sight of Karine letting her thumbs drag over the peaks of her firm, pink nipples. "Imagine it's me touching you, the way you shiver when the rough side of my thumb slides down the center of your stomach."

She did, her soft gasps coming out shaky and high. Then, he took a long drag off his cigarette, making the end burn with a bright, orange glow. His cock was thick and hard in his pants, and he did nothing to hide the visible line of his erection already bulging.

Karine's hand dipped beneath the lace waist of the thong, her pleased whine letting him know she was wet and already tender to the touch. She rubbed her clit, and then slipped a finger into herself the way Roman would have done.

But he was sure it wasn't enough.

Not quite like his touch.

Her tits shuddered as desire coursed through her body, the delicate line of her shoulders falling forward with her breathy moan. When she thrust another finger into herself, she stepped backwards, pressing against the glass.

From Roman's position, it appeared like she was flying. Soaring over sin city. And that was all his patience could take.

It took him less than a minute to shed his own clothes. She still hadn't managed to get herself off in that time.

A fucking shame.

He flicked the burning cigarette into a crystal ashtray next to the leather bucket chair, and went to her. With some force, he pulled her hand out of her thong, intent on doing the job himself, now. His hands were all over her, cupping her tits, and flicking her nipples with his thumbs until she trembled. His tongue left a wet, hot trail down the center of her torso. Her skin tasted of salt, and his pants of breath had gooseflesh blooming along her stomach.

He would have loved to do this forever.

Feel her.

Taste her.

Have her.

Once more, he was reminded just how fleeting these moments truly were for them—who knew when they'd be able to enjoy time alone like this again. As fast as the anger came and went, he'd still felt it.

It had still been there.

And it wasn't fair.

Roman wanted this with Karine as much as he wanted it for her, too—for her to always be happy like this. Carefree and dreamy when he touched her. He wanted it to last forever.

But it wouldn't.

That's why it also hurt.

He slipped her thong down her thighs. It swished to her ankles as he pressed himself into her until her backside stuck firmly to the glass under his weight.

Could people see them from below? If so, then he hoped they found themselves envious of Karine. Of how beautiful she was on display when she was being loved properly, and fucked well.

ᴛʜᴇMARRIAGE

He took her face in both his hands, searching her ocean eyes darkened with bliss. She still had that lingering smile—it was like he almost couldn't remember the Karine he'd first met. Perpetually afraid, always tired.

He vowed in that second to do everything he needed so that he would spend the rest of his life with *this* Karine.

His Karine.

When he lifted her up against the windows, Karine wrapped her legs around his hips. She was featherlight in his arms, and already shifting her hips to get even a brush of his cock along her slit. As she did finally sink down on his length, he was lost to the slick, silken heat encompassing his dick when he plowed in.

Her arms rested on his shoulders while her fingers toyed with the back of his neck, weaving in and out of his hair. He swallowed her soft moans with kisses, settling his cock deeper into her with every thrust until she was shuddering with each one.

Neither seemed to notice the thudding sounds they made—Roman drove himself into Karine, making her body rock against the glass window with a rhythmic beat. One of the only beats he knew how to keep, honestly.

He could see the sprawling Vegas city over her shoulder when his lavished attention at the spot on her neck that she loved for him to kiss, and for a moment, they were on top of the world.

What was he thinking about before he started fucking her? He couldn't even remember, his mind was already too hazy from the whimpering sounds his wife made in his ear as he brought her closer to her sweet release. It was a glorious place to be.

"*Roman* ..."

Her whisper of his name fell like a prayer between them. She watched him through lust-hooded eyes with pouty lips swollen from his kiss.

"Tell me anything," he murmured.

He didn't stop, never once breaking his pace while her breaths came out fast, and ragged. She struggled to form the words, but when she did, he hadn't been ready for them.

"Promise me you'll never leave me."

Because everybody did, he knew.

In one way or another, everybody left her.

Roman couldn't look away from her, but if he said those exact words, they would be a lie. Life wasn't that simple, and certainly not the one he chose to live. He still wasn't going to lie to Karine—or make promises he couldn't keep.

"*Promise me.*"

That time, she spoke sharper.

Desperate.

"I promise I'll never abandon you, Karine," he said, cupping her chin and dragging the pad of his thumb over her trembling lower lip. "Those are still different things."

And he knew it wasn't what she wanted to hear.

Not that she showed it.

Throwing her head back, she moaned louder, bounced harder in his arms, her cunt so tight around him that it already felt like she was milking him dry. With every thrust, she was closer to the edge and so was he.

As wet as a lake between her thighs, even the clenching of her pussy wasn't enough to stop his cock from stretching her open and stuffing her full. That's really what she'd wanted when she was against the windows, touching herself and thinking of him.

She wanted to be *too* full.

Good and used.

Fucked in the only way he could do to her. The only way she *wanted.*

"Come for me, babe," he urged, husky and breathless, already feeling the way her inner muscles were starting to spasm around him when he fucked her a little harder. "You're gonna feel this for a week, Karine."

"God, that's what I want."

Yeah, he knew.

When his hand circled her throat, and he could feel the fast flutter of her heartbeat against his palm, her final cry was loud and broken. She came with a shout, and it only took feeling the gush of warmth around his cock to make Roman empty his balls while he held Karine firm, and deep.

THEMARRIAGE

It was the pulsing jerk of his cock inside her that had Karine smiling like the cat who had gotten the cream. There was nothing that turned her on more than his seed filling her; he bet he could make her beg for it, even.

It was only once the two had crashed to the floor together—in a heap of satisfaction and happy laughter—that Karine used their mingled fluids as lubrication to keep his painfully hard cock very much alive and well. There was a sharp stab of pleasure that came with every jerk of her hand down his length, but goddammit …

He wanted more.

Karine straddled him, the slick sliver of her pussy all pink and still hungry for him hovering over his cock that she handled with two hands for a moment. "Again?"

Roman leaned up, tucking the hair behind her ears.

He wanted her insatiable.

Undeniably his.

And she was.

"One more time," he told her, his smile growing sinful along with hers as she slid down his length again, slow and tender, "and then we're eating."

Karine winked. "Deal."

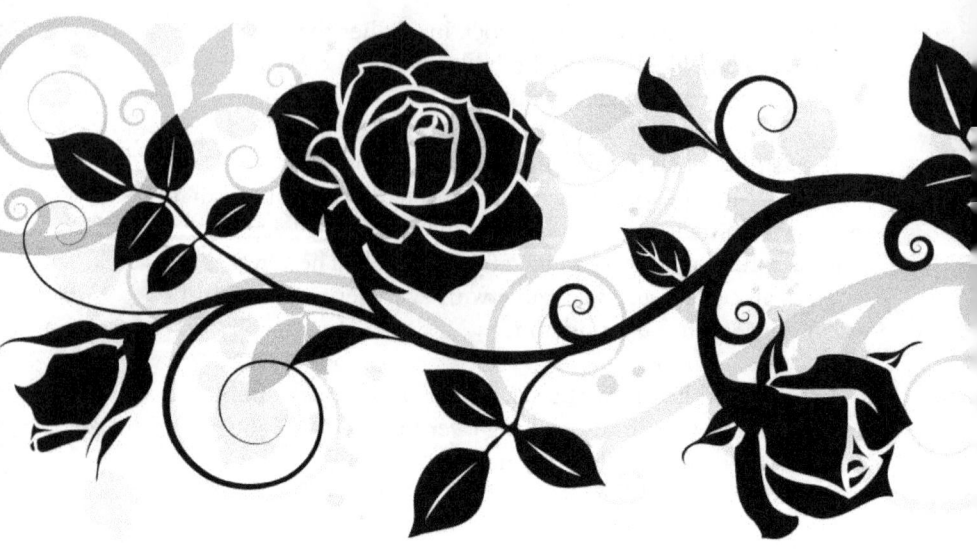

TWO

A rather large, silver platter of oysters lay uneaten on the carpeted floor between Roman and Karine where they both rested on their backs, staring up at the gold ceiling. Funnily enough, they found themselves close to the same spot where they landed on the floor earlier, only he'd convinced her to get dressed while they waited for food—even if it was only in the hotel's robe. And she ended up using that as something she could lay on naked, anyway.

The city never slept below.

An ice bucket with two bottles of champagne sat next to the platter of oysters. A treat to enjoy that mixed well with the liquor. The hotel certainly knew how to deliver on promises. They had been well worth the money.

So far.

"Let me try."

"I don't know," Roman murmured in reply, grinning all the while. "Not something you'll like, probably."

ᵀʰᵉMARRIAGE

"Well, I want to anyway," Karine said, stretching her hand toward his.

Roman hesitated to pass her the cigarette that she'd wanted to try at first, but because she didn't ask the second time—*I want to*, she said, not *let me*—he gave her the nicotine stick. Passing it carefully from between his fingers to hers.

He didn't want his bad habits tainting her, honestly. She was precious to him. More precious than money or any of his possessions ever could be. The woman also had a mind of her own, and could do whatever she wanted to do—he wouldn't control those things.

Not that he didn't like the sight of the cigarette between her plush lips when she pulled in her first drag. Or the way she watched him while she did it.

Karine had never smoked a cigarette before, and it was obvious when that first drag led to a coughing fit that melted into more laughter. It didn't take long, however, before she'd figured the task out and was passing the smoke back and forth to share the rest with him.

"You know what else we should get while we're here?" he asked, watching her take another pull from the cigarette. "Just for fun one night."

"What?"

"Edibles. You get the best kind in Vegas, I swear."

Karine snorted at that, passing him a look. "Numb and high, a state I know well."

"I didn't mean it like that."

She shrugged, unbothered, saying with a devilish grin, "I know."

She had a dark sense of humor with a twist that he sometimes didn't see coming until it was too late. Roman's dark chuckles only had her preening at him when he rolled over to reach for her, cupping Karine's cheek in his palm.

He constantly wanted to touch her.

Especially now.

"If you do want something," he told her, "all I need to do is make a call, and they'll have it brought up. Whatever it is, that's their job."

And he paid a lot for the convenience.

Karine reached for his wrist, pulling him closer to her so he could hear her say, "I kinda want to, but I don't like the idea of you leaving my side. Even for a second."

Right.

They were never quite gone from that—the fear lingering somewhere in the back of her mind, and refusing to let go. No matter how hard he tried to make it so.

Roman let out a slow breath, accepting the cigarette she passed back to him without a word. Falling to his back, he tried to figure out a way to break it to her that this wasn't going to last.

Their honeymoon, that was.

This *fairytale.*

Just because they had managed to distance themselves away from all the danger, and the reality of their lives for a few days, didn't mean it was altogether gone. They couldn't keep running—*well,* he couldn't, anyway.

Roman just needed a bit of time to make plans work before he was ready to face what would be waiting for him on the other side.

"I don't want to leave your side either, Karine," he finally said, rolling over to crush what remained of the cigarette to the ashtray on the floor. "Everything's better like this."

Karine folded an arm underneath her head and sighed, her gaze settling back on the ceiling. At least, she appeared relaxed and satisfied. Like a woman with not a single care in the world.

How she *should* be …

If only.

"How about we try the oysters?" he suggested, sitting up.

He didn't want to keep thinking about how time was ticking away in the background, minutes counting down into hours they would never get back. If they continued like this, he would have to fuck her again just to get his mind off those depressive thoughts. Not that the sex was something to complain about, but he couldn't keep using Karine like a drug whenever he needed something to help him deal.

She wasn't *cocaine.*

"I've never had oysters before, either," she admitted.

14

≡ MARRIAGE

Karine's nose crinkled in the cutest way when he drizzled lemon juice from a ready-made slice over an oyster.

"I have a feeling you'll be good at it. Now, just open your mouth wide," he said, flicking the flesh with a fork to loosen it from its shell. Karine sat up, tipping her head back a bit and jutting her chin out when he brought the shell closer to her mouth. "Trust me."

"It looks disgusting."

"Eat enough, and apparently you'll want to fuck all night."

"*Really?*"

He arched a brow, considering that. "Well, that's what people say. I don't really know. Just try it. It's going to be an ... *unusual* texture, but since you swallow me well—"

"*Roman.*"

"Swallow like a good girl."

Roman slid the oyster into her mouth once she parted those stubborn lips for him, and she did exactly that. She had a smile on her face when she faced him again, wiping her mouth with the back of her hand.

"Well?" he asked.

"I want another."

Roman chuckled.

Of course.

He was already reaching for the next shell. Anything for her.

● ● ●

They'd eaten all the oysters and drank most of the champagne by the time the television on the other side of the room stopped playing the first episode of a series that Karine had seemed interested in when he scrolled through the options. He could see she was tipsy by the way she watched him through half-closed lids where she'd perched her chin atop her hands on his hard stomach.

He had the best view of her naked body stretched out before him, *and* the reflection of her curves in the glass to enjoy, as well. Roman was a happy man—for once—in the silence.

Karine just didn't stay that way for long.

Not that he minded.

"I sometimes wonder if they ever had moments like these, you know?"

"Who?" he asked.

"My father and mother. When they first got married, I mean, before I was born."

She'd stopped looking at him, and Roman couldn't bring himself to force her to stare him in the face as she spilled her pain. Her traumas seemed hard for her to share, and he wasn't cruel enough to make it worse.

"Maybe they were in love once, too," she added, rolling her head a bit to glance up at him. He swiped at the tip of her nose with the pad of his thumb, enjoying the red flush that spread over her cheeks at the touch and his attention. "Maybe they were like us once, if you know what I mean? He never spoke about her after she died. So, I don't know anything about her but what someone might say, and they know better than to say anything. He'd—"

Karine stopped, then, shaking her head. "I don't even really remember her."

"Did he only have the one wife?"

"No, and he wasn't very faithful, either. I wouldn't say he was a good husband. Or maybe he just isn't a very good man. I'm not really sure."

Roman grunted under his breath, and at her questioning stare, he shrugged. "I don't know your father well enough to form an opinion on that. Somehow, he made friends with *my* father, though. That does make me wonder if there's ... *something* there. Someone there."

Whether it was someone *good* ... that was up for debate. Not one he particularly wanted to have.

Karine nodded, closing her eyes. "When we were kids, when Katina—when she was still around, he was a different man. I was just a child, but I have distinct memories of him being a dad. Like ... an actual dad. Does that make sense?"

Roman admired the soft smile on her face while she continued to speak with her eyes closed. "It does."

‍THE MARRIAGE

"He used to give me piggyback rides, and have dinner with us every night, and ask Katina to tell him all about her day. He was so proud of her."

She opened her eyes again, and he saw the tears she'd probably fought to hide, but in the end just couldn't. They fell down her cheeks, making tracks that he quickly swept away before she could say a thing otherwise.

Katina.

The missing link in Karine's past—the older sister who undoubtedly would have shaped a good portion of her life had she not been taken too soon. In the cruelest card the universe had ever dealt—her sister was murdered by the man Karine was supposed to marry. Roman certainly understood why all of those details made her memories all the more painful.

He still wished he could take it away.

Weaving his fingers with hers, Karine bit her lip while the tears still streaked her cheeks, more falling with her next blink. She could cry without making a sound. Not even a *whimper.* That probably cut him the most.

Who had taught her to hide sadness?

Why didn't her pain matter, too?

"I know it's kinda hard to believe," she eventually said.

"It's not the Maxim I've known," Roman admitted.

"It's not the Maxim he has been in a very long time. Not since Katina died. Well, before even … it started with his wives dying, I think, and only got worse. He buried that pain in women and work, and only brought us out when he was happy or pretending to be. He stopped pretending altogether when Katina died. Her death snuffed what humanity he had left in him. I reminded him of her in different ways; sometimes, it scared him. I … acted strangely. I changed overnight, and so did he."

Karine shuddered when Roman pulled her into his arms, trying desperately to rid her face of the tears while she apologized.

"Sorry. God, I'm *sorry.* I didn't mean to be … I shouldn't have brought it up."

"Bring anything up—*everything*. I want to hear you talk for hours about anything on your mind. I don't care if you cry," he murmured into her hair, "as long as I'm not the one making you do it. You just have to let me take the tears away, too. That's all."

She buried her face into his bare chest while he stroked her hair until her hot tears stopped staining his skin.

"I'm not sure how to explain what that feels like—to have your sister murdered right in front of your eyes, and then your father shuns you because he can't handle it."

"You don't have to explain it."

"He blamed it—they all blamed it—on rivals. Enemies. I don't even think anyone took credit, he was just *angry*."

But clearly, never at the right people.

Roman didn't say that out loud.

"Nobody will ever know what that feels like," he told her instead, "and that makes you stronger than you realize."

Only then did she lift her head up.

"I'm not strong, Roman. Please don't make the mistake of assuming that about me. I'm a lot of things, I know. And many of them are confusing, but that isn't one of them. If I was strong, I would have told everyone the truth about what I saw. What I know about … about him, what he did."

She couldn't even say his name. Some things, apparently, were still one thing at a time. And that was one of those.

Roman pulled her back down to his chest and she breathed in his scent, satisfied in his arms. "You were just a child, Karine."

That was all he could find to say. She hadn't told him more—he didn't know what Dima had said to her when he found her hiding in the closet that day, or the things that might have come after. Roman had a good enough imagination that he didn't think he needed actual details to paint a picture. Not a pretty one, either.

As a child, she wouldn't have known what to do. Could she have even understood the words she needed to say to explain to people the scene she witnessed? He seriously doubted it, considering she was broken by it. She didn't have the means to handle it.

ᴛʜᴇ MARRIAGE

And instead of telling her father or anybody else, at the time, her mind fragmented into an identity who protected her from the pain and suffering of her memories. Even her insecurities. Her weaknesses, too.

Katina clearly came later, a mirror of the sister she had lost in some ways, but she brought violence wherever she went, leading him to think she protected Karine more than anything else.

On the other side of the same coin, Katee was the child she had never truly gotten to be—an alter representative of the age where a piece of Karine was undoubtedly stuck forever.

Maybe emotionally.

"It doesn't matter anyway, right?" Karine wiped what remained of the tears from her cheeks, still content in his arms whether she was crying or not. "We're all a little fucked up because of it. Most of all, my father."

Roman had to decide whether to tell her. It was a clear opportunity for him to come clean. He knew something about her father that she ought to know—it was *her* father. It was her right to know he could be dead.

He tried to say it.

Even opened his mouth to say it.

Come on, you stupid fuck, just say it.

Karine straightened in his arms, and sat up, facing him with a weak smile. "I'm sorry for dumping that on you. I guess you know everything there is to know about me now, though. Not very interesting, am I?"

There had never been a worst lie. That was the thing about lies, though … the worst ones were the lies people told themselves. Karine was terribly good at doing that.

Roman wouldn't feed into it. He could only love her the way he wanted her to love herself; the rest she had to work out on her own.

"Well, I don't think I know *everything*," he replied, "but I want to. All of it. Even the boring shit. I might know the big picture, but it's the little details that makes it beautiful, babe. I suspect there's a lot you *haven't* done, for example. I know

19

you had never eaten oysters before, or smoked a cigarette. What else haven't you done?"

He'd been all of those firsts.

Any that she wanted with him.

The brightness returned to Karine's eyes instantly. That's really what she was for him—an instant shot of joy straight to the fucking heart, and he couldn't explain it. She drummed her fingers along his arm, considering his question before she came up with yet another answer that surprised him.

"I've never been to the zoo," she finally replied.

Roman laughed. "Are you serious?"

Karine waved a hand in differently. "If my parents ever took me, I don't remember it. I didn't exactly have the most normal upbringing."

"I know, we've established that."

"Okay," she said with a nod, "then the zoo. I've never been to a zoo."

He grinned, pressing another kiss to the top of her head. "I'll take you to the zoo, sweetheart. I'll take you to the zoo everyday, if that's what you want. Hell, Karine, I'll buy you a fucking zoo someday."

He just needed the time.

Time to get them there.

THREE

Karine didn't know the store Roman had brought her to, but considering the security at the door and the walls of glittering diamonds that greeted them, it felt important.

She walked in with him, side by side, her arm twined around his. Her hips gently grazed him as she took each step. Constantly, he kept her close, and she didn't even think he realized he was doing it. It certainly didn't help her obsessive desire to keep him in her sights at all times.

Maybe they were just meant to be in that way.

A little messed up, but together.

The heels of her stilettos clicked against marble floors as they walked past tall glass showcases protecting jewels resting on black velvet. She'd never worn heels this frequently before, but Roman insisted they suited her—well, that's what he'd growled into her ear while he fucked her from behind as she wore a pair—and now she couldn't get enough of them.

Empowerment was sexy.

For her.

"A jewelry store?" she asked Roman.

He'd only promised shopping that morning, but she hadn't thought this would be on the list.

Roman leaned in to leave a tender kiss on her temple, murmuring against her skin, "It's one of the best in the world. I thought you'd be more excited."

Karine eyed the two women that passed them by as they left the store. Dripping in visible wealth with not a hair out of place, it didn't bother them a bit to look down their nose at her on the way out.

Should she be there?

"Sorry, I've just never paid much attention to things like this before. Not that my father would have encouraged it, even though I'm sure he could afford it."

She quickly realized she was rambling when she chanced a peek at him and found Roman staring back at her with raised brows. Licking her lips nervously, she waited for him to say something—anything—even if she knew he wasn't judging her. Of all the people in the world—Roman was the only one she trusted inexplicably. The marriage proved it to be true. But being that he was her husband now, Karine didn't want to keep reminding him of exactly how naive she was.

Sometimes.

What if he suddenly decided he had made a huge mistake?

You're being ridiculous, she told herself because it was also true. Too bad that didn't fix the seeds of self doubt that had planted themselves into her mind a long time ago. It was going to be a while more before she ripped out the roots.

"Karine," he said gently.

She rolled her eyes away from his intense gaze. "Why are we here?"

That only made him tug hard on her hand, snapping her attention right back on him in an instant. There was no hiding the insecurities that he found staring back.

"What's really the problem?"

Karine shrugged. "I felt out of place for a second."

ᵀʰᵉMARRIAGE

"Your *place*," he said fast, admiring the slinky yellow dress he'd picked out for her at another store, "is wherever you want to be."

Then, he grinned in that sexy, tempting way of his. It made her own shy smile grow because it was one thing for her to deal with this man in the privacy of a bedroom, but it was another to handle him in public. She wasn't sure she could do that.

"And where I want you to be right now is here," Roman added. "Because it's time we got you a ring—proper, yeah? I didn't want to buy you something you wouldn't like, or maybe I'm a coward and don't want to hear you tell me you hate it. So, I want you to pick it out yourself."

"Oh."

"Yeah. I've set up a private consultation—they'll make whatever you want if you can't find something. Do you want to get started?"

Karine didn't answer right away. There was such a thing as being overwhelmed with joy, and even though she'd experienced it more than once with this man, it never failed to shock her all the same.

The ring *really* didn't matter.

Not in the grand scheme.

Karine wouldn't have minded waiting—and no matter what he said, she would have loved any ring he picked for her whenever he did so *because* it came from him. Yet, he'd still made this a priority, and that meant something to her.

His voice snapped Karine out of her thoughts. "Babe, you okay?"

"I'm just …" Karine glanced his way, blinking away the wetness in her eyes. She didn't want to cry, even if they were joyful tears. "I think I just realized that I'm happy."

Quieter, she added, "My life is not the same."

A sudden flash of softness reflected in Roman's eyes when he nodded, and pulled her into his arms.

"That's all I want for you, Karine. To have a happy life," he said, kissing the top of her head.

"With you?"

"With me."

• • •

A row of the most beautiful diamond rings twinkled in front of her. Each sat pretty on its own black velvet cushion, and every single one glittered like a thousand stars, blinding her with their luminescence. Karine couldn't bring herself to look away even as the jeweler and Roman discussed creating something original. They were just too beautiful, and it was a strange feeling to know she could pick out whichever one she wanted.

All of them, even.

Roman had told her so.

He still seemed interested in having her design something despite the jeweler laying out options for her to look through, but she could also sense Roman leaning towards the gorgeous princess cut with a collection of rubies around it. Right in the middle, the ring stared up at them. It was classic in its appeal, and also very *big*.

If she didn't go with designing her own ring, she was positive he liked that one the most.

Personally, Karine was drawn to a daintier one—the small gold band with a single carat diamond in the shape of a heart. It was simple, but poignant.

She wanted something that she would never have to take off, unless absolutely necessary. A ring with larger diamonds might prove difficult in that regard, but the simpler band she could wear constantly and always look down to see it whenever she wanted … well, the idea of that made her smile.

It was perfect.

"Do you have a favorite yet?" the jeweler asked from behind the counter where he stood in his very smart suit.

The man sat with his elbows on the glass, his gloved hands careful to stay out of their way, looking expectantly at both their faces. He seemed surprised by the immense patience Roman displayed while Karine stayed silent and appraised the pieces, refusing to engage a stranger any more than she had to.

ᴛʜᴇMARRIAGE

Karine couldn't even remember how long they'd been standing there, going over each piece only for her to nod politely and say nothing, but it had been long enough.

She turned to Roman, chewing on her bottom lip.

"I know this is the one you want for me," she said, pointing toward the larger ring he'd been eyeing, "if I don't decide to have something made."

He picked up the princess cut and held it up to the light. It shone even more brilliantly, the cuts of the diamond so pristine and amazing. Even she had to admit she *did* like it. Just not enough.

"It looks like it was made for the madam," the man added to the conversation.

Neither paid him any attention.

Roman studied it closely while Karine slipped the other one she preferred on her finger. As strange as it was, she felt an instant connection with it, and like she hoped ... looking down at where it sat on her finger only made her smile.

It didn't have any embellishments. What you saw was what you got. Perfect, in its own way. Much like Roman.

"But this is the one that is calling to me," she continued. Roman turned to look at the ring on her finger.

Of course, he wanted to get her the best ring the store had to offer. She was supposed to be his queen, and he wanted everyone who looked at her—or the ring on her finger—to see it was true. *Only* the biggest and best would do. He wasn't even the first bratva man she'd met who thought like that—they were who they were.

Karine decided she would get the one he wanted if he looked at it again ... but he didn't. Roman curled his fingers over her hand, encasing the ring that sat there, and holding tight enough to make her heart skip a beat.

"I told you, Karine, you should get the one *you* want."

Her smile was wider than ever.

"I'll never take it off," she promised fiercely against his lips when he pulled her in for a kiss that made even the jeweler turn away.

Someone would have to take it from her dead body first.

• • •

Roman paid for the ring—and while Karine was given a tour of the rest of the jewelry the store had to offer as he did so—he stayed all the way on other side of the room. Despite being surrounded by three ladies who were running a constant stream of commentary, Karine kept glancing over her shoulder to keep her husband in her sights.

It felt *better*.

She wouldn't apologize for it.

Obviously, the ladies in their black dresses and sensible heels had decided she was a valued customer—she bet anyone spending money in the place was—and clearly hoped to impress her while they had the chance to make a few more sales.

Unfortunately for them, Karine was more interested in the phone call Roman was making. She hadn't noticed him speaking on the phones he bought them since they arrived in Vegas. As far as she knew, he had gotten rid of all modes of communication so the outside world couldn't trace them except for their disposable phones. So, why was he currently on one of the burners, keeping his back turned from the man ringing up the order a few feet away?

From the expression on his face, she could sense the topic of conversation was serious. And he made an effort to keep his voice down as he talked fast.

Roman ended the phone call almost as quickly as he started it, and if Karine hadn't been watching his every move to quell her nerves, she would have missed it. She looked away with a jerk, hoping he hadn't caught her trying to eavesdrop. Even if she was too far away to actually hear anything useful.

They were married now.

A team.

She trusted him, yes, but he encouraged her to have a mind of her own, and that meant Karine had questions. Whatever Roman was discussing on the phone had to be important, although she opted not to ask what it was for when he

ᴛʜᴇMARRIAGE

walked towards her with a warm smile, making the sales ladies scatter.

Not too far.

They still wanted to make money.

"Do you see something else you like, babe?" Roman asked, wrapping one strong arm around her waist. "Just point."

She did.

At his chest.

"I do now," she whispered in his ear.

His laugh was thunderous and dark, making Karine shiver on the spot, and alarming the people who were apparently waiting on her answer. He dragged her closer, making Karine stare up, and the rest of the room disappear before he dropped a sweet kiss to the tip of her nose.

"Well, then we'll just have to get the thing I picked out for you."

"What?" she asked.

"I think you'll like it."

Karine couldn't hide her bubbly, nervous laughter as Roman gave a nod to the man who produced a velvet box from thin air. The same jeweler who had helped them earlier.

In his hand, the man popped open the clasps of a navy velvet box, opening the top. In front of her waited a six-strand diamond necklace—each rope delicate and glittering under the lights. Compared to some of the larger, less functional pieces in the glass cases, the necklace was like her ring, simple but beautiful.

A statement.

"Oh, it's beautiful," she said, reaching for it.

Roman grabbed the necklace from the man, and slipped it around her neck. He clasped it without much trouble at all, and then took her hand in his, leading her toward a free-standing, floor-length mirror off to the side.

It wasn't lost on her that since their arrival, the store had not allowed entrance to other customers. It was just him and her—and the few staff, keeping their quiet distance—as the two came to a stop in front of the mirror.

She toyed with the bottom rope of the necklace, admiring the way it sat powerfully on her neck, hugging her collarbones, and dipping low down her exposed cleavage.

Roman picked the right outfit for her earlier. It showed off the necklace without much effort at all.

"A custom piece," she heard the jeweler say.

He also mentioned a price.

She tried *not* to hear that, and failed. The large number made Karine pause, though she didn't take her hand away from her throat.

"I ... don't know. It's very ..."

Karine fumbled with her words, staring at herself and the unfamiliar reflection that stared back. She wasn't used to seeing that smile, those clear eyes, or the happiness. The necklace was really just a bonus.

A beautiful one, sure.

Roman stood tall behind her, then placed his hands on her shoulders.

"I do. It's perfect, and made for you," he said. "Look at you."

She did.

Again.

She—and the necklace—looked better with him behind her. The whole world looked better through that view.

• • •

Karine finally understood what it felt like to be walking on clouds by the time they had returned to the hotel room, and Roman decided to run her a bath. She couldn't close her eyes without seeing the piles and piles of bags and boxes from department stores all over Vegas. She could make her own store in the hotel closet, if she wanted. How were they going to travel back with all of it?

She didn't ask.

When he said shop, he meant *shop.*

Karine hadn't been ready.

"Did you have a good day?" Roman asked.

THEMARRIAGE

She sat on the edge of the marble bathtub, while Roman slipped the straps of her dress down her arms.

"I had an amazing day," she replied, looking up at him. "But I'm tired, too."

His rumbly chuckles had Karine laughing, too. When it was just him and her, alone like this, when *she* was happy, his smiles held pride. She had figured out a while ago that there was a small piece of Roman he kept well hidden from everyone—insecurity was his own monster to beat, but she seriously doubted he showed that vulnerability to anyone.

Except her.

The dress slipped down to her waist, revealing her small breasts. He came around to stand in front of her, staring without shame. She still had the necklace on, and had no intention of taking it off. Oh, *someday*.

Not today.

Scooping her hand into his, he helped her up the steps that led into the bathtub. As she sank into hot, bubbly water, Karine asked, "Are you getting in with me?"

The tub was big enough for it.

And she wanted him.

Roman didn't bother to reply. The lavender scent of the bubbles filled her every breath and immediately relaxed her muscles while she enjoyed the sight of him stripping from his clothes piece by piece. The man really was a *sight*—sin in the flesh. Impressive in size, dark hair dusting the most tempting places on his body, and his gaze locked on her.

Yeah.

How could she not stare?

"I just don't know if I deserve all of this," she said, running her fingers over the necklace but meaning much more overall.

Roman's clothes had come off and now all her attention was on his cock. He wasn't hard—*yet*—but the size of him still made her mouth water.

She wore his ring now. The weight of it was not substantial, but she felt it constantly even so. He possessed her. Happily *his*. The very fact that they belonged to each other turned her on.

"You do deserve it all, Karine, and much more. I'm working on it," he said.

"I know you are."

Even if he didn't tell her *everything*. Even if she thought he was too used to her not asking questions. Karine did think he had the best of intentions.

Before he joined her in the bath, he kneeled down and grabbed her chin, tilting her face up so he could kiss her again. Holding her there, he pressed two harder kisses to her lips before saying, "And don't ever doubt whether you deserve my love and attention, or the gifts I give you. I want to spoil you, and I *will*. As often and with whatever I like. For the rest of our lives."

She couldn't fathom why he loved her like he did—but she was done trying to figure it out. It wasn't a terrible thing to live with the fact that this man loved her unconditionally.

Roman sunk ungraciously into the tub, splashing water everywhere and making her giggle.

He grabbed her by her hips, pulling her into his lap where he rocked her sensitive clit against his growing erection under the water. When his words were husky in his throat, and his cock hard to the touch, she lowered herself over him, taking inch by glorious inch of him slowly until she was tight and deep and *settled*.

A grunt fell from Roman's lips when she tried to stay steady—if only for a second, she wanted to feel him stretching her open—and she had to give him what he needed instead. Her breasts bounced lightly as she rode him, the ropes of diamonds now wet against her chest catching the light around them.

Glazed, dark eyes appraised her.

Loved her.

She used her palm to swipe away some foam on his beard, and he caught her hand with his. Kissing the side of her palm, he yanked her closer and kept her hand immobile as he worked her body faster and harder against his. His wicked words made her crazy. Every praise that left his lips took her higher.

She had control on top of him.

℠MARRIAGE

Except he took it away, too.

Made her wild.

The water splashed over the edge of the tub the closer she came. She sank into him, taking the kiss he rained down on her without warning until her lungs burned and all she could do was whine against the seam of his mouth for mercy. The orgasm finally swept through, the current so violent she thought she was drowning.

Could you drown on air?

Either way, he fucked her through it.

She was tender and raw while he finished, but every final stroke of his cock reminded her of exactly who she belonged to. *The man she chose.*

A man she loved.

Roman groaned when he shot into her, holding a trembling Karine tight to his cock as he filled her with hot spurts. His pulsing cock made her shiver.

She pressed her eyes together, her cheek pressed to his chest, and then felt him release her arm. When she looked up again, Roman was staring at her, smiling. Sly, and content. His blissed gaze was half-lidded, but still locked on her.

"I don't think you know how beautiful you are," he said.

She clenched around him.

"I never felt beautiful like this before," she replied, touching the necklace again.

He shook his head. "You don't need diamonds to make you beautiful, Karine."

"But you've still bought them for me."

"Because I want you to have everything I can give you."

Karine wanted to ask him if he wanted a family— or a house of their own to fill? Would that make their marriage complete? She thought about the fact that she could feel him inside her now, his cum thick and mingled with hers.

Instead, she laid her head down on his chest where she could hear his heartbeat. He stroked her damp hair, and she kissed his skin, tasting salt and man while he was still thick between her aching thighs.

"I just want you," she said in a sigh.

Roman said nothing, only took a deep breath that lifted and lowered her with his chest.

Hot water and bubbles surrounded them like a soft bed. Karine could lay like that with him forever, if the world would let her.

But how long would their forever last?

Even though she tried not to let her mind go there, she knew her past was going to catch up with her soon. Roman had to know it, too. Unless they kept running … was that the plan?

Would they use her new, forged identity to escape somewhere? Leave the country, maybe?

Something told her—Roman wasn't the kind of man to run away. He wouldn't leave his family behind. Not even for her.

FOUR

It was five days of bliss.

That's what he gave her.

Five days of him—of life without restraint or worry. She didn't have to do or be anything but exactly what she wanted and who she was.

Paradise, really.

No doubt, it wasn't the honeymoon she had been expecting. Instead, she was handed a dream, one she'd never forget.

It was like Roman had somehow peeked into her mind and figured out those fears and insecurities that sometimes kept her up at night. All she really wanted was to be alone with him—just because she loved him didn't mean she *knew* him. Parts of him, yes. And the peeks of the man under his exterior had kept her close for this long.

It just wasn't enough.

She wanted all of him.

That was exactly what he gave her, tucked away in a Vegas hotel suite with the heart of a city below acting as their nightlight in the midst of those conversations in tangled sheets.

To top it off—he'd showed her Vegas. A feverish dream of a city, bleeding life out of every bright light. Chaos in neon, just like her mind. The melting pot of people and culture welcomed her skittish oddness even when she walked down the street. She didn't want to miss a thing. For the first time in her life, she'd found somewhere that sort of felt like home. She'd never wanted to *go back* anywhere. And one couldn't quite call their prisons home, right?

Here, Karine felt like nothing could go wrong.

She may not have had the wedding of other women's dreams, but she certainly had the man they all fantasized about. Wrapped around her pinky finger, content to be warm in her bed, deathly gorgeous, and entirely hers.

It was all that mattered to Karine.

On the fifth day, she woke up in their hotel bed because the smell of delicious food was the only thing besides Roman between her thighs that could pull her from her dreams. Lately, anyway. Happiness seemed to bring calm to Karine's otherwise chaotic mind. Finally, she was *resting*.

Her first instinct was to reach for Roman as she awoke. When she couldn't find him in the soft sheets of empty space next to her—Karine's eyelids fluttered open in an instant.

He wasn't in bed, but the door to the bedroom opened just then. Roman, stark naked but for a sexy smirk and a white silk robe that he left open—walked into the room pushing a silver trolley of food.

"What's all this?" Karine asked, smiling as she sat up in bed while he positioned the trolley on her side.

He uncovered the plates underneath the silver domes without a word. A pile of breakfast danishes, French toast, waffles and stacks of pancakes sat artfully displayed under the biggest. More fruit than she had ever seen or eaten, a big bowl of chocolate chips, a variety of different sweet syrups and cakes waited under the others.

"And don't worry, I got the coffee," he added with a chuckle.

_{THE}MARRIAGE

There was a tall carafe of freshly brewed coffee and two mugs with flared bases that allowed someone's hands to hug the cups from the bottom up. Karine shook her head in disbelief at Roman.

"Do you really think we're going to eat all this between the two of us?"

Roman shrugged before slipping into bed beside her. "You don't have to eat it all, just promise that you'll take a bite out of everything. Try anything you haven't before. Figure out what's your favorite so I can make it for you on Sunday mornings, or something."

That made her laugh.

Karine made two plates, filling them with most of the offerings on the trolley. She handed one to Roman, and tore into hers while taking the occasional bite he offered to her. Making sure to let her lips linger on the tips of his fingers every chance she could. Even better when she was able to lick some chocolate syrup from the side of his thumb.

The waffles were divinely sugary, topped with maple syrup and a mixed berry jam. She moaned with genuine pleasure at every bite.

Roman had a plate of food practically identical to hers, but he paid it very little mind. More interested in watching *her*. Eventually, his lingering attention had her blushing. No matter that she should have been used to it by now.

"Are you just going to sit and stare—what about your coffee?" she asked.

"I just—" Roman's gaze darted to the window for a second where it paused before coming back to her. "Trying to remember all of this. You."

There was something about the way he said that—maybe it was how his gaze didn't stay right on hers at the end—but it gave her a bad feeling in the pit of her stomach.

"Is something wrong?"

Roman's jaw worked as he chewed on his thoughts, and she thought he might actually tell her what it was. Just for a second, she *really* did. But then he breathed in deeply, and shook his head.

"You have nothing to worry about, my beautiful girl. Come here," he said, tugging on her wrist until she was close enough for him to kiss. It was too quick, but it still took her breath away all the same. Only, it hurt a little more. Roman smiled lopsidedly, lifting one shoulder when he added, "It's not like I can really forget this anyway—I couldn't forget you if I tried."

That, she did believe.

• • •

After breakfast, Karine headed for the shower, needing to wash off the remnants of the night before. With her back turned to the bathroom door, she didn't see Roman come in, and his footsteps were so quiet she hadn't heard them until his last one.

By then, she was already engulfed in his embrace. Her giggles muffled into the crooks of his arms as he nuzzled her head to the side, getting access to her throat that he loved with his mouth in the best kind of way.

She melted into him while the rainfall shower overhead inside the large, tiled stall shot down in a steaming, steady stream. Her toes just touched the threshold to step inside the stall, but he'd caught her before she did.

Roman's kisses ended on the pulse point in her throat, and then he rested his chin on her right shoulder. Letting his arms fall around her waist, with nothing but his silk robe between them, he said nothing.

"You know, for nothing being wrong," she said quietly, "you're broodier than usual."

He kissed her neck once more, then slowly flipped her around so she could see him.

"Are you getting in with me?" she asked, looking down to find him semi-hard already.

Roman cocked a brow. "Likely."

"Hmm."

"Let's not pretend we're fucking sad about it."

Fair point.

^{THE}MARRIAGE

"I just wanted to touch you," he added, quieter. "I came in, you were there—there was a time not too long ago when you could barely run yourself a bath without someone being right at your side. Do you realize that? I saw you and thought ... *I don't think she knows how many days it's been.* So, yeah, I just wanted to touch you. I've never really been amazed at something before, but I am with you. Obsessively, maddeningly, constantly amazed with you."

"Roman—"

"I don't really think I deserve you."

He didn't give her time to absorb the impact of his words before he'd moved on to his next task—dropping the robe and stepping past her into the large stall. Karine followed him in, letting him tug her under the waterfall of water for a kiss that melted her into his arms all over again.

When he released her, moving to grab the hotel's provided bodywash and the fresh washcloth on the tiled shelf, she searched his face for answers to the questions she didn't want to ask. There was something definitely different about today. Like he wanted to tell her something he didn't have the words for. Was their time in Vegas coming to an end?

"How about we do something adventurous today?" he suggested, breaking through her thoughts.

"I've never been bungee jumping."

But it sounded like fun.

Roman threw his head back and laughed. *Hard.* "Do you really think I'm going to stand back and watch you being pushed off a fucking cliff? Honest question."

She rolled her eyes. "Okay, so what kind of an adventure are you talking about?"

"How about a spa day?"

It was Karine's turn to laugh now.

"You're not serious."

"What's wrong with that?" he asked.

"A spa day is Roman Avdonin's idea of a big adventure?"

Her giggles had his face darkening just enough to make her wink. He shrugged back. It wasn't often Karine got a rise out of Roman, and she enjoyed it.

Very much.

"It's not like we'll have the opportunity to keep doing shit like this—spending the day together at a spa, relaxing. Not when we have to go back soo—"

She cut him off, pressing her palm brutishly to his mouth to keep him from finishing that sentence.

Karine didn't want to hear it.

That made it real.

"Okay, yes, let's go. It'll be fun," she said quickly.

Roman sighed as he took her hand away with two kisses to her palm. "I really just want you to have a nice day, Karine."

She smiled as she took the bottle of bodywash from his hand. "I always have a nice day when I'm with you, Roman."

• • •

The private property where they had to travel outside of the city to reach looked like a resort, but Karine hadn't seen any large signage on the outside of the gates as they'd driven through. The small plaque was too small for her to discern the writing when Roman pulled beyond security. She didn't know where they were but the weaving, long driveway that led to the welcoming lobby style entrance was a beautiful distraction.

Karine didn't mind the long drive. There was nowhere else in the world she'd rather be than with Roman, the top down and wind in her hair. If she closed her eyes, it was almost like she was flying.

Free.

Roman had watched her closely during the drive, smiling the whole time. He even joined in when she started singing to a song on the radio that she had heard enough times to at least know most of the verses. He had a good singing voice. Deep and sexy.

Unsurprisingly, he ignored her compliment when she told him so.

His only comment had been a teasing, growled threat of, "If you mention this to anyone…"

All it took to quiet his grumbling was Karine leaning into him, pressing her red lipstick-painted mouth to the shell of his ear while her hands wandered over his muscular thighs, asking. "What Roman? What will you do to me if I tell the world about your secret musical talents?"

He'd taken his eyes off the road to stare at her, a sinfully dark promise at the ready to make her shiver.

"If you want it to hurt—I can do that. And you'll like it. Test me."

She bit down on her lip at that, and he had turned away with a smile. The urge to do just that—*test him*—teased her self-control, but she had to quell it. They'd arrived at that point.

Roman parked right at the front door's steps, under the large carport. A valet appeared, offering to take the car to a designated parking spot as Karine stared through the wall-to-wall glass that looked into a modernly designed black, white and navy-blue lobby. A uniformed man helped Karine out of the car with a smile and a hello—he also used her first name, but she didn't think much of it. This felt like exactly the kind of place that would want those details ahead of time for guests to be welcomed.

The sprawling grounds featured white pebble walkways, and water features with designated sitting areas at each, and left its guests soothed by the quiet, calm atmosphere.

The place was as impressive—and likely as expensive—as their hotel suite back in the city.

Roman offered her his arm, and she took it as they walked to greet the others who had come to the doors in their basic black dresses that seemed strangely uniform.

The one said her name was Mel—she did seem sweet—and that she was one of the managers. Roman introduced the others to her, only giving her their first names.

Mel brought them into the lounge area that was innately serene while soft piano played somewhere from up above. There was something crisp in the air—something that had Karine breathing deeper the second time—that added to the space.

While Mel spoke—giving them a guided tour of the various rooms on the ground floor, Karine leaned towards Roman.

"This was a good call. I definitely need a massage. You're a work out."

The smile on his face was weak and almost half-hearted. That sinking pit in her stomach returned fast. Like he was keeping something from her.

"Don't you like the place—you booked it," she said, too quiet for their guide to hear.

Roman forced a happier expression on his face, shaking his head. "No. Of course, I don't want to leave. This is good. It's great, babe. We both need to relax a little, right?"

"Only if you want to."

"I do," he assured.

So, why didn't it feel like it?

• • •

One of the final rooms on the ground floor that Mel brought them to was one she said could be used for meditation, and immediately Karine's mood brightened.

She hadn't meditated since she'd left the lodge in Vermont, opting to spend her mornings on top or underneath Roman. Not a bad trade, all in all. Even so, she still missed it.

"Maybe we can do it together. I can show you," she said, turning to Roman. He looked apprehensive as she knew he would be, his feet stuck like cement to the ground even as she tugged on his hand. "Come on, it'll be fun. There's no wrong or right way of doing it. Either way, you'll feel better after, I promise."

Roman looked away from her, and Mel interjected their conversation.

"We have instructors and other residents who would be happy to join you in your meditation sessions," she suggested.

Karine smiled politely but shook her head. "I didn't come here to be around other people. Thanks, but it's okay. We're not staying long enough for that. And why do you call your guests residents?"

"We find people respond better to that than patien—"

⁼MARRIAGE

"Karine, I don't want to meditate," Roman said abruptly, the firmness in his words startling her attention back to him.

Mel cleared her throat when she heard Karine say, "Okay, you don't have to do it. Relax. We can just go to the spa. You booked something, right?"

When he didn't answer right away, she looked over her shoulder to the only other person in the room for one. At first Mel's confused gaze darted from Karine to Roman, but then she smiled and nodded. "Of course."

When she thought Karine wasn't still staring, the woman turned her glare back on Roman. It was like they had some secret between themselves that they were trying to communicate without words.

That's when Karine got a feeling …

One she didn't like at all.

Putting a hand on Roman's arm, she pulled him slightly toward the corner of the room for some semblance of privacy. Her voice dropped to a whisper.

"Roman—"

"Babe, calm down," he murmured.

Calm down?

That didn't actually make her want to calm down.

"What is this place?" she demanded. "You said a spa. I figured massages, or saunas … except I don't think you—"

Over Roman's shoulder she could see Mel staring at them. She could likely hear some of their conversation, but Karine didn't really care.

He reached for her, putting his hands on her shoulders. She always delighted at his touch—it reminded her of who she was now; his *wife*—and this time was no different.

"Yeah, I got us a spot, which was what I said, and I didn't lie about what this place looks like and basically is," he said quickly. "And no, I haven't changed my mind about this. We're not going back to the hotel."

Somehow, Karine had gotten this all wrong.

She felt it in her bones as he stared at her, being very careful to choose his words and not lie, but cutting her deep all the same.

"Karine," he said softly.

Roman had been studying her every move with his eagle eye, and maybe he'd seen the lightbulb switch on inside her head, too.

God knew it was bright.

Blindingly so.

"Roman, *what* is going on?" she snapped.

FIVE

Roman wished for nothing more than the ability to be completely honest with Karine. She was his wife, after all—it was the very least she deserved. The woman, maybe the only person, whom he owed anything to. His father and grandfather had both set the precedent, as Avdonin men, to treat their women right. In a way that they would want to be treated by their wives, too, because if they could demand *so much* from the women they proclaimed to love, there was no excuse.

He hoped she would always tell him the truth, but on this, he had not offered her the same respect. Her clear, burning anger was justified.

Roman wanted to tell Karine the truth from the beginning about the private psychiatric facility, but he had to hide it from her for her own sake. There was no way that disclosing his plans to her would lead to anything good. More like, an incident he couldn't handle alone.

That's what concerned him the most. In order for their Vegas trip to work, they couldn't afford to be put into a situation where they might draw attention. What would have happened if Karine had a meltdown that ended badly simply because he didn't think she could handle the truth?

The last five days had gone exactly the way he'd pictured their honeymoon together—or rather, what he hoped for. He wanted to give her a taste of what a normal life with him might have felt like. What he wanted their marriage to look like when all of this was over, and he could finally give her the world.

He hoped he'd been successful.

She'd been so happy. Blissfully unaware. He gave her every breathing moment of his days for as long as he possibly could—but now it was time they faced reality.

Was it going to hurt?

Yeah.

Just a little.

Roman was so fucking sorry for that.

His main duty was to keep her safe—this place offered exactly that. Michelle had helped to find the right facility because that had really been the most troublesome part in the whole equation when they needed a mixture of things. Therapeutic help for Karine, should she want to continue down that path with another doctor. Privacy not just for her sake, but also safety. It helped that the doctor who would be working with Karine here knew Michelle, and promised to tie up paperwork and anything else she could just to extend the stay as long as they needed.

Was that what he wanted?

No.

The idea of leaving Karine here, locked behind the high, stone walls that surrounded the property was killing him. It'd been killing him ever since he got word from Michelle that everything was a go. He didn't sleep. *Couldn't.* Not that she had noticed because he made a special effort to keep it from her. Instead, he let guilt chew him alive every single fucking night that she slept peacefully beside him during their stay in Vegas.

^{THE}MARRIAGE

Roman was willing to spend as much money, and use all his resources for this—to make it work. It was a treatment and rehabilitation facility with a luxury feel, yes, but it had a larger purpose for Karine's stay.

Who would look for her here?

Who would even *know*?

Where was a better place to be—if the only thing she really needed was to be safe until she could be happy again—than here? As it was, her mental illness had already scared the men around her in to hiding her from the world, ashamed of what someone else might think. It was highly unlikely they would look here to find her.

The people who ran and managed the facility were trained professionals, and according to Michelle, the best in the business to manage her in his absence. He'd actually flinched when Michelle used that word—*managed*—like Karine wasn't entirely her own person with her own mind.

This was the kind of oasis she could use in order to make progress with her own issues, and he couldn't have her waiting like a sitting duck for Dima and Leonid to attack. Not in Vermont, not in New York. Not *anywhere*.

It worked twofold.

Well, it should.

The reality of it all actually terrified him, though. Roman wasn't sure how long he could keep her safe from them without outside help, and this was truly his last resort. However, he didn't for a second think she would be happy about it. Roman banked on her lashing out and refusing his plan because the same undertones of the situation that bothered him would undoubtedly hurt her.

That's why he didn't tell her.

What he didn't expect was for her to view it as a betrayal.

"*Roman!*"

Her hiss yanked him violently from his thoughts—the only place that actually saved him from the sight of her rage leveling on him. The second that damn light bulb had gone off for her, he'd already known it was too late …

She knew what he did.

What could he say?

"You need to tell me, right *fucking* now, exactly what is going on," Karine said, every word high and strained. "Don't lie to me—don't feed me anymore bullshit. Don't *touch* me. Just tell me what you did."

Roman stood in front of her, squaring his shoulders so that Mel, the floor manager, wouldn't see the full extent of Karine's anger in that moment. He needed to be able to handle her himself—at least this one last time before he left.

She'd been right about one thing.

He did this.

No one else.

"I'll tell you all of it, Karine, but you've got to stay calm. You know you're safe," he tried to say. "I wouldn't do anything to fuck that up."

Her eyes narrowed to two, dark beads. Face flushed, her hands started to shake at her sides, but she made no effort to hide it. When he reached for her she tugged away from him sharply, snarling, "Don't you dare touch me now."

Roman winced. "Come on, ba—"

"*Don't* call me that, either."

All that anger inside her came rushing out in a hateful hiss of words that cut him deep. To have her so close, but not be able to touch her … comfort her, *God*, it stung. Bad.

That's when Mel decided she needed to step in.

"Okay, Miss Karine, let's take a moment to resettle and reset our feelings and conversation. Please, we are here to help you," the woman said.

Karine turned her fiery gaze on Mel. "It's *Mrs.* Avdonin. I'm not a child, and I won't be talked to like one. Address me accordingly, thank you very much."

Each word came out calm, and *flat*. Yet, the rage simmering inside Karine, twisting her pretty mouth into a bitter sneer and vibrating through the rest of her body was still so clear to him. *Worrying* him, really.

Katina could show, and everything would be over at that point. There was only so much the staff here could or would do for Karine's violent alter—they'd made that unfortunately clear to him before arrival. Everybody had to be safe. Every doctor, nurse, or any other staff member on the property.

ᴛʜᴇMARRIAGE

Safety was a priority when it came to residents. He *tried* to understand, even if it was hard, when they explained procedure after procedure in case of different events.

This was *not* what he'd wanted—yet, what other choice did he have to keep Karine safe when time was running out, and Roman had to go back? Nothing about this was easy.

Fuck.

"My apologies, Mrs. Avdonin," Mel was quick to say, "but this experience isn't meant to be traumatic. We're willing to do anything we can to help during your stay with us, truly. We strive to make this environment one you feel at home in with us."

That didn't make Karine happy. At all.

"Who in the hell are you, and why do you think you're going to help me?"

"Because that's my job."

In an instant, Karine's gaze snapped back to Roman, wild in a blink. She might attempt to bolt; her darting gaze taking in the windows and doors said that she was considering it. He wouldn't let her get far—even if it broke his fucking heart, he just couldn't let her leave now.

"You have to relax," Roman said in a murmur, "and let me explain, all right?"

He didn't help the situation either.

"Why am I here?" she screamed at him. "Explain that!"

Roman swallowed hard. "Babe, just—"

"Roman, *why* am I here?"

From the corner of his eye, he watched Mel speak into a white radio that he'd noticed was strapped to every employee's waist. She was probably requesting someone else join her, just in case, and he didn't blame her. Not a single person here was willing to put the entire facility at risk because of one unruly newcomer.

He also wanted to make this as least traumatic as possible for Karine, but Roman seriously doubted that was going to be the case.

Christ.

He'd fucked up.

Again.

"Karine, listen to me," Roman told his wife who was becoming more and more agitated by the second. "This is only about keeping you safe—that's all I wanted to do."

But he should have known.

The *label* of it.

An entire facility.

His secrecy.

All of it.

Roman did know better, but *fuck* ... he had to do what he had to do.

He held his hands up where she could see them clearly, not willing to touch her if she didn't want him to, but still itching to do it all the same. He wouldn't let anyone else touch her, either.

Mel had thankfully stepped back, giving them some space, but that didn't stop Karine's quick, sharp gaze from slicing back and forth between the two.

"You lied to me," she hurled at him. "You brought me here under a pretext."

"Actually, I don't think I did lie to you, Karine. Not technically."

"Fine. Twist your words however you want to—you didn't tell me the whole truth. You told me we were going to spend the day at a spa. Something *adventurous.*"

She practically spat that at him.

Roman didn't even blink, or move a muscle. "This is sort of like that—for both of us. Neither of us know how to do this, babe. It is an adventure, but it's not an easy one. You wouldn't even let me talk about going back to New York, how in the hell was I going to tell you *this*? I just ... I didn't have a choice. I had to figure out something without a whole lot of time to do it, and no matter what choice I made, we were still gonna end up apart. At least here, you can get more—"

"*Fuck you.*"

That burning retort didn't blow by him quite like the rest had. In fact, it felt like a slap against his face, and all he could do was stand there and take it.

He deserved it.

ᴛʜᴇMARRIAGE

Karine shook her head, lips quivering. Tears rolled down her cheeks, leaving wet tracks she didn't even bother to wipe away, and Roman wished he could hold her. More than anything, he hated when she cried.

Why did he have to be the one to make her cry?

"I'm sorry," he settled on saying, "but it was looking like I couldn't take you back to New York. Not safely. This option came up, and fuck, it works. Okay? I get it, I know what it is, but *it works.*"

"You lied to me. You manipulated me. *Again.*"

"Karine—"

"How can you say you love me and then do this to me?" she cried. "Do I even get a say—what, will you pay them to stay quiet and lock me away?"

She was too loud, now.

Even he knew it.

Mel cleared her throat, a clear attempt to grab his attention, but he didn't look away from his wife. No matter what, he wanted one thing clear.

"That's not what this is," he told Karine. "That's not what it will ever be."

Karine glared with cold eyes, clenching her palms into fists. Any moment, he expected Katina to appear. The blank flicker in her eyes and the way her stare darted away to nothing sometimes said she was there. Mad, already fighting, and causing chaos inside Karine's fragile mind.

Still, Karine kept staring back. As fast as he had all of her attention, she took it away. The tension tightening his spine and shoulders left almost instantly, but his heart dropped when she spoke.

Because she didn't speak to him.

"Is there somewhere I can go right now?" Karine asked Mel. "To be away from him?"

Mel, startled by the reaction, didn't answer right away.

"Please, anywhere?"

She seemed too rational.

In control.

Even he didn't know what to do with that.

So, he did nothing.

Roman stood back and watched her walk out of the room with the floor manager who had regained her composure, and with a tight nod, made a beeline for the exit with Karine on her heels.

Nobody said shit to him.

Whatever.

He wasn't going anywhere.

No way in hell was he leaving this place before he told Karine everything she needed to hear from him—because that was the thing she didn't seem to understand. There was a big difference between want and need.

Sometimes, it also meant life or death.

• • •

Roman sat in the corner of the entrance lounge for over an hour—waiting to hear any news on Karine.

Katina hadn't appeared, or he sure as hell would have heard about it by now. The only information he had been afforded by the staff was that Karine headed to the meditation room by herself. They weren't sure if she was actually meditating or not, but they didn't want to disturb her, and she made her wishes about him clear.

She didn't want to see him.

Not yet.

Roman was willing to wait as long as it took for Karine to be ready to speak to him again. He hoped there was a part of her that would understand why he had to do this, even if that was selfish of him.

Didn't she realize he wanted a normal life, too? That the past five days with her had been a heaven he'd never known before now. It was only a slice of what they could be together.

If life wasn't in the goddamn way.

That was the thing, right?

The world kept moving.

And now, leaving her here, knowing when he walked out those doors he was going back to New York to solve this mess with Dima and Leonid—it was the hardest thing he would ever do. But maybe ….

God, maybe if he did it now, then they wouldn't ever have to do it again.

All because he was in love with her. Because nothing meant more to him now than that woman who wouldn't even speak to him. Hadn't what he did showed her exactly that? It was *proof.* He'd do anything to keep her safe, even if it meant she hated him for it, too.

She could hate him alive.

Karine couldn't love him dead.

The only thing he was concerned about was keeping Dima away from her. So far, in fact, that she was only a figment of his imagination. If it was possible. Something he thought was real but couldn't find a scrap of her existence. That Karine didn't exist anymore, anyway. The little girl whom Dima had hurt and silenced, terrified and terrorized … Karine wasn't that person, now.

Dima was the cause for everything, Roman was sure. A catalyst, certainly. The reason Karine was who she was—and that was more than enough. He'd done *enough.*

Never again would that man lay a finger on her. Roman would make sure of it, but while he did, she had to stay here.

There was no other option.

He couldn't keep her safe himself.

Finally, after the third glass of water was offered to Roman, Mel decided to make another appearance. She was smiling wide, too.

"Good news?" he asked, daring to hope.

Mel nodded. "Your wife has requested you join her in the meditation room whenever you're ready."

Now.

He was ready right now.

Roman jumped up from his seat, and followed her down the hallway past the swinging, heavy double doors. There wasn't another woman in the world who could make his heart race as fast as it did at nothing more than the thought of seeing her again. No matter how many times he saw her.

It was always the same.

He entered the room alone, and Mel shut the door behind him with a tight smile and barely a glance inside the space.

The room had all white walls and navy-blue accents from the thin yoga mats on the floor to the framed art hanging from hooks by twine. Soft music played in the background, and a wall of floor-to-ceiling windows overlooked a calm, beautiful part of the property. Other than that, the room was quite bare.

Minimalist.

Karine sat cross-legged on one of the mats with her back turned to him. As he approached her, she didn't move a muscle or say a thing, not even when he came to a stop beside her.

"Are you going to speak to me now, Karine?"

She took a breath.

And then another.

He let her have those few seconds before she peered up at him. Roman searched for Katina there, but didn't see her staring back. This was all Karine. Stronger, even if she was mad. Still beautiful, all the same.

Despite her aggression towards him, Roman was proud of her. Of who she was, and who she could be. Who she wanted to be—he wanted her, too.

All of her.

"Actually, it's time for me to speak and you to listen," she finally replied, soft-spoken and calmer than he expected.

"I'm listening," he replied.

She breathed in deeply, squaring her lungs like she could taste the air in the room.

"I trusted you, and you used that. You lied to me. Again," she whispered.

Roman was fast to open his mouth, ready to correct her because he had only really lied by omission and that wasn't quite the same, considering the circumstances. Then, she held her hand up to interrupt him, and he opted to say nothing at all.

This wasn't about him.

Even if he was frustrated.

Even if she didn't hear him.

^{THE}MARRIAGE

"Please don't talk, Roman, I just …" Karine looked down at her hands, neatly folded in her lap but still trembling like they had been earlier. "I really need you to listen."

As strong as she was being, he could hear evidence of her quivering voice. She'd been crying, clearly. He knew this was difficult for her.

Karine wasn't accustomed to putting her foot down, and expressing her feelings. Not without suffering for it, anyway. She was still learning to handle the roadblocks put in front of her without defaulting to the way she coped before—through medication and a fractured mind.

He reminded himself of that.

This wasn't easy for her, either.

Roman was not the kind of man who clung on to hope, but he did more times than he could count when it came to Karine. He had hope for her.

"You manipulated me into coming here. You're having me admitted to this place that I haven't even agreed to come to," she said, apparently deciding to just say it and get it over with. Roman stayed silent as she continued. "They're filling out paperwork for a seventy-two-hour psychiatric hold. Do you know what that means?"

"Only at first, to get the quick admission. It was just semantics, babe, that's all."

"*Still.* I'm not even a danger to myself. I haven't been. This is bullshit."

Roman let out a sigh. "Yeah, I know. But it gets you in the door at first. Fast, that's all I can say."

And no matter how many times he tried to explain all of those details were nothing more than surface steps to a grander plan, he didn't think she would care to hear it.

"I thought we were going to have another great day together, but instead, you're leaving me here. You're abandoning me again. What do you think that is going to do to me? You can't keep telling me you won't do something, and then turn right around and do it. What is wrong with you?"

He'd never been asked that before.

Not quite like she asked it.

Roman stared at her, unsure of what to say, so he stayed silent.

"I don't expect you to actually give me an answer," Karine muttered, not looking away from her lap where she picked at the frayed knee of her skinny jeans. "I expect you to turn around and leave me here, like you planned to do, anyway. So do that, then. *Leave.*"

Roman didn't.

He couldn't just leave it at that.

"You know why this place bothers you the most?" he asked quietly. She wouldn't even entertain his question, never mind that he spoke in the first place, and continued to refuse to look at him, even when he uttered a low, "*Karine.*"

Still, nothing.

Fine, he thought.

"The truth is that you don't want to be within a mile of a place like this because a part you knows this is what you needed a long fucking time ago. And maybe when you're not drugged and dazed, you've got a little more control, babe, but that doesn't help you *deal*. If Michelle gave you enough insight to understand what's going on, then imagine what a team can do. Take the fucking label off it—stop hearing other people in your head because that's what it is, isn't it? You hear your father saying you're a lunatic, or some other stupid shit. It's not about him, okay? It's about *you*."

Karine let out a shaky exhale before asking, "I thought you said this wasn't even about that? Earlier, that's what you said to me. I wasn't here for that. It's about—"

"That's not a lie, either."

"But which is it—is it to keep me away from Dima and his father, or for my mental health?"

Roman threw his arms wide. "Karine, it can be both."

"Except it wasn't … until you got me through the doors."

Karine's jaw clenched, and while her gaze remained lowered from his view, he didn't miss the tears tracking down her cheeks. Guilt gnawed on his bones, killing him from the inside out.

Slow, and painful.

Just like he deserved.

_{THE}MARRIAGE

"The thing is," Karine said, her bottom lip trembling as she spoke, "I know I don't get a choice in the matter, Roman, so just leave. Because you see, that's the only choice I do get here—the very least you can do is let me make it."

"Karine—"

"I want you to go."

Dull and flat, her words stabbed at him. The heat of disbelief flared up the back of his neck when she still wouldn't look at him the longer he stood there, waiting for even a goodbye. A simple *bye*.

Hell, a *fuck you* would do.

She wouldn't even give him that.

"What, you won't look at me now—you won't say goodbye?" he asked, hearing the hurt in his bitter tone.

The thing he didn't think anyone could understand about him and Karine was the fact she adored him, and he absolutely needed that. He wanted her idolization—her unyielding love just because she wanted him to be hers. She could spend her entire day staring at him in amazement, and she left him with just as much wonder. They were not exactly the kind of people who were meant to be, but damned if the universe didn't just make it so for them both.

It probably wasn't healthy.

Very few things he loved were.

"I want you to say goodbye to me," he murmured, doing his best to keep the anger out of his voice.

And failing.

Miserably.

What he needed was to touch her. Wrap her in his arms, hold her tight, inhale her scent, and pray to a God he didn't even believe existed that he'd be able to do that again someday. Just to help him last for the time they were going to be apart.

But she wouldn't give him that, either.

He already knew it.

Her nostrils flared in rage. She shook her head once more, and the calm composure she had carefully cultivated came apart at the seams when Karine let out a screech of frustration, standing from the floor in a blur of wildly waving arms. Narrowed eyes turned on him, and for a second, he wished she *wouldn't* look at him.

Not like that.

It hurt, too.

"Why won't you just go? *Leave!*"

Mel and another member of the staff came to stand in the doorway at the sound of Karine's raised voice. He didn't even glance their way, refusing to break his wife's stare now that he had it.

"I really do want to keep you safe," he told her.

"Mr. Avdonin, I think maybe you should leave now," Mel insisted.

"Karine, let me hug you before I go," he tried again.

She shook her head.

Again.

Because they both knew the truth ... and once he put his hands on her, she was going to feel better—good again. She always did in his arms. And God, he wanted to do that for her right now, even if it wouldn't last and it was only a lie. *He* needed to say goodbye, too.

Yet, there they both stood.

An invisible wall remained between them, and he couldn't close that distance unless she let him first.

She didn't.

Karine allowed herself to be coaxed away by the woman who had joined Mel in the doorway. The tears crept down her cheeks as she passed him by, not looking away to hide those blatant tears, but she didn't give him a thing.

Didn't say a word.

"*Karine,*" he shouted at her back.

Her dainty shoulders tensed, but she continued walking until she was at the door. One more step, and she would be gone.

He had no choice but to let her go.

Heart *dying.*

The outburst of emotion came from Roman before he could stop it. Without thinking, he drove his fist into the closest wall, driving his hand wrist deep into plaster. He heard the sound of bone crunching when the skin of his

^{THE}MARRIAGE

knuckles split against the beam it found inside the wall. His blood stained the pristine white paint, but none of it helped.

None of it changed anything.

Nothing would now.

SIX

Karine was sure Roman was long gone by the time she had
found a bathroom to hide inside. She quickly realized the
door couldn't be locked from the inside unless someone had
a card for the electronic reader, and it was just one more
reminder about what this place really was.

How stupid could she be?

How many cameras did Karine overlook? Why hadn't she
thought to ask about the heavy doors, and the locked
corridors that hadn't been open during the tour?

No, she'd been ... all too willing to follow Roman like a
lost puppy. Straight into a new cage, with prettier bars.

The woman who opened the bathroom door to peek
inside at Karine wore plain white scrubs, and a lanyard
around her neck with an ID badge that Karine suspected
controlled things like the card. At the sight of Karine sitting
on the bathroom floor next to a row of pedestal sinks, the
lady said nothing about the outburst earlier.

Karine's face still burned with shame all the same.

≣MARRIAGE

"Do you just need a minute?" she asked.

Karine nodded, but didn't look up from where she picked at her fingernails. "Please."

"Not a problem. You're not going to be forced to do or take anything here that you don't want, Karine. Not unless you're a danger to yourself or others. You're welcome to your privacy, but I did have to check. I'll be out in the hall whenever you're ready."

The door clicked closed without the woman waiting for a reply. Not that Karine had one, anyway.

For a long while, she simply sat there alone in her heartache. Silent and *angry*. Didn't she have a good reason to be, though?

Why did it have to make her feel guilty, too?

In the meditation room, Karine had decided she would be as calm and controlled as she could be—she *had* to be. It took mere minutes for her to figure out the plan that had unfolded around her by her husband's hand.

There was no way out.

No other option.

Karine had never once found herself in an institution. Despite the threat of it sometimes lingering over her head when Maxim thought she was getting out of hand, she'd managed to avoid it. She had enough knowledge about places like these to know once she had been involuntarily committed, fraudulently or not, leaving was not as easy.

But that was the thing …

Once she understood why they were really there, she didn't need to know anything else.

Roman had already made the decision. When she thought they were creating something real—when her traitorous heart believed they had a shot at love—he was actually plotting to lock her away.

Essentially.

The other details didn't really matter—his reasons weren't as important as what he'd done in the end. She wasn't convinced this was the best option for her.

How was keeping her far from her husband, somewhere she didn't know with people she couldn't trust, the right step to take?

Karine cursed herself for opening up to Roman. She shouldn't have told him so much about her past. Nonetheless, despite being aware of her triggers—he still chose to abandon her.

And not like before ...

Not like the lodge when she was still fresh from Chicago, and scared of her secrets that were no longer hidden. No, this time he'd let her wrap him around her heart only to squeeze it to death so slowly that she hadn't even realized she was dying.

Roman made her love him.

And then he did this.

Didn't he know how difficult it was going to be to keep control of the fractured parts of her mind that had already started screaming between her ears? Once again, she could hear the echoes of voices.

It would be easy.

To give in, and go to sleep. Let them handle all the fears, and the darkness beginning to creep through her mind.

She didn't, though, instead forcing herself to meditate and clear her mind as best as she temporarily could on the tiles floor of an unfamiliar bathroom with a row of silver stalls facing her.

And she thought of him.

Roman.

She'd gone into that last conversation wanting him to understand what he had done, what he was *really* doing to her. She had needed him to know there was no coming back from this.

His betrayal.

But then she saw him.

He'd looked almost afraid—like he was falling apart, too. Just like her.

Karine had tried hard to keep from giving into her weakness for him. All those thoughts and the pain she wanted him to hear her say jumbled together, stumbling over her racing heart, and nothing came out right.

As much as she had tried, she couldn't get him to see the damage he was doing. He apologized and made excuses, but she didn't think he could see how he was breaking her. All the progress she'd made, the trust she had in him—everything fell apart.

Just like that.

She didn't even bother asking him how long she'd be here. Where he was going, or if they would see each other soon. Could she call him?

Nothing.

She didn't ask him anything.

Karine had to make herself walk away from him because he didn't deserve her affection. She wanted to despise him.

If only she didn't already love him.

• • •

Eventually, Karine did leave the safety of the bathroom. They brought her to the room that was supposed to be her living space indefinitely—only big enough to fit the dresser, bed, two-person dining table, and a small sitting area in front of big bay windows that faced the dry land outside. There was a flatscreen behind glass inside the wall, and a camera in the corner.

She would later discover another camera in the bathroom. The place had every inch covered, no matter how humiliating. The women who escorted her to the room, Mel and the nurse from earlier, ran through the rules that Karine didn't care to hear. It was only once she sat on the rubbery sheet covering the bed and realized it was like that so someone couldn't use the fabric to make some form of ligature, that she really shut down.

She could have asked Mel how long she would be there for, but she didn't bother—why when she would either be refused an answer, or lied to. Clearly, there was something at stake for the staff handling her. Money, reputation … freedom, even.

What was the point, anyway.

Even if not knowing *did* both to her ... even if not knowing made her dark thoughts worse, and her self-hatred spiral. Maybe Roman had committed her for life. Maybe he couldn't deal with her just like her father.

Perhaps, had she known that the last few days would be her final days of freedom, Karine might have done things differently. Now, she was a prisoner to somebody else. It was starting to feel like she was nothing but a scrunched up piece of paper being passed around from one pair of grubby hands to the next.

Each one left her more used, and dirty.

The wrinkles weren't coming out.

"Do you like the room?" A voice interrupted her thoughts.

Karine winced, and turned to look. A middle-aged woman stood by the door, her hands clasped together and her head tilted gently to the side as she regarded the young woman resting in the bed, lost to her mind.

When she didn't say anything, the woman continued, "I asked for you to have this one because of the view—I hoped it would allow you a place to meditate without interruption. We don't typically see much movement out there."

She gestured at the windows.

Karine didn't bother to look.

She couldn't help but wonder what it was with all these women—first Masha, then Michelle and now this lady. Why did they all think they were going to fix her? They couldn't.

"I'm Sylvia. I'm going to be your therapist here. I know it's your first day, but I would really like it if we got to know each other, Karine."

Her soft voice and quiet demeanor only added to her friendly smile. She wasn't trying to hurry Karine in to doing something—so, at least that was a relief. That didn't mean she wanted to talk.

When Karine still didn't speak, Sylvia continued.

"I promise it won't take you very long. At the start, it can all be a little overwhelming. It's a new place, and you don't see anybody you recognize, but that will all change soon. I always like to give people as many days as they need to get accustomed to their new environment. Don't worry, we don't have to start working any time soon."

She made air quotes with her fingers as she said *working,* and the smile never left her face.

Ugh.

No, thanks.

Karine gritted her teeth.

Why was she being spoken to like she was a child? Did these people here assume she was incapable of having an adult conversation?

Karine jerked her face away from Sylvia to look out the window, hoping her displeasure and disinterest was finally crystal clear.

"It's okay," Sylvia said. "We don't have to talk right now, either. There's a button next to your bed, your door, and in your bathroom so you can reach a member of our staff at all times. Don't hesitate to use it, okay? Anything you need."

Karine almost laughed out loud at that.

Did she really want to know what Karine needed?

Free will.

A different *life.*

A future.

Roman.

She squeezed her eyes close to drive those thoughts away. She didn't want to think about him. She wanted to forget about Roman, hoping that would help with the pain of his betrayal.

"Is there anything I can get you right now?" Sylvia continued.

Karine opened her eyes, narrowing them at the woman who was still smiling.

That only annoyed her more.

"Yeah, you can," she said.

Sylvia brightened. "And what's that?"

"You can fuck off."

Karine rolled over, back facing the door.

That was that.

· · ·

They came for her the next morning.

At least, she was grateful the staff gave her the night. Karine had spent the past twelve hours in relative peace, if one could consider the hellish state of her mind peaceful. Regardless, they left her alone other than stopping long enough at her door to leave a tray heaped with food. It did look good, but she couldn't even force herself to move let alone *eat*.

Her room had everything she could possibly need, so technically, she had nothing to want for. And seemingly nothing to use should she want to end her misery. While it wasn't a thought in her mind, really, Karine was disturbed by the rounded edges on every piece of furniture and how not one single thing could be moved. All of it was bolted down.

On the surface, the room seemed clean, modern and inviting. Like a standard hotel room, not cheap but not expensive, either. Except when she looked closer, the bright white walls meant to be welcoming were made of stone and felt like they were going to swallow her whole.

This was exactly the life she had led at her father's home, too. Only with different walls and familiar faces keeping her company. He made sure she had everything to stay alive, which included a woman to care for her closely, and always under a watchful eye.

That wasn't what Karine wanted anymore.

She wanted a life—to really live. Because hers thus far had seemed to consist of being a pawn someone else moved from here to there. Tiring, honestly. She wanted freedom, possibly even an adventure.

The man who said he would give it to her had been just another liar.

Karine spent the night oscillating between grief and rage— the constant rollercoaster was nearly too extreme for even her to manage. Except it never stopped. It didn't give her the chance to get off the goddamn ride. She battled the voices in her head that were threatening to leap out. She wasn't sure how much longer she could keep them at bay.

It would have been so much easier to just switch off.

64

Karine started to *want* to.

Sylvia knocked on her door the next morning, but entered without waiting for an answer.

Karine was still in bed and barely even glanced at the woman. She didn't have the energy or interest to, and it wouldn't make a difference. The therapist would still see the dark circles under Karine's eyes and the bloodshot, dead stare stained with dried tears.

What a way to spend a night.

Fuck him for doing that to her.

"Looks like you didn't eat anything last night," Sylvia noted, her tone grating on Karine's nerves for no particular reason. "Would you like some breakfast now? We have a large menu, and you're welcome to mix or match anything you like. Our chef can prepare whatever you want, and you can take it wherever you'd like within your room, the halls, or the property."

Karine lay still, with her back turned to the woman just like she had ended their conversation the night before.

She didn't want to eat. She had no appetite. She missed Masha. And she seriously doubted any of that would mean anything to Sylvia.

"How about some pancakes? Are you a tea or a coffee person?" Sylvia continued.

"I'm a person who wants to be left the fuck alone," she hissed in response.

"I understand that you're frustrated and angry with your husband. I was hoping we could talk about it? A conversation could change your whole perspective, Karine."

Karine wanted to scream.

Or laugh.

Hell, maybe both.

Why would she want to talk to this stranger? It took her so much to open up to Michelle, and even that felt like a waste now. Especially when Michelle's name had been brought up as a facilitator to her committal here.

She would probably never see Michelle again, but that might be for the best.

"How about meditating? I heard you have a special interest in meditation. It's actually how I like to spend my mornings, if I can. Would you join me?"

Enough.

Karine rolled over fast, and sprung up in bed, dragging the dense, heavy rubber-like sheet off her with a clenched fist. "I get you're doing your job," she told the woman, not hiding the venom in her voice at all, "but I want to be very clear with you. I don't need your help. I won't *use* your help. Or anybody else's in this fucking place. Leave me alone."

Sylvia's smile dropped and for a split second, Karine thought the woman might lose her kind facade. No such luck. She breathed in deeply instead, suggesting quietly, "Maybe talking to your husband might help."

Jesus Christ.

No.

Definitely not.

Karine rolled her eyes, and fell back in bed again.

What else needed said?

• • •

The bitch wouldn't *give up.*

By the end of the day, Sylvia was back with a phone she tried to hand over to Karine. Except she still hadn't moved from her spot on the bed, and even the buzz of her husband's voice on the other end of the phone couldn't entice her.

"Roman would really like to speak to you," she whispered to Karine.

Oh, did he?

All the curtains in the room were closed, leaving Karine cloaked in darkness. Just the way she always liked it. Except when they were in the hotel suite—she'd loved the way the sunshine poured in through the glass walls, spilling over her body in the mornings.

Karine rejoiced in daylight then, but it didn't last long.

ᴛʜᴇMARRIAGE

"She's fine—surface-wise, I mean. She just hasn't eaten since she got here, and she's refusing to speak to anyone, leave her room, or engage in anything else."

Sylvia spoke with a very matter-of-fact tone into the phone. All over again, Karine could feel her cheeks burning with anger. Flushed hot and red. Once again, she was being treated like a naughty child in this place.

They'd report her bad behavior back to her husband, and what? The idea of him knowing she wouldn't eat or talk might shame her into doing it?

That was a joke.

What would Roman do about it?

He was fucking coward, too.

"Karine, please talk to him, and you'll feel better, I promise. Even if you're still mad, you will feel better in a way. He's been waiting all morning to speak with you."

While Sylvia pleaded, Karine simply wedged both her arms between her thighs, bringing her knees up in the fetal position. This wasn't a conversation. Only one person was speaking, after all.

"She isn't giving me anything—yeah, I'm sorry Mr. Avdonin," Sylvia murmured, her voice distant a bit like she had turned away.

Karine blinked at the wall. She didn't care what they thought of her. They could write as many reports as they wanted, come up with plans for therapy if it satisfied them— but she wasn't going to comply.

How far would they go when she continued to refuse? Restrain her if she got violent? Force medication down her throat?

She couldn't care less.

"He wants to know when he can call you next, if you don't want to speak with him now," Sylvia said.

Karine sighed, saying softly, "He can call when I'm dead."

That's not what the therapist told her husband.

"I suggest we call you when she's feeling more up to it, Mr. Avdonin," Sylvia whispered into the phone before ending the call.

Karine's throat felt dry, but she wasn't interested in drinking anything. That meant moving. Breathing more. *Being.* The only thing going through her mind was how close she had been to freedom, that he'd dare to let her live, and now it was all over.

And it was all Roman's fault.

"Karine, we're trying to help you here. I hope you come to that realization sooner rather than later." Sylvia's happy-go-lucky demeanor hardened a bit when she added, "For your own sake."

"Who do I have to call to wipe my ass?" Karine hissed in response.

• • •

She walked out to the Zen garden two days later.

Several more attempts had been made by Sylvia—and other members of staff—to try and bring Karine out of her shell. None of it worked, and she only did what she wanted when she wanted to do it. She refused all contact and conversation, too stubborn to give everyone else what they wanted when she didn't have anything at all.

Apparently, Roman had called several times since that first phone call. She'd refused to speak to him, too.

At the garden, she stood over a small pond, watching the colorful fish swimming around. The scaly bastards had the right idea. Short life span. Their only purpose in life was to feed, reproduce, and then die. A simpler cycle.

There wasn't emotion involved.

Pain was primal.

"Drink this."

Karine sighed at the new voice behind her. It was Sylvia. *Surprise.*

Not.

She was the only one who continued to make normal conversation with her at this point. Everyone else had given up and were trying to either force her, threaten her, or bribe her into submission. To no avail.

ᴛʜᴇMARRIAGE

Karine looked at the cup the woman passed to her hand, and rolled her eyes. "Probably not—who knows what you've put in there?"

"It's just chamomile tea, don't worry. We don't believe in drugging our residents without explaining we're doing it here. Besides, we've been given a history of your past experiences by your husband. Although, he's admitted he may not have the full picture himself. Anyway, the point is, we're not going to play around with drugs. You've been told you won't be forced into anything, and you won't."

"Except talking, apparently."

And living.

Karine continued staring at the fish. Her stomach rumbled, and she worried Sylvia would hear. She'd eaten nothing but some dry toast and crackers since her arrival with water to wash it down and keep her stomach from eating itself. It was one thing to be hungry, but it was another to feel like she couldn't actually eat. She was sure if she put anything of substance into her stomach, she'd throw up.

Even the toast and crackers were a lot.

Too much, really.

Karine refused to speak, staring down at her reflection in the mug of tea. She knew what these people wanted from her—the same thing her father had demanded of her every single of her life.

To obey.

Once Katina died, he couldn't bear to look at Karine's face anymore. It had only added to the insecurity she already felt whenever she stared into a mirror. She wondered if he wished their places were reversed. If the supposedly unknown murderer had killed Karine instead of his beloved older daughter.

Most of the time Karine wished for exactly that, too.

Katina was the one who deserved to live a full life and didn't, while Karine knew she wasn't capable of having one in the first place. The universe seemed determined to prove it, too.

"This will help calm you, it might even increase your appetite," Sylvia continued.

Karine felt herself snapping.

Every last nerve burned.

She didn't want Sylvia to be nice to her.

She didn't want sympathy or pity.

She just wanted to be left alone.

Before she could control her actions, she threw the mug of chamomile tea to the ground. It crashed, smashing into pieces and spilling over the cobblestones, startling Karine.

She hadn't meant to do that.

But *God*, she'd wanted to.

"I'm sorry. I'm sorry," she cried.

Sylvia looked upset, coming towards Karine with open arms like she might hug her.

Karine was already backing away.

"Look what you made me do—just leave me alone! Why won't you leave me alone?"

She cried the whole way back to her room, and slammed the door behind her when she was finally alone again.

Funny.

Karine thought she'd run out of tears.

SEVEN

Roman could barely fucking stand it—returning to New York City as a married man, but *alone*.

Leaving Karine at the new facility, seeing the pain and anger in her face—when she refused to even look at him—it broke him. He'd known the second he walked out of there that it was the wrong choice. It was also the only one he had, and it was already too late. What was done was done.

He had no one to blame.

This was all on Roman.

That's what made it worse.

Marky met him at the airport with a car, and Roman's hand shook like a junkie's would when he lit his cigarette. He'd needed to stay a couple extra days in Vegas just to finalize a few minor details that would keep Karine safe, and erase any of his footprints that he might have left behind that could lead to her, but then he was gone.

And *broken*.

"You all right, man?" Marky asked, taking the airport's exit ramp without a glance over his shoulder as he merged. Someone behind them blew their horn, but his friend only laughed and hit the gas harder.

Roman pasted himself to the passenger side door, glaring out the window at the familiar streets that didn't quite feel like home. He'd never been so unhappy to see New York. "No. I feel like someone's broken every bone in my body. I don't think I've physically hurt this much before."

He felt hungover, and exhausted, even though he hadn't touched a drink in more than twenty-four hours. There wasn't a drug in his system to do the deed, either. Shame, really, because getting high or drunk might have made this slightly more bearable.

Roman was desperate for numbness. That was the terrifying truth. He craved that blissed, unfeeling place he had spent most of his teenage and adult life more than he ever had since he put that shit down.

Marky glanced at him from the driver's side, taking in the way Roman had awkwardly slumped against the door.

"Come on, man, you did what you had to do. There was no other way," Marky tried.

Roman scoffed.

No.

That just wasn't true.

"I can think of a hundred things I could have done differently. For starters, I shouldn't have left Karine there. I should have just taken her out of the country like I wanted to at first."

But they'd needed a little more time for a decent passport forgery that would pass in some of the world's largest international airports. He just couldn't make it work, not without risking getting flagged somewhere overseas— because they sure as shit wouldn't have stayed on this continent.

Marky shook his head. "And what, leave your father here—your *ma?* I mean, fuck, Demyan will handle business regardless, but that doesn't mean it'll end well."

Roman didn't reply.

^{THE}MARRIAGE

His friend didn't really need him to.

"That's not gonna happen, Roman. You wouldn't be able to stay away from Brighton Beach if there's a war happening anywhere near it. You know what your duties to your family are."

"Karine is fucking family now, too," Roman snapped back.

He didn't mean to be a prick.

Shit was just … *bad*.

Everything was bad for Roman right then—like his entire world had somehow flipped over on its top and no matter what he did, he couldn't feel right. Everything was wrong. Bad all over.

Marky clutched the steering wheel hard. Maybe he'd already run out of things to say, or the sight of Roman was enough to tell the man he wasn't going to get anywhere.

"What have I done."

He wasn't actually looking for an answer.

It wasn't a question.

He already knew what he'd done.

Roman rubbed a hand over his face, feeling his fingers tremble again; his nerves were totally fucking shot.

It was impossible to ignore the what ifs constantly dancing around in his mind. What if Karine never spoke to him again? What happened if she became unmanageable at the facility in Vegas, and he wasn't there to help her?

"You've done what you needed to do. You're the only one who has done anything for that girl. You took her out of Chicago. You rescued her from a marriage to that motherfucker. You're keeping her safe. You have literally given her a life, man."

Roman had his face covered with his hand, and he finally took it away so he could look at his friend. A cigarette had burnt down quickly between his fingers, but he'd forgotten about smoking it.

"Do you think it looks that way from her perspective—behind those walls? So what if I showed her what life looks like, I also took it away."

He sank into the seat and closed his eyes.

Only her beautiful face floated up.

73

She would be the only thing on his mind.

• • •

The person he didn't think would be waiting for him the moment he walked into his parent's home was Masha.

She stood at the front doors with her arms by her side, her eyes piercingly dark and sharp on him. Almost like she'd been standing there for days—weeks, even. However long it took. Just waiting for him or Karine to show up.

Marky had dropped him off and drove away. Roman dragged his feet all the way across the driveway and up the steps to the entrance of his parents' house.

"Ma brought you back from Vermont, then?" he asked.

Not that he'd had any expectations on the topic—Masha had served a purpose at first with him and Karine, but the second she became his wife ... well, it was all on Roman. He'd never given Masha, or what to do with her, a second thought.

Masha said nothing for several moments, just stared before she let out a heavy exhale. He couldn't remember the last time he had seen her standing this straight. Shoulders high, back like a rod. The woman wanted something, and guessing by the way she stared at him, she'd found the man with the answers.

Great.

"Where is she? What have you done with her?" she hissed.

Roman had already slipped his wedding ring off. He wanted to be in control of the narrative, of what people knew or didn't, and decided he would tell those who needed to know about the marriage. He hadn't yet decided if Masha was going to be one of those people.

Nor would he apologize for it.

"All you need to know right now is that she is safe, and I would never hurt her."

A cry, one a stray cat might make cold and alone in a dank alley, escaped her lips. He almost reached for her—to steady her.

However, Masha didn't need his help, and he knew it. She was capable of looking after herself. She had spent all her life striving to keep herself alive, and see the next day. The woman didn't need him offering her any kind of comfort.

"I don't know anything," Masha practically spat at him. "All I know is you manipulated her and took her away from that place. She was happy at the lodge. Safe there. She liked the people. She was getting better."

Masha's voice became sharper with every word that left her mouth, to the point Roman found himself wincing as her voice echoed in the entry hall.

Roman clenched his hands into fists. He was ready to punch the wall again, but his knuckles still hurt from the first round in Vegas. He hadn't done anything to help his hand recover, even ignoring the one swollen knuckle that was probably broken. Instead, he just left it to heal as he usually did with all his physical injuries.

Nothing new.

"You don't know everything, Masha. She was safe there, yes, but she wouldn't have been for very long. Nothing is forever—not right now, anyway."

"There is nothing you can tell me that will shock me."

"I'm sure your life has been difficult, but I don't have the fucking time to exchange stories."

"I'm not looking for a *story*." Masha's eyes grew harder. She wasn't pleading. Neither did she sound subservient anymore. She glared openly at him, letting him see exactly how she felt about what he'd done. Even though she didn't know the full details, Roman still felt the shame as if she did.

"I need to know where she is. I need to be with her," she added.

Roman weaved a hand through his hair, muttering, "You need to drop it, Masha, because it's not going to happen. You're not going to see Karine until I've decided it's safe to do so."

"Until *you*—"

"Yes, *me*," he snapped back fast, tired of arguing with a woman who he owed nothing to. "I make the calls here."

He wasn't sure how certain he sounded because he hadn't even been able to convince himself yet of it. How was he going to stay away from Karine?

Masha's mouth parted in surprise, the facts of the matter finally beginning to sink in for her. Several times, she made attempts to say something, but she couldn't form whatever words she wanted.

Roman lost his patience.

Fast.

"Excuse me," he said, moving to step past her in the entry. "I need to speak to my father. You can just ... chill."

"You're going to pay for this."

She hurled the words at him when he walked past. It made Roman stop in his tracks and turn to her again.

"What did you just fucking say to me?"

He'd given Masha chance after chance to back off—to recognize that yes, she was given more freedom in her place, but her *place* was a privilege here—but it seemed like she was only growing more bold with time.

"You *will*. You'll pay for doing this. For keeping us apart." Masha trembled as she spoke. He could see it wasn't an easy feat for her to take a stand like she was, but he was losing all sympathy considering the circumstances.

Many, she didn't even know.

"And you'll be kicked out on your ass if you want to keep walking this fucking line with me," he snarled at her, adding darkly, "I can make you disappear if I want to. Don't forget it."

Just to be clear.

Because apparently, it had to be.

Masha blinked in shock. What did she expect? He'd tried to be friendly with her. He didn't want to handle her the way she had been treated by the Yazovs.

She had nothing more to say to that. He had put her firmly back in her place. For now, it was good enough.

Roman strode beyond the entry, deeper into the house with a nagging feeling that he would have to do something about Masha soon. Before she became a real problem for him.

ᴛʜᴇMARRIAGE

He just didn't know what.

• • •

He wasn't expecting his mother to be in his father's office with Demyan.

Two bulls led him inside, and shut the door behind them. Demyan and Claire were sat across from each other at the big oak desk. Each had a glass of vodka on ice in their hands.

They turned to look at their son. While Claire was in the room, Demyan paid her the respect of not filling it with cigar smoke. It was the only time Roman remembered his father not smoking in the space. It didn't stop the smell from lingering on the walls, though.

"Roman!" Claire jumped off her chair and came over to give him a hug. He let her engulf him in an embrace that felt like home. For a moment, anyway. "We were so worried. Why would you do that—we didn't know where you were, or what you were doing, why?"

She stroked her hands over his face affectionately, tucking the longer strands of his dark hair behind his ears. It reminded him that he needed a damn haircut because his distractions lately had caused him to put it aside. Roman pulled away from her, still fuming from his latest interaction with Masha and not wanting to show it to his ma.

She didn't deserve that.

It wasn't on her.

"I'm fine," he assured. "Everything's fine."

"Where is she? Where's Karine?" Claire asked, looking over his shoulder in the hopes that she'd somehow missed Karine behind him.

Fuck.

Maybe he should have explained before just showing up on them. It might have made this easier, but honestly, he doubted it.

"She's not here, Ma. You had to have known I wouldn't bring her back here. It's not safe."

Claire stepped away, her knowing gaze looking him up and down before finally asking, "So, where is she? Where did you take her?"

"Somewhere she can be safe, and can get the help she needs," he replied.

When Roman met his father's eyes he was unsure of his reaction. Demyan seemed calm. He always seemed fucking calm—that was the damn problem. He wasn't able to gauge shit from Demyan when he needed to the most.

Why couldn't *he* be like that, too?

"Getting help where? What are you talking about?"

His mother's cluelessness about the overall situation pleased Roman. It meant his father hadn't given anything away regarding Karine's new location. The less people who knew, the better.

Loose lips sank ships.

Every fucking time.

Even if it was his ma.

Demyan was the only person who had some idea—a few details because Roman couldn't make it all work on his own—but not the full picture.

"Claire, sit down, let him explain. He's not going to give you any information he doesn't want to share. Clearly, he's gone to great lengths to keep a lot of it hidden from the world. For good reason, I promise."

Demyan's voice was firm, and while Claire was usually the one who had the upper hand in their relationship, his father also worshipped the ground his wife walked on. However, it only took a tone of voice for his father's position in the bratva—in their *family*—to be clear. While they were in his office, his mother would listen to his command.

So, she took her chair again—while still throwing darts at Roman with her eyes, and saying nothing all the same.

"She is in a place where she can get real help with her treatment. More help than Michelle could offer at the lodge by herself. But she's also safe where she is, and that's what she needed more than anything else right now."

Claire shook her head like she didn't understand, but she didn't ask any questions. That would be a defiance of her husband's orders, though he could see how his mother struggled to keep her emotions and questions under control.

Demyan cleared his throat, and nodded when Claire glanced his way. She seemed to take that as permission to ask those questions her son had seen in her eyes.

"So this place where you took her, she went in willingly? She knows it's a place where she'll get help—where she's safe?"

Roman shoved his fisted hands into the pockets of his pants. He wasn't sure how to even begin to answer that question. "Karine is not always in a position to make her own decisions. I'm sure we can agree on that."

His mother didn't like that.

At all.

"What does that mean?"

"Ma—"

"You didn't answer what I asked. You talked around it. Are you telling me—or not—that she didn't want to go in there?" Claire demanded, her gaze fiery.

Roman looked his mother's way knowing his frustration with everyone and everything was undoubtedly written all over his face. He couldn't be bothered to hide it anymore. Karine as a topic of conversation with his parents was last on his list at the moment. More important shit waited at the top.

What were they going to do about Dima and Leonid? What about the fact that Roman was almost killed by one of the bastards?

Karine was *fine*.

Or rather ... safe.

It was time to handle business.

"No, I wouldn't say she was particularly excited about it, but it had to be done," Roman settled on saying to his mother. "She couldn't stay at the lodge anymore—hell, look how close Dima came up on me. She couldn't live *here*. Where else was she supposed to go? Where was I supposed to take her?"

"Well—"

"I am the only one who is fucking responsible for her. I made a choice, that's all. I know where she is, I know she's okay … and I know they can't get her there if they don't know she's there in the first place. That's all that matters to me."

He wouldn't admit his feelings for Karine. Not openly to his parents—except he didn't really have to anymore. They knew what this meant.

Claire's nostrils flared, a sure sign of her disapproval. She didn't have an answer to his question, though.

He had thought about his actions long and hard already—agonized over his final choice in the short days and hours leading up to her admittance to the Twin Rivers facility in Vegas. If there was any other option for Karine, he would have taken it.

This was it.

At least she was safe.

Roman had to keep telling himself that.

"I hope you've explained it to her, and that she understands your point of view here because … Roman, she was making such good progress. She trusted you."

His nerves were already pulled taut.

Ready to snap.

Roman just needed a reason.

"I don't need to fucking listen to this," he barked at his mother. "I can't do everything right—I can only get it done, Ma."

"Don't you push it," Demyan growled from behind his desk, a single finger pointed like a gun at his son.

It was a warning Roman knew he couldn't take lightly. Rubbing his temples with his fingers, he tried to soothe the throbbing ache at the back of his skull.

No such luck.

"What happened to your hand?"

His mother's horrified question had Roman rolling his eyes and waving the concern off when he replied, "My hand is fine. Or it will be. I'm not sure about the rest of me."

The silence in the room echoed. Maybe they didn't know what to say, but he wished somebody would figure it out. He was fucked. In every way possible.

"I married her," he said.

ᴛʜᴇMARRIAGE

He had to tell them; planned to, actually. He didn't mean for the words to just slip out like they did, though.

"You ..." Claire started to say, trailing off as her gaze darted from him, and then back over her shoulder to her husband.

Roman filled in the blanks for her, saying, "We got married six days ago. Now she's officially *mine*. Dima can't claim any right over a married woman."

Claire covered her mouth with both hands, her gaze widening. He couldn't tell if she was still horrified, or overjoyed.

"But he can kill her for it," Demyan murmured, drawing his son's gaze to his.

Roman didn't reply.

"Well, son, I suppose now you need to do whatever you have to do to keep your woman safe," his father advised.

He was trying.

Wasn't he?

• • •

Roman called Twin Rivers—again—as he took the stairs down to the entry of his parents' home. The woman who answered the call said she would try and get a hold of Sylvia, who was Karine's primary counsellor, and there he stood on the stairs, waiting like an idiot on hold with no promise of anything.

He'd been calling the facility almost hourly. They knew him well by now, expecting his calls to the point where a couple ladies actually greeted him by his first name, and they probably also knew he wouldn't give up until he'd spoken to his wife.

His meeting with his parents hadn't gone according to plan, either. There was no chance to discuss anything work-related with his father while his mother remained in the room. They hadn't made any plans.

The only thing on everyone's mind seemed to be Karine, and the decision Roman had taken on her behalf. Like it wasn't already done—it *was*.

It was clear he wasn't the only one putting the weight of blame on his shoulders.

Marky was the only one who didn't want to burn him at the stake for the choice, apparently.

"Hello, Mr. Avdonin," a familiar voice said through the phone. "Sylvia here. I just went in to check on your wife, and she doesn't want to talk."

Right.

The same answer he'd been getting.

"To me, you mean?" he growled into the phone.

"To anyone. She's been quite hostile towards us pretty much since you left the facility."

"So, she's refusing treatment?"

"We haven't even broached that subject yet, Mr. Avdonin," Sylvia replied with a sigh.

Roman flattened a palm to his face, seeing white dots floating in front of his eyes as the anger bubbled beneath his surface.

Maybe this was how Karine felt, too. Like she wasn't in control of anything. If she wanted to give him a taste of what she experienced on a daily basis, then she had succeeded.

"I just want to speak to my wife, okay? Can you get her to do that? Fuck the treatment. Fuck the program. I just need to hear her voice."

It took the woman on the other end of the call a minute to respond, and when she did, it wasn't at all what Roman wanted to hear. "I can't make any promises. This entire thing has been traumatic for her in a way I'm not sure you've truly realized … It's on her, now. Some people need a lot of time, and let's hope she is just one of them. Hopefully, she'll come around."

He also heard what she didn't say.

Or didn't want to say, rather.

You made your bed—lie in it.

Roman ended the call.

He didn't want to listen to any more.

As he headed out of his parents' house, he texted Marky to meet him at Poe's.

It was code that Marky would recognize.

ᴛʜᴇMARRIAGE

Everything was just too much, and Roman swore he was starting to fall apart at the seams. There was only one thing he could do to get himself under some semblance of control, even if it would leave him numb.

He just needed to feel alive.

If only for a second.

Even though he was the one who'd admitted Karine into a facility, it was as though she had been the one who left him for dead. He didn't even think she knew it.

How could she?

EIGHT

Marky was late, and by the time he got to Poe's—well, the deed was done. Roman was already sniffing hard, and rubbing his nose with the back of his hand.

"What the fuck did you do, man?" Marky asked, rushing to where Roman stood at the mouth of the alley beside the dive bar known only as Poe's to the men who liked to frequent the place.

His friend didn't bother to lean against the wall like he was. With a cigarette burning to dust between his fingers, he couldn't actually remember whether or not he'd taken a drag off it before it was practically gone.

"Nothing. I didn't do anything to help her," Roman replied.

That wasn't what Marky asked, but it was the only thing on Roman's mind. The entire reason why he was standing there sniffing what coke remained in his nose straight up to his fucking brain. Too bad he'd never been able to take enough to end it all.

^{THE}MARRIAGE

Somehow, he'd never found a threshold.

"Fuck that. And I want to know what you're doing here, Roman. This is the last place in the city you should be—what are you *doing?*"

Roman threw the spent cigarette butt to the ground, and grabbed his friend by the shoulders. "That's what everyone seems to think. Including my parents. They think I abandoned her. I married her, for fuck's sake."

"Roman, look at me," Marky snapped, shoving out of his friend's hold.

"I am looking at you, man. I'm telling you exactly what's going on. I married a girl, and then abandoned her. I should be shot in the fucking face."

At that point, despite the somber tone of his voice, Roman broke into a loud cackling laugh when he made a gun with his fingers, pointed it at his head, and pretended to pull the trigger.

Unsurprisingly, Marky didn't find it funny. His suspicious gaze swept the street to see if anyone was watching them. No one was.

Roman pulled a pack of cigarettes out of his jacket and lit another smoke. The ache in his chest said he didn't need another one, but fuck it.

He was already dead.

One more wouldn't hurt.

"Yeah, yeah, okay, I heard you," Marky said, shaking his head. "I'm not going to stand here and give you a fucking speech right now, but you don't need me to, either. You know what you're here for, and I can see it all over your face. Your eyes get black like coal when you're high on coke, Rome, do you even realize that?"

Roman blinked, licking his lips and smirking a bit. "Do they?"

The coke made his mirth insatiable. Things that weren't at all funny became one long joke to him. He couldn't stop the urge to see everything as *good*. Because it was better when he was like this.

Even if nothing was good at all.

His relationship with Karine, his life, all of it was falling apart and there wasn't anything he could do about it.

Marky groaned as he put his back to the wall, standing beside Roman. "You've been clean for months, man. You were so fucking close."

The sky was the brightest of blues.

"It doesn't even matter," Roman said quietly.

"Nah, it does. You know it does."

"Yeah, well—"

"And you're a married man, now. You have a chick who cares about you. What are you doing getting fucked up, huh? How's that gonna look?"

"She won't even talk to me on the phone. She fucking hates me." Roman pushed away from Marky and the wall, throwing that cigarette to the ground, too. He really didn't need it, and he'd lost the urge for nicotine, really.

His friend took small steps, keeping his distance but still following behind. Marky knew better than to think he could get Roman to actually do what he wanted.

That's not how any of this worked.

"Where are you going?" Marky asked

Roman shrugged, throwing his hands wide. "It's over. It's fucking over, man. I thought I could save her, but I can't."

Or was he talking about himself?

Hell.

Even he didn't know.

• • •

It felt like an entire day had passed when Roman woke up next. He couldn't remember anything from the previous night, but he woke up in the same jeans and button-down shirt that he'd been wearing the night before.

Alone.

The last thing he was able to bring to mind was going to the place where he knew they'd hand a baggy over to him with no questions asked. Just the sight of his face alone would guarantee him his drug of choice.

He was still Little Odessa's Devil, after all.

ᴛʜᴇMARRIAGE

Spoiled beyond rotten.

Unquestioned, and unchallenged.

After that, everything was a haze.

Did Marky show up? Yeah, he did remember *that*. Everything after, though? Roman couldn't be sure.

Did they drive around for hours?

Did he steal a car?

Who the fuck knew.

Roman couldn't remember anything.

Somehow, he'd ended up in his own bed in his loft. The same one the cops had raided in Odessa before he'd been sent to Chicago. *Fuck*, he missed that place like nobody knew.

For that, he was grateful to Marky. This was exactly the reason why he'd texted his friend. Even if the prick did feel some kind of way about Roman's drug use, he'd still watch his back no matter what.

Sitting up in bed, Roman scrubbed a hand over his face. He hadn't trimmed his beard in days, leaving his face dry and rough under his touch. In fact, he couldn't even remember the last time he took a shower or changed out of these clothes.

Had he put them on yesterday?

Or the day before?

They reeked of alcohol and cigarettes either way, and he couldn't ignore the disgust he felt at himself as he tried to pretend like the room wasn't spinning in his line of vision.

Jesus Christ.

Roman didn't bother to move at that point. He needed several minutes before he could get out of bed, and face the damn day.

It was what it was.

In the shower—he stood under a steady, beating stream of hot water. It stung his skin, pinking it from the heat, just the way he liked it. When he placed his hands on the cold tiles, his knuckles hurt, reminding him that unfortunately …

Well, he was still very much alive.

You can fix that, you know. It doesn't matter when you're high. Nothing matters when you're high, Roman.

Just like that, his monster was back. Gnawing on his shoulder, clawing at the back of his brain. He thought about the sweet relief a pill would bring—one that would take away the pain, and keep the high going. By tonight, he could take a little something else to keep him from falling asleep if he didn't want to dream.

It would be *easy*.

A little something—anything—to keep his mind off the fact that he still hadn't spoken to Karine.

Once out of the shower, he changed into fresh clothes, but didn't bother to take the time to trim his beard or even wrap his swollen hand that ached even more when he was out of the heat.

Roman's mind was on one thing—making it all go away.

But the smell coffee halted those plans, for the moment, and he stepped out of his room, and peered down the hall. Through the glass wall that made up the loft of the garage, he could see Marky down below.

"You want some coffee?" he called up when he noticed Roman descending the stairs.

"What time is it?"

"Too late to wish you good morning," Marky replied.

At least, his friend was less grumpy than he had been the previous night.

"I'm heading out, actually," Roman declared, still doing up the buttons on his shirt.

"To where?"

"You my warden or something now?"

Marky wouldn't approve of the pills he planned to go find, but at the same time, Roman didn't feel like he owed the man shit. He owed no one nothing.

Except Karine.

"I need you to stay on track," Marky said. "For Karine's sake. You remember? Your wife who is currently receiving treatment for her mental health condition. A choice *you* made for her, Roman."

Hearing her name was like a punch in the gut.

He didn't need the reminder.

God.

ᴛʜᴇMARRIAGE

"She doesn't want to talk to me," he said under his breath, leaning against the railing at the bottom of the stairs.

"Give her time."

"She fucking hates me. What part of that do you not understand?"

"The part where you seem to forget you're not a child, I guess. You don't get to just act out because you're mad or hurt. She needs help. *You don't.* You have the ability to help yourself. So just fucking do that, man."

Marky stood steady and calm as he delivered those words—a final blow—to Roman. He wouldn't be able to physically stop him from going out and doing whatever the fuck he wanted if it came down to it, but he also didn't need to.

He'd called Roman out—that was more than enough.

Rightfully so, too.

It pissed him off like nothing else, but Marky made damn good points. Roman glared at his friend for a full minute before he walked over to the coffee machine, and poured himself a cup.

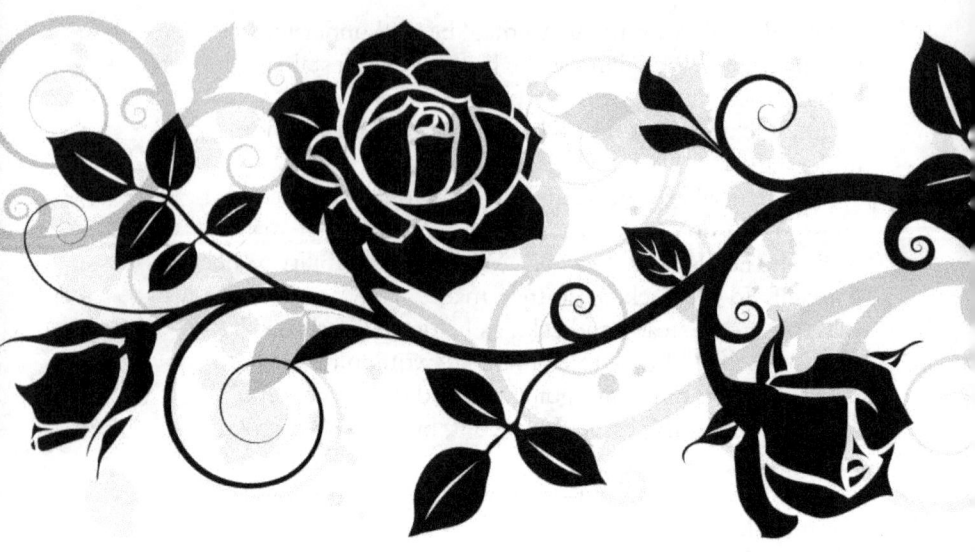

NINE

Demyan found himself lost in his thoughts and unwilling to open his eyes after waking from a night of restless, non-existent sleep because it meant a new day. Of uncertainties, of exhaustion ... *of worry.*

He wasn't *that* man—decades of position and power had allowed him an arrogance a man like him needed to be who he was. So, when he found himself worrying, well, it was hard to swallow.

There was too much to do.

Who *could* sleep?

With Dima and his men making their presence known in New York, Demyan moved to protect his assets and keep the business running smoothly first. He hadn't spoken to Leonid yet, the man who was supposed to have taken over as the new Chicago boss, despite Demyan's many efforts to reach out.

The man's son, on the other hand, was apparently freely raging around New York—and God knew where else—like a maniac, without reprise from his father. None of this shit would have happened with Maxim as the boss of his organization.

If their two families ever encountered a problem in the past, they would have met up in person and talked it out. That came with mutual respect, but Demyan supposed they had all lost that façade a long time ago.

Maximum outcome with minimum casualty—that was how he liked to run the show, but with a flock of headless fucks running around doing whatever they wanted ... Demyan doubted this would end well.

When did it ever?

"Are you awake?"

He heard his wife's soft voice beside him and finally opened his eyes. Other than his children, Claire was the only person in the world he'd start his day for when he didn't particularly care to.

The effects of exhaustion in his limbs from only a few hours of sleep made them heavy and needing stretched. When he did, eyeing his wife standing beside their bed, the rushing blood made him lightheaded. It wasn't just his body that was tired, but his mind, too.

Mental and physical.

He couldn't fix one without fucking with the other.

"I am now," he murmured to Claire.

"Sorry, I made you some French toast and didn't want it to go cold. I wasn't sure how long you'd want to sleep."

Demyan sat up in bed, letting the soft cream-colored sheets fall down his bare chest while his wife placed a tray on the bed. With a gigantic mug of coffee in her hands, she slipped in beside him under the covers.

All it took was her side-long look tossed his way, and Demyan could tell she had something on her mind. Nearly three decades of marriage with this woman, relearning what it meant to fall in love time and time again, gave him that privilege.

He had a pretty good idea what had his wife quiet, and yearning to talk.

"You're thinking about the girl," he said.

Demyan picked up a triangular piece of French toast, and inhaled the scent of vanilla and cinnamon sugar. His mouth watered. Nobody cooked like his wife.

"Our daughter-in-law, you mean," Claire corrected, arching a brow.

At least, she was amused.

"I knew he was taken with her, but I didn't realize he would take it so far that he'd marry her," he said.

Claire sighed, and sipped her coffee. "She's a sweet girl who has endured a lot. If you ask me, she makes a nice addition to the family."

"You like her."

That's what she should just say.

His wife only lifted one shoulder in reply to that, and then said, "More importantly, our son seems to love her."

At one dark point in his life, Demyan would have said love wasn't worth the pain that sometimes came with it. But he'd come far enough—or rather, lived long enough—that his scars had been numbed over the years.

And his wife helped.

With the *love* deal.

"She's also a lot of work," Demyan replied, then groaned around a bite of French toast that was worth waking up for. After chewing, because he knew damn better than to talk with his mouth full around Claire, he added, "He'll be lucky to come out of this alive. Sometimes, I think you overlook what scares you to see what pleases you, sweetheart. You know that's going to make reality harder to handle when it catches up, huh?"

The only unfortunate part of having tied himself to this woman for life was the fact that sometimes, Demyan was the only one who told her the harsh truth. Everyone else was too scared too—worried they might upset the one woman he'd likely kill for.

So, the task was always left to him.

It was what it was.

Demyan loved her enough to do it.

Claire said nothing, chewing on her bottom lip while she stared out of the window in their room. Letting him eat his breakfast in peace, Demyan was nearly halfway through his plate when she spoke again.

"I am proud of him, Demyan."

He didn't reply.

She shrugged, adding only, "I didn't know if he was truly capable of it—but he can stand up for what and who he believes in, as long as it's what he wants. That's better than nothing, Demyan. At least he stands for *something*. And you're right. Karine is a lot of work, but it looks like he's the only one who makes her happy, so who are we, or anyone, to take it away?"

* * *

"He wants a meeting," Pavel said.

Demyan, shuffling through the pages of the documents relating to a shipment of weapons he had to proverbially sign off on, glanced up at the sound of his spy in the doorway. "Who?"

He hadn't been paying attention.

Work had to keep moving, too.

When Pavel started shuffling his feet from one to the other—he knew it, then. Demyan expected uncomfortable news. Older than dirt, Pavel had once been an enforcer for Demyan's father but eventually worked his way into the highest ranks to become his boss's best spy. Collecting money, or keeping an eye on all the men in the organization and reporting back if something needed handled. He knew the man well, and his mannerisms.

The feet shuffle meant bad news.

"Dima. He says he wants face time."

Demyan cocked a brow—all this time Pavel had been trying to get a word through to Leonid in Chicago, or *someone* that would get New York a direct line to the boss, and *Dima* was the one who finally answered?

"Fucking Dima? What do I want with a pup?"

His youth was the only excuse Demyan could really give the prick, and feel like it might be justified. No man with any age or sense in this business cared to go on like Dima apparently did. Not unless there wasn't another option.

There was *almost always* another option.

Demyan hated to think about it, but even killing Roman when he had the chance could have ended all of this. What reason would New York have had to keep the girl if the reason for her being there in the first place was dead?

But he hadn't killed Roman.

And his warning rang loudly.

Was the asshole just having *fun*?

Pavel eventually shrugged at Demyan's lingering, questioning stare.

"Where's Leonid?"

"Apparently he's not in New York," Pavel said. "Nothing's showing up anywhere—any associates of his in the state say he's not been in contact."

"Then, I'll wait until he gets here," Demyan replied, bored, dropping the papers down with a swoosh on his desk. "I'm not sitting down with Dima without his father."

"Kinda seems like it's not just associates *here*, boss. We don't know where he is. Nobody's seen him recently—even people in Chicago are whispering about it."

That made Demyan pause.

"How recently? When was the last time anyone outside the immediate circle saw him?"

It wasn't Pavel's fault, but Demyan had never been known for his patience, and it was starting to show.

Shoot the messenger.

There was some truth to the adage, he thought, as Pavel eyed him warily.

"What is it?"

"Well, people say different things but—"

"Pavel, I'm fucking serious. *Talk.*"

"A common theme seems to be that he hasn't been seen since the fire," Pavel replied.

Demyan sat back in his chair, spinning around slowly as he tried to think.

ᵗʰᵉMARRIAGE

Was that why Dima was doing all the work—his father had hidden away all this time, and there was no one to check the cocksucker for his behavior?

What was Leonid hiding from?

Or *who*?

Whatever he was—in their limited interactions through the years when Leonid served as Maxim's second in command—Demyan had never viewed the man as weak or afraid. Not one to cower, he was like every bratva man that enjoyed using their special brand of intimidation to their benefit.

Why did he refuse to be in New York?

Why was he afraid to show his face to anyone?

"You can tell Dima to fuck off," he finally said.

That was his final decision. It had to be, regardless of the consequences. Demyan didn't know what game these men wanted to play with him, but he'd just made one that would force their hand either way.

Pavel's jaw clenched at his boss's command, knowing what the results of that choice would likely be. Dima would retaliate.

He'd have to.

A slight like Demyan's, well, it was a personal offense—being refused a meeting with the boss.

"He wants a boss-to-boss meeting? Then the bastard better bring the boss over here first. That, or he gives me a legitimate reason why Leonid can't be here."

Demyan needed answers.

He wanted *everything* clear.

"I'll communicate your decision through the man he sent," Pavel said.

Demyan didn't have the interest to go through the paperwork anymore, and the shipment of guns heading to Russia was the least of his problems. Maybe work could wait. He wanted to get to the bottom of a different kind of business.

More importantly, he wanted to know what really happened to Maxim.

"And while you're at it," Demyan threw at Pavel's retreating back, his frustration making his voice gravelly,

"Get in touch with the two agents from the FBI. Invite them back—tell them I wanna have a chat."

• • •

Agent Packard and Agent Mahon stood with their arms crossed over their chests in silent reflection of each other. Demyan remained seated in his chair across from them.

Their hardened expressions seemed forced. Like they had a discussion before the two entered the home of the bratva boss. Perhaps about how they were going to present themselves to him, guessing by the postures?

It made him smirk.

They were still convinced they could somehow control the narrative, but Demyan knew better. The very fact these agents were willing to damn near ask how high when he said jump—or rather, *let's meet up*—told him the truth.

They were looking as hard as he was.

Maybe for the same thing.

Likely for different reasons.

"I would offer you some vodka, but I'm not sure what the FBI protocol is on the matter of drinking on the job," Demyan said, deciding to keep things light at the start.

After all, he had no beef with them. The agents, and the bureau, hadn't laid a finger on Demyan's business as of yet, so what would be the point in causing trouble?

He knew they were still in their feelings about the fact that Roman hadn't given away any information they could use— but hadn't he helped them enough? He'd given them a different and more innovative direction to look in.

That was more than another man in this life would do for a *cop*.

At best.

"Why don't we get down to business," Agent Packard began.

Once again, he was the one taking the lead here, so Demyan focused his gaze on Mahon instead when he said, "You know I don't do business with the FBI. Let me make one thing very clear to you, the only reason you're here is because I want some information from *you*."

Honesty was the best policy, right?

Mahon had to look away, glancing at his partner for direction. Demyan's suspicions were confirmed in that moment. Still green around the ears. Was he a new recruit? How many years had he been engaging criminals of Demyan's caliber?

Demyan smirked again.

"I'm sure we can help each other," Packard replied.

"It depends on what you're giving me, actually."

"What do you want, Mr. Avdonin?"

"All the information you have on Leonid. Everything you know about Maxim Yazov. Preferably, anything about the two together that I would find useful, do you understand?"

Even though Packard managed to stare at him blankly, the way Mahon shifted his arms behind his back to clasp his hands told Demyan everything he wanted to know.

The FBI had uncovered something about Maxim they hadn't shared publicly yet.

"And what are you giving us in return?" Packard asked.

Demyan leaned slightly over the table, weaving his fingers together with a bored shrug. He even shook his head, half disappointed, a bit apologetic.

"I apologize for the misunderstanding, gentlemen. I was under the impression that you understood what it means to keep an open conversation going with me. Or didn't you get the memo?"

Packard still didn't blink. "What makes you think that, Mr. Avdonin?"

Demyan stood up. The shift in the air was immediate, and he was sure the other two could feel it. With a wave toward the door, he said, "You're welcome to walk out of here today and never come back, or you could tell me what I want to know, and my door stays open. Just for a little while longer, yes? Imagine the kind of brownie points on your report card you'll get for that."

Still smiling, although he knew his tall frame was intimidating, Demyan waited his hand outstretched for the other two men to make a move. It was their call; he was willing to let them make it.

Mahon fidgeted under the pressure, looked like he was about to shit himself, while Packard managed to hold it together. It was amusing, at least.

"Why should I tell you anything when your son refused a real interview?"

"He told you everything he knew," Demyan told the older agent. "Anyway, it looks like you're ready to go. I won't take up any more of your time."

Demyan nodded to Pavel who had come to stand at the door.

Packard clocked the gesture and cleared his throat before saying, "There is something you should know."

If they were expecting Demyan to show enthusiasm—they weren't getting any. He remained silent. That was always the better choice when you already had the upper hand.

"The remains found in the fire at the Yazov mansion— they may not belong to Maxim Yazov."

Demyan dragged in a hard breath through his nose. It was all he was going to allow himself in the presence of these men.

"And maybe we can meet again, to discuss any other information we have that could help you. Or if you have anything to share with us," Packard continued, tipping his chin in a nod.

Demyan gestured at Pavel again, and this time the spy had an enforcer waiting in the hallway behind him to guide the two agents out of the house and off the property.

Good riddance.

Demyan was done with them.

• • •

He found his wife blow-drying her hair.

Demyan couldn't help but stare at Claire's reflection as she brushed thick strands of hair while simultaneously running a dryer over it with one of those large barrel brushes he thought could be better used for torture. The sight of her bent over in a silk robe had him standing back and grinning, unwilling to interrupt her just yet.

Gray had started to streak through her hair.

Her curves were softer.

Deeper lines found their way around her mouth and eyes when she smiled, and he loved knowing that so many of those happy moments had been because of him. He'd dared to love her, after all, and wives of men like him tended to suffer a great deal for it. Demyan made a special effort to make sure his wife never did.

She'd been his second chance ...

Everything good.

When she caught him standing at their bedroom door, she blushed before turning to him.

"Hey, you."

"How do you do it?" he asked, stepping into the room.

Claire turned the dryer off and tossed it to the bed with the brush before smoothing her hair with her hands. "How do I do what?"

"Get more beautiful every day."

Claire shot him a rueful smile as he came closer. "How do you still manage to make me feel like the good girl with a crush on a bad boy?"

Demyan towered over her, placing both his hands on her silky soft hair. Then, he kissed the top of his wife's head.

"You look like you've got some good news," she said.

Demyan knew she would figure it out. Claire could always reach inside his mind to find what he was thinking—his eyes were her windows to his soul.

"I don't know what I've got yet, if it's anything."

"Care to share?"

"The remains they found in the burnt down Yazov mansion—well, it isn't Maxim."

Claire pressed the tips of her fingers to her lips. "Then who was it? Where's Maxim?"

She reached for her husband's wrists, clinging to him because, no doubt, Claire knew all at once those were the same questions Demyan had. Since they met—Claire made him feel like *he* was the one with all the answers to her questions.

The truth was that she saved him.

"Leonid is missing. Nobody's seen him since the fire. Dima is in New York and demanding to see me, but he's here without his father. There has to be a good reason for that."

"Leonid is dead?" Claire asked.

Demyan remained silent because this was just a theory without actual proof.

But it was a good one.

TEN

Days went by without any difference in the way Karine woke up feeling. In unseen agony from heartbreak, but visibly numb to anyone who looked her in the face.

She'd been helplessly trapped the very moment when Roman first brought her to this place. The same thought invaded her head every morning she cracked open her eyes—that he had abandoned her.

Why hadn't he taken her with him?

What had she done to deserve this?

One morning, she woke up in the same bed, with the same sheets, and accidentally looked at her hand to see the diamond ring he had given her. The one she had picked out that day at the jewelry store with that small diamond that sat daintily on her finger but couldn't be missed all the same.

Impulsively, she smiled at the memory of that day because it was a beautiful one.

In those ignorant seconds of happiness, she had dared to think that was how the rest of their married life together would be.

He made her feel like every blushing, blissed bride should on their honeymoon, gifting her with an experience she never thought she would have, and he did it effortlessly. Like he didn't even have to think about it. He just ... *did*.

Karine had thought that they somehow just brought out the best in each other—*together*.

Ever since she could remember, she expected the worst from Dima, honestly. To be in a marriage full of hate and rage, subjugation and abuse.

But now she was married to Roman.

Even though she was trapped in this institution, that didn't change what was. Her marriage to Roman was still very much real. It didn't change that, for a moment, he had made her feel that unimaginable happiness, and she didn't think it was entirely a lie.

Not all of it ...

It couldn't be.

The ring reminded Karine of the necklace. One of the few items Sylvia and a male nurse had provided with Karine the day after her admission because, as they explained it, the chain was too delicate for her to use as a weapon. Whether against herself or otherwise. They had nearly taken her wedding ring, convinced she could use it as a sharp object to self-harm but because she didn't have a history and threatened to throw an unholy fit, she kept the ring.

For now, the therapist warned.

Right.

Karine toyed with the idea of taking the necklace out and wearing it. He'd picked it out for her. Would it help to close the emptiness in her heart, even if it didn't soothe the anger—would wearing it make this *bearable*?

Did she even want to feel closer to Roman?

There was that voice, never far from the back of her mind; familiar and vicious, reminding her every day that he had let her down—just like she said he would.

THEMARRIAGE

Katina had been so used to taking over when things got too difficult for Karine to handle that it was hard to shut out the high-pitch ring of her warnings. At least, Karine had learned to pay attention. To try and understand why she was saying what she did.

Pressing her eyes closed, Karine reminded herself the voice and person it belonged to was a part of her own thoughts.

Michelle had helped her with that—understanding the core of the disorder she had lived with daily for a decade.

Those thoughts of Michelle quickly brought with them the faces of the other women who had broken down the walls Karine hadn't even realized she'd erected around herself over the years. Claire.

Masha.

Where was Masha?

Loneliness was the worst kind of prison for Karine. A personal hell she had lived in for far too long, leaving her constantly clinging to the scraps of attention she was sometimes given. It made the deep sadness in her heart all the more cruel and painful when she thought about all the people who were taken away from her.

People he took away from you.

Karine shook her head, ignoring that invasive, sharply hissed thought. Not that it stopped that fractured part of her mind from fighting to fill her mind with *more*.

Why couldn't he leave you in Vermont, huh? You said it—you were happy. You couldn't have a life there, Karine? What does he expect you to do now? Start over?

With people she didn't know or trust, Karine finished herself.

Not fucking likely.

The urge to pull the ring off her finger and throw it as far away from her as the room would allow was strong.

Karine ignored it.

Somehow.

She wondered if it was some sort of karmic irony that now she was married to Roman, she found herself wondering if she had to escape him.

He'd done exactly what her father did, after all. What Dima would have done if she married him instead—eventually. Once he'd likely had his twisted, sick fill of her and had enough of abusing every piece of her that he could.

Roman was a different man, sure. It didn't change what this was, though. Keeping her imprisoned, without any real choice, and creating only the illusion of freedom.

How is it different?

Katina demanded her answers, slinking into Karine's thoughts to warp them to her own advantage when she had the chance, never missing the opportunity.

She hated that.

Didn't want it.

Karine could be angry all on her own—she didn't need Katina's violent emotions warping her own, too.

"Shut up!" she screamed, cupping either side of her head.

It was just unfortunate that Katina's voice had grown too loud too fast, taking over every thought and movement.

Telling her she was better off without Roman.

You need to get away. Run.

That their paths should never have converged—the universe had gotten it all wrong.

No.

"No, no … *no!*" Karine snapped. "Stop it right now!"

The thing was, well, the voice was wrong.

She couldn't stop loving Roman, even though she didn't understand him. Or entirely why he decided this was his only option for her.

He had kept her safe—a promise he hadn't broken. Didn't that mean something? Didn't that count for *anything?*

Didn't that prove it was real?

To her, yes.

For Katina … not so much.

That was the hard part.

"Karine? Are you okay?"

It was Sylvia—again; she was never too far away from Karine, it seemed. Her calm disposition only rattled slightly as her tone of voice raised an octave when she came through the door of the private room to stand just beyond the threshold. Lines creased her brow when she added quietly, "I heard you yelling. I was just next door speaking to Miss Tanny."

Oh.

Yeah.

The lady who'd apparently hoarded so many animals in her bungalow home that after an unfortunate incident with a five-foot pile of paper the old woman had been saving for forty years fell over ... Karine winced, still able to hear the women crying as she told the story from where she sat playing cards just outside of her room in the hallway the day before.

It was an unfortunate thing.

Her family decided to step in, then.

Didn't really want to keep being here, just living, after that, the woman had admitted while she'd gathered her cards before leaving. But it was the way she'd spat out the words—*just* living. As though the idea was simply unthinkable.

And that ... well, Karine did understand.

Not that she'd engaged the woman.

She didn't want to talk to anyone.

Nothing personal.

"Do you need some help?" Sylvia asked, moving towards her bed with careful, slow steps.

In her gaze, Karine could see the therapist expected rejection. For good reason because she'd offered nothing more and nothing less.

Still ...

"Maybe I do," Karine replied.

• • •

"I don't want to eat in my room today," Karine told Sylvia.

She noticed the way the woman's eyes brightened, but she kept outwardly calm.

"Of course, you don't have to. You could eat with some of the others in the dining room, or you could eat outside if you want. Wherever you'd like. There are lots of little nooks around the place you are welcome to enjoy."

With someone right at her back, she bet.

Sylvia had been helping Karine arrange her clothes in the wardrobe. Something that should have been done upon arrival, but Karine hadn't touched her bags since she got there. Just seeing the bags was enough to make her want to rage all over again.

She still couldn't get over how Roman had secretly packed all her things—even the beautiful clothes and shoes he'd bought her—at the hotel.

Without even considering asking her, he'd planned a future for Karine when her back was turned—maybe even when she lay naked and asleep beside him in their hotel room under the illusion of happiness.

It was the little details of betrayal that really got to her when she thought about it. And that was the thing ... *here*, all she could do was think about it.

The last thing she expected from the man she had agreed to marry—was oiliness. A man could be a lot of things, but she didn't want one who was slick or slimy.

"I don't think I want to eat with anybody else. I don't want to meet anyone new," she said, going back to her conversation—and plan—with the therapist.

Sylvia nodded. "Sure, you can eat outside. Do you want to look around the premises and decide where you'd like to sit by yourself?"

She had that pathetically hopeful look in her eyes. The same one Karine remembered seeing in Michelle's too in the beginning. It was how she could tell they had their fingers figuratively crossed, hopeful that perhaps she was finally coming around.

God.

To what?

All these expectations they all had for her ... it was just too much. Karine hated it.

She never should have left Masha behind. She shouldn't have agreed to Roman's plan that night he convinced her to get into a car and drive to him.

Why could she so easily walk back through every single one of her mistakes?

ᴛʜᴇMARRIAGE

Masha was the only person who truly understood her. In all the years they had spent together—she had never once tried to change who Karine was.

In fact, she'd still cared for her despite it.

"Yeah, maybe I should have a look," Karine said with a nod. "Or go for a walk."

Sylvia was pleased.

For a moment—her hands started to lift as though she might grab Karine and give her a hug, but she managed to stop herself in time.

Which was just as well.

She'd hate to start screaming today.

"Okay, yeah, that's great. I can show you around. We can go now if you want."

Karine smiled.

It was her first smile here, and it seemed to melt Sylvia's heart by the way she beamed right back at the younger woman.

She couldn't believe her luck.

Karine had news …

There was no such thing.

"Let's go," Karine said, striding over to the door.

Sylvia came over to unlock it with her keycard. Depending on who was in the room, what hours of the day it was, or what might be happening in the rest of the wing, Karine had no real control over whether she could open the damn door.

The woman was still smiling at Karine when the door did open.

When they stepped out into the hallway together, she made a run for it.

• • •

"Why did you do it, Karine?"

Sylvia tapped a pen on her notepad as she sat on a big white couch across from her.

Karine had been given a gray chaise lounge to sit on. With her legs tucked in under her and her hands wedged between her thighs, she asked, "Why did I do what?"

"Try to run away?" Sylvia's patience *now* was one of a saint, even though she'd screeched like a little girl when Karine ran.

She couldn't remember laughing so hard.

Too bad the humor was long gone.

"I don't know the answer to your question. Frankly, I don't know the answers to most of your questions."

Sylvia made a note, and Karine tried to ignore her rising frustration. Between the conversation, she had to carry outwardly, and the one she refused to have internally … focus was tough, and anger was easier.

The voice she had become so profoundly aware of recently—the one who called herself Katina—floated on the surface of her consciousness almost constantly. It was Karine's strong-willed desire to keep her alter subdued that forced Katina back, but that didn't mean she liked it.

Katina's sharp hiss told her that she didn't need to answer any of these questions. A reminder that she didn't actually need, but that didn't stop her from saying it and more. *You did right by running,* she heard Katina muttering. Apparently, the next time she was serious about escaping—well, she should have a plan in place and be prepared to take extreme measures if she wanted better results.

Karine forced the lump down forming her throat. She hated hearing Katina's voice in her head, and without the drugs she used to take to fade that voice, it was growing louder and louder. The only thing about fading the voice was Karine also inhibited her own control.

There was no way to win.

"Why don't we take it one question at a time?" Sylvia asked, lifting her shoulders under the white silk blouse she wore. Her pencil skirt was so tight that Karine wondered if that was why she'd taken a second to dart after her earlier. Or was it because of her teetering four-inch stiletto heels? She *really* hadn't expected Karine to run.

She almost felt bad.

Almost.

"You can think about your answers, and I want you to know there are no wrong ones," the woman continued.

_{THE}MARRIAGE

"You can even just tell me the first thing that pops in your head."

"What is the question?" Karine snapped.

Soaked in anger, her words made Sylvia wince. Her tone was charged by Katina's voice, and she closed her eyes.

Stop it, she said silently.

"It's okay, Karine, you don't have to suppress anything. It's okay if someone else wants to come out and speak to me," Sylvia insisted.

Was it really?

Karine's nostrils flared.

Sylvia had no idea what she was asking for. She wouldn't want to meet Katina—no one did. Katina didn't introduce herself to the world because she wanted to make friends. She came along to burn everything down.

When she opened her eyes, Sylvia was still staring at her, searching her eyes for proof of a switch.

"Is it still you, Karine?"

"Are you still alive?" she asked back in a murmur.

Sylvia's brow dipped. "I beg your pardon?"

"Yes, it's me."

"Okay, that's okay, that's very good."

"What is your question?" Karine asked, doing her best to modulate her anger.

She wasn't going to do it—no matter how much that voice told her to lash out. It wouldn't be what Roman wanted, and while he was the last person who deserved anything from her, he wasn't *here*. She didn't think letting her frustration explode would do her well, considering that.

"Why did you run when you knew you wouldn't be able to escape?" Sylvia continued.

It was a good question.

She had actually thought about it already.

There was no way she would have made it out of the facility without being tackled to the ground by security before she even hit the stone wall. And yet, the moment she was out of that door, she felt the urge to make like wind, *and go*.

For a second, that's all it was. And she'd laughed, too.

Then, it was over.

Like everything else.

"Because I wasn't running from anything or going anywhere," Karine said, meekness returning in her tone. The tears blurred her vision as she continued, whispering, "I have nowhere to go."

• • •

When Karine woke up the next morning—for the first time since her arrival at Twin Rivers—something had changed. She couldn't quite figure out what it was. Her first instinct was to check the ring on her finger. It was there, of course.

She was still married to Roman.

It wasn't all just a dream, even though it sometimes felt like it.

Before Sylvia knocked on her door, she had showered and dressed for the day already. There was even a rumble in her stomach.

She didn't remember the last time she'd been hungry—*ravenous*. Not since she left the lodge in Vermont.

"What do you want to do today, Karine?" Sylvia asked. "Hopefully something less strenuous than yesterday."

The therapist even smiled, though it was hesitant. She stood at the door to Karine's room, blocking it with her slender body.

If Karine wanted to, she could have pushed past her and run out. Undoubtedly, there were guards standing close by. Waiting for any rash decision Karine might make because she wouldn't risk another event where she might run.

"Maybe we could go on that walk we talked about yesterday."

Sylvia didn't appear as hopeful today. Who could trust Karine to make wise choices—who could trust her at all?

Karine knew all about that.

Who did she really trust anymore?

She thought she trusted Masha, but did she really?

She thought she trusted Roman, too.

"A walk sounds perfect," Sylvia agreed, "but I want you to know that we'll have some security with us."

Karine shrugged. "I'm used to that."

It took the other woman a second to absorb that admission.

"Are you?"

"Usually, yes. I'm not sure how much money this place is going to get for keeping me here, but I'm sure you've figured out already that I don't come from great people."

Good people.

"Well, I know a little. Just enough, anyway," Sylvia replied. "But it's not really about *you*. There is so much about you that I'd like to know."

"I'm not sure there's much you'll like hearing about," Karine replied.

Sylvia's smile had faded, but there was a softness in her eyes that made Karine think she might actually care.

But she was one burned, twice shy, and wouldn't be falling into that trap again.

"I don't make judgements, Karine. Sometimes hearing the worst about humanity is a part of my job, and you should know I am very good at it," Sylvia said. "If only you'd give me a chance to show you."

Karine went to the door, and Sylvia stepped aside.

Outside in the hallway, she was surprised to find there were no guards. She was certain they would follow them outside but for now, Sylvia had chosen to trust her. Or at least, extend a show of it for the moment.

She glanced back over her shoulder at the woman to find Sylvia had raised her brow, a silent question hanging between the two of them—like she was asking, *well, now what, Karine?*

"I don't know what you want from me."

"Just to talk," Sylvia said. "You *can* do that."

"I *can't*, actually. I've never been able to, mostly. I don't know if maybe I don't want to. There's so much … a lot has happened, and I—"

She couldn't make a coherent sentence. Thoughts and feelings became one big jumbled mess at just the idea of discussing her past.

Sylvia reached over to close the distance between them, touching Karine's shoulder—maybe for the first time, she couldn't honestly remember.

It was soft, though.

Light.

"Your husband believes in you. He told me all about the progress you made in a short time—he knew all you needed was a *chance*, Karine. You don't know how strong you are, but I know you can do this. Even if the way you do it is by taking it one day at a time."

Above everything, the emotional whiplash was the worst for Karine. One second she was angry at the world, the next she wanted to cry, and right then, she found herself longing for the man who'd put her here.

Irony was a bitch.

A cruel one.

The women walked down the hallway side by side, and Karine wished Roman was there with her. At the same time, a part of her was glad he wasn't.

Like spiritual warfare, she was being ripped apart. Karine didn't know how to stop it.

• • •

"Did he call today?" Karine asked Sylvia.

It had been a few days since the first time they went on that walk together—a step in the right direction, Sylvia said after they had headed back to Karine's room.

Karine didn't think she would be admitting as much, but she was actually beginning to feel like she could trust Sylvia. She wasn't at the same place of trust she'd reached with Michelle or Claire, but maybe she could get there. At some point in the future, if she was still stuck here staring at the same four walls.

So to speak.

What option did she have?

"No, we haven't heard from him today," Sylvia replied.

Sitting in the gardens next to the small fish ponds, Karine had a paper bag with a sandwich and a banana for her lunch.

ᴛʜᴇMARRIAGE

Sylvia was eating a protein bar beside her on the bench. She could have opted for something tastier—crepes had been on the brunch menu—but she only wanted easy today.

Karine had woken up that morning with the sudden urge to hear Roman's voice. It was the first thing she asked when she laid eyes on Sylvia, and it hadn't been far from her mind since.

However, he didn't call.

When she asked Sylvia to find out *why*—she was told that he hadn't called in over four days. He'd called repeatedly, several times an hour, for days. Then stopped without warning.

Because he'd given up—was he angry?

She didn't know.

It broke her heart.

She couldn't blame him for the silence—mostly. It wasn't his fault. Karine didn't feel like she deserved any better than that.

"I'm sure he'll call soon. Your husband sounds like a busy man," Sylvia continued.

Karine blinked away the hot sting of tears in the back of her eyelids. She could picture him standing right there in front of her, if she leaned over and stretched her hand out she was sure she'd be able to touch him.

Her imagination had always been vivid.

Far too real.

That was part of the problem.

"Yeah, that's probably it," Karine replied, shrugging as her grip tightened on the paper bag. "He's busy—he's got a lot of things to deal with."

"There you go. I'm sure he'll call soon."

Karine shook her head. "Or he's too busy to deal with me. I'm a nuisance to him, I think. I keep fighting him, I'm always in the way. I don't even know why he married me."

Sylvia ate the last piece of her protein bar, then stuffed the wrapper in her jacket pocket. She gave Karine a look from the side as she said, "We talked about this already, didn't we?" You shouldn't doubt the positive things that happen to you because they happen for a good reason. Do you consider your husband to be a foolish man?"

She thought about that.

"Not usually."

Sylvia grin. "All men have their moments. Do you consider him to be a liar?"

"He lied to get me here."

"And that's what hurts the worst."

"Shouldn't it?" Karine asked.

Syliva hummed under her breath. "You know the circumstances that found you here—did he have another way?"

She didn't answer that.

The therapist seemed fine with her silence.

"You just have to trust him, and understand that he married you with good reason. He married you because he loves you, and it's exactly what he wanted to do. That one thing can exist and be true outside of the other things he's done, Karine. You can hate the sin, and love the sinner. They don't have to be mutual or exclusive."

Karine didn't add the fact that Roman may also just have married her to keep her safe from Dima—so he couldn't claim her as his property.

She'd rather believe Sylvia's version instead of the poisonous doubts that constantly left Karine floating in uncertainty and pain.

Sylvia smiled, saying quietly, "He *will* call. I'm sure he has a valid reason for not doing so in a few days. Give him a chance to explain it."

Which meant waiting.

But for *what?*

Even though Karine nodded her head, she wasn't feeling as confident as Sylvia did. Maybe she had pushed him too far. Maybe, like her father, Roman wanted to wash his hands clean of her entirely.

She hated the part of herself that understood why.

• • •

⁓MARRIAGE

Nighttime was the worst.

She used to never dream—or rather, she never remembered them come the next morning. Lately, she couldn't escape the nightmares. Constant and vivid, they trapped her between sleeplessness and memories she didn't want to relive.

It was even worse when she couldn't tell the difference between being asleep, or awake. Karine gasped for air as she peered through the crack between the door of the closet. The faint ringing in her ears deafened all other sounds.

Katina and Dima's voices were muffled. She couldn't even hear her sister crying anymore or the crack of his fist when it fell against her skull for the final time.

Katina must have slumped down to the floor, but there was a blinding white light splashed all over the bedroom.

No, that's not right.

Karine hadn't been in the bedroom.

She blinked rapidly but still couldn't see anything, but that was the first moment she'd come back into awareness, and left the nightmare. Not that it mattered, she still knew what happened. She had seen it so many times that she memorized every detail of the scene. Even the smell of her sister's perfume.

She cried out for Roman when her body jolted awake all at once. She sprang up in bed, realizing her nightclothes were damp from her own sweat and so were the sheets surrounding her.

Where was she?

Where was Roman?

She shouted his name again.

Nothing.

No one answered her back.

The room was dark, and she jumped out of the bed searching for a switch along the wall. Stumbling in her fear and confusion because she couldn't remember where she'd fallen asleep. She was blind in her dream and now that she was awake—she was blind still.

"Roman. *Please.*"

Her whispers disappeared into the darkness until her fingers felt the shape of a switch. A harsh yellow light flooded the room, and that's when she remembered where she was. *Finally*, Karine could breathe, but her chest was still tight.

She stared around the sterile bedroom, realizing that the faint hope she would wake up to the hotel room had been another part of her nightmare.

Tears filled her eyes when she realized she was alone. It'd been a long time since she last saw him, and she was starting to forget what it was like to hear his voice.

When she searched her quiet mind, expecting Katina's eager and commanding voice to ring through, she heard nothing.

Karine ran to the bathroom to stare at her own reflection, finding tear-stains streaking her cheeks and droplets still hanging from her lashes. When she blinked in the mirror, the tears fell. At least, the visible color in her cheeks that had been missing from her face for days was starting to return.

Not much else could be said for the exhausted, crying girl staring back at her in the mirror.

"You're always beautiful, babe. Even when you cry."

Karine's eyes shifted to the reflection of Roman in the mirror. His figure stood behind hers in the doorway of the bathroom, his handsome chiseled face was set in a soft expression as he regarded her. His beard was neat and freshly cut. Even the longer part of his hair on top had been brushed into a high quiff. With his hands thrust deep in the pockets of his pants, Roman stood with his legs apart, firmly planted on the tiled floor.

With authority and power.

Just like she remembered him.

Karine clutched the edge of the sink, and shut her eyes. *You're still dreaming,* she told herself. *It's not real.* She took in two deep breaths, slow and steady, the only thing that helped when she was starting to lose control.

"It's just in my head. This is not real," she muttered out loud.

‎ᴛʜᴇMARRIAGE

"It's not just in your head, Karine. Turn around and look at me."

His deep voice filled her soul. She opened her eyes, and stared at the mirror again. He was still there in the reflection. Standing behind her, *waiting*.

Was she getting worse?

Her dreams were turning into hallucinations, taking over her life. Fear was her constant companion. The only thing she counted on.

Then, he came towards her, his smile growing as he reached out and touched her shoulder. She felt that—the pressure of his big hand, and thick long fingers wrapping around her before he spun her around in a flash.

That was real.

He was really there.

Roman hooked a finger under her chin, leaning down until their lips nearly touched, and she felt that, too. "I'm sorry—for everything. You really thought I could stay away from you?"

ELEVEN

Roman was still high when Marky knocked his door down. No, literally, the asshole kicked it open when he didn't answer.

He hadn't heard him knocking or his phone ringing because the music was too loud in the loft.

The first thing Marky did was turn the music off.

Roman was in nothing but his gym shorts, unbothered by the sight that greeted his friend. His place was a mess. He hadn't bothered to pick up the takeout containers or bottles from the night before.

What did it matter?

"Cut this shit out," Marky barked at Roman. "Who plays music that fucking loud, anyway?"

It made him laugh.

The music was the problem?

Hilarious.

THE MARRIAGE

"You want something?" he asked Marky, throwing himself into the couch where lines of coke were neatly arranged on a broken shard of mirror.

He couldn't even remember how it all got there. Did he do this all himself? Because it was exactly what he was looking for.

Pressing one nostril down, he held the mirror up to his face so he could snort with the other one through the rolled-up hundred dollar bill he'd left on the glass. Marky's voice droned on, but it was nothing more than a buzz in his ears.

He pinched his nose because it tingled for a few seconds—burning right before adrenaline shot through his body like his veins were on fire.

There.

He'd be up for another eight-hour run, at least. Who fucking needed sleep?

He grinned at Marky.

"Do you even see yourself, man? Why don't you hold the mirror up and take a good look at yourself," Marky snarled.

His friend even dared do swipe out at the piece of glass with the remnants of powder in Roman's hand, but coke made him faster—*better.* Tossing it aside, he threw his arms out on either side of him, getting comfortable again.

"What is your problem, bro?" Roman asked, laughing even though he knew it would only piss his friend off more. He just didn't understand why.

Who cared if Roman destroyed his life?

It was already gone.

"Why are you here and why won't you leave me alone? I don't remember telling you to come over." Roman looked over at the door and the damage Marky had done by making his way through, pointing at it as he said, "And shit—you better fix that door before you fucking leave."

"I'm not going anywhere until you answer my questions."

Excuse me?

Roman cocked a brow. "I don't have to do shit, actually."

"No, you don't have to do anything, at least nothing I ask. But your father isn't too far behind. Everyone knows something is up with you, Rome. You've been out of the picture for over a week, man. Your parents are asking questions, and I'm running out of excuses here."

"I was in a fucking car accident that nearly killed me. How about that? Maybe I just need some time to recover from it. Huh?"

That good feeling was settling in, the coke *really* getting to his brain and shutting off those overworked, overactive nerves. He wasn't heavy or light, just weightless. Just *there*. He wasn't angry or sad, he felt nothing.

He was finally numb.

Couldn't they let him be numb?

Best of all—he didn't have to worry about Karine when he was like this. She was a distant memory, and he wanted to keep her that way for the moment because otherwise—well, that hurt.

"That is not what this is about. You're getting fucked up because of your wife—pretty pathetic you're willing to lie about it, man."

"I'm getting fucked up because I can," Roman retorted.

Too hotly.

Not able to stand the scrutiny of his friend, Roman jumped up and went looking for a beer. He could feel Marky's eyes on him, following his every move. Like a bug that needed squashed.

"And you need to get the fuck out of here before I kick your ass out myself."

He popped a can open—one of the ones he'd left on the coffee table; it was still warm. Gulping the beer down, he didn't even mind. It did nothing to quench his thirst, but he didn't care.

"I'm starting to think us being friends fucks with your head," Roman added. "You forget your place. Who are you and who am I—can you tell me that?"

Marky's cheek twitched as he glared right back, while Roman felt nothing.

He couldn't even remember why they were still friends, in fact. Who gave this guy the liberty to break down his door, run his fucking mouth, and call Roman out on anything?

ᴛʜᴇMARRIAGE

"Okay, yeah, I'll leave. I don't give a shit," Marky replied, pointing his finger like a gun at Roman. "I *shouldn't* give a shit. I just wanted to ask you when was the last time you called Karine?"

Roman didn't like the way he asked that—or maybe it was the answer in his mind that made him shout, "She won't talk to me—what do you want me to do?"

Marky nodded. "But you haven't called in a long time, so you don't know if that's still the case, Roman. You've been doing this for days—you've been up for *days*. Don't you realize it?"

Roman swayed a little where he stood. The alcohol made him tired, brought him down from the floating feeling the coke had given him. The beer was a bad decision because all of a sudden—Roman could feel things. He could actually hear what Marky was saying, not just what his coke-addled brain wanted to hear.

He returned to the couch, and sat down again. Scrubbing a hand down his face, he avoided looking at Marky.

"You need to go and speak to your father," his friend said quietly. "The two agents were there to see him a few days ago. Some shit is going down. You're gonna miss it because you're too busy numbing yourself to the world around you."

Roman dragged in harsh exhales, letting the air out slower than he took it in. From under his lashes, he kept a firm glare on Marky.

"The same agents who tried to interview me?"

Marky shrugged. "I guess so."

"What the fuck is up now?"

"Dima wanted a sit down with your father, but he refused. He doesn't want to meet anyone from the new organization in Chicago who is not the boss."

"So where the fuck is Leonid?"

Roman heard the way his voice pitched darker. Marky had messed up his high. *Big time.*

"Nobody seems to know. I don't think the agents knew, either. I wasn't really told a lot, to be fair. Just enough to pass it on to you."

Roman raked a hand through his hair wishing he could go back to the day before when he didn't care that he needed a shave, a haircut, and a solid night's worth of sleep. He liked being selfish—it was easier.

That was over, it seemed.

There was time—a period of over a week—that he had just wasted getting high when he could have worked towards finding Dima.

He didn't know if Karine would ever speak to him again, or if their marriage would even work now—but he had to do something to make this world a little safer for her to survive in.

Roman owed her that.

At least.

• • •

His parents were eating when Roman barged into the dining room. At least, he'd taken a thirty-minute stop at his barber's before showing up. He didn't look *as* fucked up as he did when Marky walked in on him that morning. It was all that could be said for him, and even he knew it.

His mother stood behind his father's chair with her hands on his shoulders. They were in the middle of having a light-hearted conversation if the laughter in the air was any indication.

Usually, a scene like that would have him turning away, making some internal comment about men being wrapped around their woman's finger. He'd never admitted it to himself before, but that misguided pride had always made up for the emptiness he felt. He'd not known what romantic love really was—how vulnerable a person became once they were in love. Degrading it was just another way for him to deal with what he lacked.

But the sight of his parents together warmed Roman's heart because it reminded him of how strong the bond was between them, and how well his family thrived from the roots they'd planted. And just as fast, it pissed him off.

It reminded him of what he didn't have with Karine.

THE MARRIAGE

Not yet, anyway.

Too bad they were having a good time.

Just the sight of Roman ruined it.

"Where have you been?" Demyan demanded.

At least, his mother kept smiling. "Take a seat, Roman. I'll get you a plate."

Roman didn't even pay her any mind. His gaze didn't leave his father. "The agents came back to speak with you? And you didn't think to let me know?"

Demyan put down his spoon, and drew in a deep breath. "I would have told you if I knew what you were up to, but you keep fucking off—"

"Why don't you eat something before fighting?" Claire tried interrupting with frankness, however, neither were interested in the food anymore. Even Demyan, who never turned down his wife's food—seemed to have lost his appetite when he pushed his bowl of stew away.

"I don't need to give you a report of all my actions, and my every move, Papa."

He'd made sure to make the distinction with his father right then—he wasn't interested in talking to his boss.

"You do need to check-in when you have a history of landing your ass in trouble."

"Why don't you just come out and say what you want to fucking say?" Roman asked, opening his hands wide. "Fuck her feelings—*say it*."

Demyan stood up at that.

Claire stepped back, clasping her hands together. He could count the number of times he'd gone to blows with his father in his lifetime—once when he was eighteen. Because if he could walk and talk like a man, then he could get hit like one, too. Or that's how his father justified it. After spending two or three years, completely wild, on the streets, rarely at home, finding all kinds of trouble, he thought he could do this once with his dad.

Back him up against a wall.

Let lingering anger spill between them.

Forget who they were.

He'd been too young. Threw the first punch, too. Demyan kicked his ass that day—rightfully so. On the wet grass, he'd beat a lesson into Roman with three punches to the mouth that left him swollen and bloody.

Roman had been high that day, too.

He didn't like who coke made him be.

He also wished he wasn't aware.

"Get out of my sight before I get Pavel to drag you out," Demyan demanded, jerking a pointed finger at the door. "That is the last time you speak like that in front of your mother."

Roman didn't move a muscle, but his gaze darted to his mother. Claire had turned her face to the side, but he didn't miss the swipe of her sleeve under her eyes to wipe away tears she didn't want him to see.

Just like that, the tunnel vision his rage had created vanished, leaving him loosening his stance and glancing away.

He shouldn't be doing this here.

"Sorry, Ma. I didn't mean to just—"

"Why don't you tell him what you know?" she said, offering the words to his father like Demyan would know exactly what she was talking about.

The change of topic didn't give him a chance to breathe.

Roman searched his father's face for a clue. Demyan gritted his teeth and shook his head. In that moment, Roman realized he still hadn't become a better son to his father. He had tried to—in the months that he spent in Chicago.

It didn't last.

Demyan sat down again, picking up his napkin to tap the corners of his mouth before tossing it to the table. Something he would never do carelessly, yet didn't think twice.

"Maxim is still alive."

Roman thought the ground was shaking under his feet until he realized it was just his fast-tapping foot, and he had to cross his arms over his chest to stop the nervous tic. His parents could clearly see the effect this news had on him, as much as he tried to hide it.

_{THE}MARRIAGE

"The body they found in the fire wasn't him. Leonid is missing. Dima is pretending to be the boss and keeping his father's absence hush-hush. I don't have proof. Nobody has proof. But that is the only explanation."

Roman could feel his feet moving. He was headed to the door before his brain had even arrived at the decision to leave.

"Don't go anywhere, Roman. Don't do anything that'll jeopardize the bratva or the girl's safety. You need to be here. Little Odessa is the safest place for you. And you know she's where she needs to be."

His father was right.

But she had to know.

Not even the devil would keep him from Karine now.

• • •

When Roman got there it was the middle of the night.

They made a big show about how it was unauthorized access, and it didn't matter if he was her husband.

Blah fucking blah.

He was ready to shoot up the place if they kept him from her a minute longer—in fact, it did take him showing his gun, on top of Sylvia and another floor manager getting on the phone, to get him through the first set of doors.

He had to see Karine.

He had to tell her everything he knew about her father and hadn't had the balls so far to come clean about.

One of the women at the front desk was there the day Roman checked her in—she was the one who agreed to show him to Karine's room herself after the initial uproar.

That solved the problem because he really didn't want to have to kill anybody tonight. Probably wouldn't be very conducive to his purpose in being there.

He didn't ask anything about Karine or if she'd made any progress as the young woman led him through the bottom floor to a rear wing where Karine was housed. He wanted to witness it for himself.

There was a part of him that expected the worst—that nothing had changed and, in fact, had deteriorated. That his parents were right when they warned him of the consequences of admitting Karine to this facility without her consent. That he was destined to have a wife who would hate him forever.

He didn't expect her to even want to speak to him, but he wanted her to see that he came for her. Just like he promised he would.

The woman showed him to the door, and he knocked before stepping in after she had swiped the badge the security guard had given her earlier to unlock it.

It was the middle of the night, but the light was switched on. Karine wasn't in bed, but the sheets left spilled half on, and half off the mattress said she had been there. At some point.

He might have panicked had he not noticed the bathroom door was open. There she stood at the sink, staring at herself in the mirror. Angling his body toward her, taking that first step, he hadn't been ready for the tears he saw falling on her cheeks or how she stared so hatefully at her reflection, disgusted at what she was seeing.

Didn't she know?

She was the most beautiful thing he'd ever seen.

His next breath ached.

In the best way.

"You're always beautiful, babe. Even when you cry."

Karine's gaze darted to where she could see him standing behind her in the mirror. Just as fast, she closed her eyes. Those seconds crawled by. One too many.

"It's just in my head. This is not real," she said in a mutter.

That was a knife in his heart.

"It's not just in your head, Karine," he replied. "Turn around and look at me."

She did look at him then, the very moment he opened his mouth and told her to do so. That didn't make her move, though. She didn't turn around, only stared at the reflection of him in the mirror.

ᴛʜᴇMARRIAGE

He went for her, then, grabbing her shoulder to turn her around like he wanted and sliding a finger under her chin. Tipping her head up as he leaned down, he felt her breath kiss his lips while those big, clear eyes of hers watched back.

"I'm sorry," he said fast, wanting that to be first, "for everything. You really thought I could stay away from you?"

It took her more than a few seconds to register the truth staring back. That he was really there with her. Her mind wasn't just playing tricks on her like it used to in the past.

Then, she fell into his arms—sank right into him all at once—and he would have been happy to melt and fuse together forever in that moment with her.

Roman weaved his fingers into her silky dark hair, molding himself to her soft supple body.

This was where he belonged. She was his home.

He'd found that in her.

She was *his.*

"I'm so sorry," she mumbled into his chest, her fingers tangling into his shirt and jacket. "I'm sorry I pushed you away, Roman. I don't see anything when I'm scared. I'm just *scared.*"

He didn't want to hear it.

Slipping his hands in around her chin, he forced her to look up at him again, saying only, "You don't ever have to apologize to me for *anything.* Ever."

She was who she was.

He'd loved her more for it.

Because she loved him crazy, too.

When he kissed her, it was soft and slow. He took his time while their tongues met and grazed, and her hands explored. She tasted just the same. Her sweetness soaked from her to him with every touch.

When they pulled away, she rested her head on his chest, and he rocked her slowly back and forth.

"I'm not okay without you, Karine," he whispered hoarsely into her hair. "I don't like who I am without you."

"You're mine—you promised."

Her soft proclamation had him nodding. "For as long as you want me."

It was when the door clicked shut that Roman realized the woman had left them alone. He didn't really consider that it was probably locked again, or even the cameras he knew were overhead, peering into the darkness.

Karine wrapped herself around him, her legs trapping his waist as he lifted her up and carried her to the bed. Neither of them spoke, their lips talking for them with fast kisses that turned hungry in a flash.

It didn't matter how much time they had together—or what the next day was going to look like—they had something else that needed to be done first. She touched him, and it set him on fire.

The teasing drag of her fingernails along the column of his neck had him groaning into her next harsh kiss.

He laid her down on the bed, and she reached for him, so he stretched himself over her, covering her completely with his larger, stronger body. He could feel the smallness of her underneath him. She widened her legs, telling him with her body what he needed to know.

Nothing had changed between them.

Not like this.

She still wanted him the same way she did the first night they were together. Only now, she was his wife. Her pleasure belonged to him.

Roman undid his pants, and she helped him pull them down his legs. The shorts she wore—slipped off easily with a hard tug of his hands.

They were still clothed on top, but naked from the waist down. Their heavy pants of breath matched the other. Everything happened so fast, and in total silence.

When her hand fisted into his shirt, popping a button, he asked, "What do you want, babe?"

"Just love me."

He would.

He *did*.

Roman watched the way Karine's hand skirted under her nightshirt to squeeze her breasts while he pumped his cock until it was achingly hard. Her greedy little whines urged him on when he slid the head of his dick along her slit, finding her wet and hot already. He thrust himself inside her, and she sighed so *softly*.

It was like wet silk had wrapped around him in an instant, and the punch to the chest took his breath away.

Karine rolled her hips, arching her back so she lifted herself up towards him, meeting his body in desperation. She wanted him deeper—*fuck*, he'd already seated himself right to the root. He stayed higher above her, his hands splaying out along the curves of her stomach where her shirt had ridden up so he could hold her tight.

Squeezed her in every flex of his hips.

He could consume her completely—lose himself in the way she felt milking his cock, and he became happily drunk on every sound she made.

Karine bit down on her plump bottom lip, opening her eyes wide when his fingers dug in hard enough to leave behind red marks.

"Watch this—*watch me*," he told her.

He pinned her down to the bed by her hands when she'd grabbed his wrists. The pillows at her back gave her enough incline to see the way his cock looked stretching her open. Every stroke found his length wetter than the last. He loved being coated in her, knowing soon she was going to be full of *him*.

The first time she came, she did it with a whisper of his name. Unable to move under his hands, she went still with eyes blown wide as he fucked her through it.

The second time, he'd managed to get her bent over the pillows while his hands were on her hips, pumping his cock in and out of her in quick succession until every last drop of his seed was buried deep in her.

She'd pushed back into him when he came, too, using her hands against the bed to steady her trembling form as the waves of her hair tickled his chest, and she sat hard on his cock to *take it* the way he demanded.

Karine's cheeks were flushed as she stared back at him. Sweaty, and pinked.

He pushed some stray strands of hair off her shoulder and out of the way, then kissed the tip of her nose.

"You promised," she repeated.

He did.

Still hard and jerking inside her with every jostle of their bodies, Roman said, "I am hopelessly, completely in love with you, Karine. I will never abandon you."

Her breasts heaved after he'd pulled out of her, and she yanked him down on top of her on the bed again. She reached up to touch his face, tracing her finger along the sharp lines of his cheeks and jaws, not complaining about his weight on her.

Though it was substantial.

"I know that. I have always known that. You don't have to teach me to trust you," she finally whispered.

Didn't he?

Trust like that was always earned.

• • •

Sylvia D'Souza, Karine's head therapist in the Twin Rivers facility, stood beside Roman the next morning with a coffee in her hand. He had his own brown paper cup which he'd been sipping from while she droned on about policies and bullshit—and his complete lack of disregard for all of it.

"You know, we have strict rules in place regarding family contact, and we have them there for a reason. While we encourage family members to keep in touch regularly, and we are very happy to coordinate meetings—spending the night in a client's room—well, it shouldn't have happened."

While Sylvia spoke, Karine was in the garden across from them. She was tucking some bulbs of something into the dug up soil, though he hadn't thought to ask what. Even though she was probably aware of being watched, she chose to ignore them. She had to have known they were talking about her, too.

He admired her for that—for her ability to accept the fact that her life was the subject of discussion to the people around her whether she wanted it that way or not.

Roman took a sip of his coffee and shrugged. "Did they learn something?"

THE MARRIAGE

That question had the woman's cheeks burning red. "They deleted the camera footage if that's what you're asking."

He actually hadn't been.

"Yeah, listen—I know it's against the rules, but I'm sure you get that these are unusual circumstances."

Sylvia looked at him with an almost indulgent smile. "Each of our guests are here because of the unusual circumstances of their lives. We cannot make exceptions. For the sake of your wife's recovery—*follow policy*. Otherwise, we'll have to discuss removing her from the program."

Threats now?

"Look at her today. Does she look like a woman who needs any of this after spending the night with her husband?"

As if on cue, Karine turned her face up at the sun and shielded her eyes to look. They could clearly see the smile on her face, the pink in her cheeks—the *life* in her eyes.

Sylvia cleared her throat, muttering, "I'm sure she was delighted to see you, and I'm very happy that you were able to put aside your differences. Hopefully, that'll help us here as well. However, Mr. Avdonin, you are going to have to leave again, and I sincerely hope that … well, last night … hasn't taken us too many steps back in her recovery process."

He knew she had a point.

They hadn't had much of a chance to talk last night. Karine had fallen asleep in his arms after letting him lavish her with all the attention and affection she craved from him for as long as he could keep his eyes open. Only after she closed hers did he allowed himself to drift away, too.

It was the first night in over a week since he relapsed— that he hadn't used just to stay awake, and was able to sleep. It was like his mind had been running on full gear and top speed, and Karine had a slowing effect on it. She made him push down the brakes, and his spinning mind came to a screeching halt.

Before he came here he wasn't sure if he'd want a line, or if his hands would start to shake come morning. He didn't want her to see him like that, but so far, he'd managed without a single craving clawing at his back.

Maybe that was it …

That's what he needed.

She was the drug he missed.

"I won't leave this place until she's calm. She won't be back where we started," he replied.

Sylvia appeared to be ready to argue, but she took one look at him and relented nonetheless, only nodding in silent reply. Frankly, she could only ask for so much. He couldn't offer anything different than he did. Their hands were both tied.

"How has she been? The last time we spoke, you said she was resisting all help."

That brought a smile to Sylvia's face.

"I'm happy to say that has at least started to change—she's made what I would consider to be immense progress in regard to just being here. Thankfully, she did only need time. I'm sure seeing you is going to have a huge positive impact as well. I see great potential for recovery in her."

Roman's heart dared to feel a little lighter at the thought. Drawn to even simply staring at his wife, he did just that. She was so tender and delicate with her work as she crouched in the soil on her knees. Her hair fell around her shoulders, and she worked with her gardening gloves on, inspecting each bulb before she put it into the ground.

He wanted to see her working in their garden. A big, beautiful blossoming garden where she had planted and flowered every bed herself. Adjacent to their warm home filled with children.

It took him a second.

The image ripped away his breath.

He bet she would make an amazing mother—the kindest and most caring. He wanted her to be the mother of his children; to see their little faces and find his wife's familiar features staring back.

"Has she had any … episodes?" he asked.

"There were a few times when I thought she came close … I think the lack of medicinal cocktail and time away from her most stressful triggers has allowed her a bit of clarity and control of her disorder. I would have liked to speak to the others if I could, but I won't say it's a bad thing if she can halt them from coming forward for now."

"So ... does that mean she's oka—"

Sylvia shook her head. "It's not about that. What's okay for one person is someone else's beginning, Roman. I'm afraid this condition is not as simple as that. Mental health rarely is. This is going to be a lifelong struggle, but with time and therapy, she will learn to keep her alters in check. They may even eventually merge into one. Merge into her. It takes time, and none of this might happen at all, too. You just never know."

Roman continued staring at Karine. He was back to thinking about their house again and what a life with her was going to look like—how the very picture of it make his heart beat harder. Would the professionals tell him to keep her from being alone with their children even though he couldn't imagine doing something like that to her?

That was far away, sure, but ... it was on his mind, all the same.

"As much of a struggle as it will be for her, you should be prepared for what that will mean for you, too," Sylvia said.

"All I want is her," Roman returned. "The rest is details, and I don't care much for those."

"Then that's all she needs."

He turned to the therapist who was smiling again.

"I have never wanted a normal life," he said with a chuckle. "Or a boring marriage, for what it matters. She challenges me. Keeps me on my toes, and reminds me every day that she needs me, that I have to strive to be a better person. I can't fuck this up for her. Is that messed up? That I need her more than she needs me."

"No, it's not. It's just a little co-dependent, is all. It could also be that you are both incredibly lucky to have found each other. I'm not here to judge the whys, Mr. Avdonin. Only figure them out, lay it bare, and let you do what you wish with it. Keep that in mind."

Right.

Karine stood up, then, and waved at them.

Roman shook Sylvia's hand before he walked over to his wife so he could take her in his arms and kiss her one more time.

They only had a little time—the rest could still wait.

• • •

"Is Sylvia pissed with us?" Karine asked as he held her in his arms, enjoying the heat of the sun beating on his face. The weather in Nevada in the colder months was nothing like New York.

"Fuck Sylvia," Roman uttered, bending his head down to run his mouth over her neck with quick, peppered kisses.

She shivered with a giggle.

Standing in the garden, in the open for everyone to see, he didn't care if it was inappropriate.

He was paying these people a lot of money to have Karine here, and he was done being lectured on what he could and couldn't do with his wife.

How did this hurt her recovery? She couldn't help herself but lean into him, to *want* him. And given how viciously he'd ripped himself apart over the last while at the idea she didn't want him, he was all too happy to soak this up.

Karine did eventually pull away from his mouth with a breathless laugh. "I'm already embarrassed enough by last night—the girl who handles the desk blushed at me earlier. *Stop it.*"

"Don't really want to."

She gave him a half-hearted glare. "Well, try."

"Or … we can go somewhere else. There's a path, let's walk."

That seemed to work for her. Roman weaved their hands together, and they started down along the cobblestone path.

Karine couldn't stop peeking over at him, each time making her grin bloom even wider. Happiness gleamed in her eyes. He still couldn't believe how much he loved her— how *right* she felt beside him.

With him.

"I thought you would be disappointed in me," she said.

^{\tiny THE}MARRIAGE

"I'll never be disappointed in you, Karine. I'm proud of you, and I know I hurt you by bringing you here. The way I did it … no excuses, babe, that was wrong. I should have had a conversation with you about it."

She nodded. "Maybe. And maybe I would have still resisted. I didn't really want that week to end, you know?"

He pulled her hand up to his mouth, and kissed her wiggling fingertips.

"I didn't want it to end either, and I promise we'll go away on a vacation. Somewhere far away with beaches and palm trees—white sand and ocean for days. Just as soon as all this is over."

"You mean as soon as Dima stops looking for me?"

That stopped him in his tracks, and her, too. She turned to him, offering only a shrug to explain what she'd asked.

"When he stops looking—he'll be dead," Roman said frankly. She drew in a quick, shaky breath and he thought, *now or never.*

"Karine, there is something you need to know. Something about your father."

Her smile sagged for a split second as she searched his eyes, and didn't find something to calm her worry.

"What is it?"

"It's nothing to be—"

"Just tell me, Roman. What about my father?"

"There was a fire—at his home. They found a body. The FBI thought it was likely your father, and no one led them to believe any different."

"He's dead?"

The wetness in her eyes made his chest clench. Despite the complications that colored their relationship, he thought there was a small part of Karine that had to love Maxim because he was her father.

Maybe that part of her would never forget the father he used to be before her sister's death.

Roman wished he'd prepared something to say, but he hadn't bothered. He didn't start thinking until he got there, and saw Karine again.

"No, he's not dead," he admitted. "Your father is still alive."

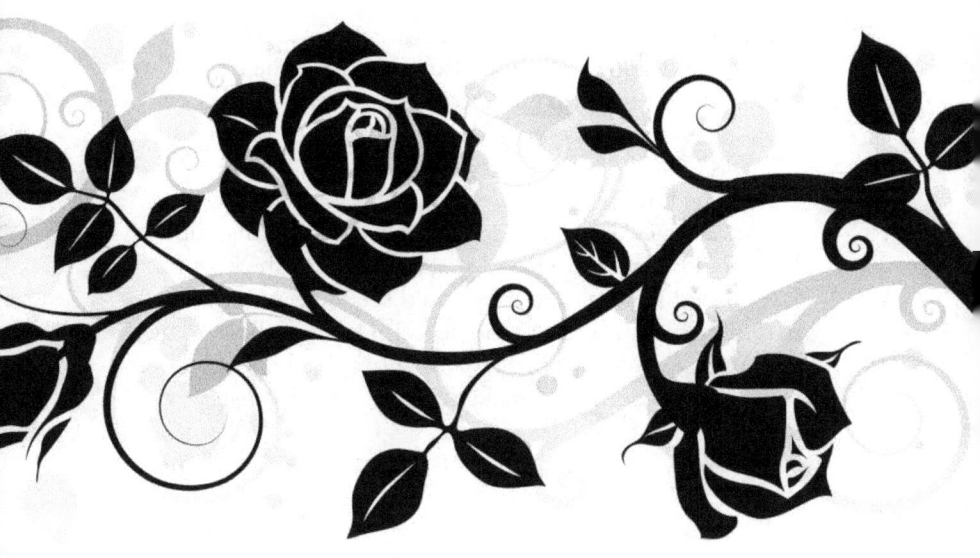

TWELVE

"I don't ... I don't understand," she finally settled on saying. "I thought Katina had—"

"Her plan—" He didn't miss the wince Karine gave at that statement; Roman bet knowing her alter having a major hand in plotting the death of her father had to be a big blow. "Doesn't seem to have gone through—at least, not how she expected."

Roman had made his mind up to tell Karine everything this time. No matter how difficult that conversation would be, a part of her had played a big role in the events leading up to what he believed might have happened in Chicago. And she deserved to know how it could affect her *now*.

The hardest part was telling her about the hand Katina had in all this. No matter what her relationship with her father had looked like over the years—or the fact that she had been unfairly treated by him—Karine would not want to hurt him.

"I didn't want to have to tell you this, Karine, and I tried to shield you from it as long as possible. Just until we had everything figured out because it was clear something wasn't right from the start. It's likely Leonid died in the fire, Dima's been hiding it to use a false position of power and move around—nobody knows where Maxim is."

It was a lot.

Even he knew it.

Karine stayed quiet while he held her in his arms, rubbing her shoulders with slow and steady pressure. She kept her face turned from him, but he could see the way her stare darted maniacally around the peaceful view of the garden. As if the small fish ponds would somehow give her the answers to Katina's actions, and make sense of what Roman was saying.

"You flew all the way across the country just to tell me that?"

"You had to know—it could mean he's coming for you. We don't know that, or anything different, but we have to act like we do."

"You could have told me on the phone," she insisted.

"Could I, really?"

How well would that have gone over?

Karine didn't argue that; he was more grateful than he would admit about it, too.

And he had more than enough money to burn so what was another four-hundred-k on a chartered jet? It was the paper trail risk that concerned him more than anything else, but he was always careful in that regard, anyway.

Karine shuddered as he held her, and she sniffled before covering her mouth to hide a soft cry. The sound alone was enough to cut him deep.

"I want to say he deserved it—that he deserved what she wanted to do to him, but he didn't. Nobody does. It makes me just as terrible as Dima. It makes me a monster."

Oh, this sweet woman.

She truly was too good for the world.

Their world, anyhow.

He took her face in his hands, stroking her silken cheeks with his thumbs and quickly swiping away any tears that dared to fall, saying fiercely, "Never, *ever* make the mistake of comparing yourself to that man. You can't take fault for the actions of something you never had control of, to begin with—Katina was never *you*. She doesn't think like you or act like you or even want the same things you do."

"But she *is* me—in me. They're like little doors. All these memories, and people, and *things* … the feelings I don't like or the images I can't forget, I put them behind doors. And some of them won't open again after I close them, and others never had a door to start with. She didn't like it when I put one in front her. She's still there, though. *Always*, there, Roman, and it takes so much to—"

"I know," he murmured fast.

He bet that scared her the most, too.

Roman held her face a little tighter, adding, "But you know now that she's only one piece, huh? And it doesn't make a difference to me, anyway. This is the woman I love. This is the woman I kiss."

He took her mouth in his, without warning, and bruisingly. She sank into the kiss instantly, gasping hungrily for breath, and tugging his lip with her teeth as she kissed him back ferociously.

He trailed his hands down the delicate line of her throat and over her trembling shoulders. Crushing her tighter against him when his hands splayed across her lower back, he whispered hoarsely, "You're all mine, Karine. No matter what."

"You'll always tell me, won't you? That you love me, remind me that I'm yours—you will, won't you? Because I hear one thing in my head, but it can't change what you *do*, Roman. Okay, so I just need you to keep telling me—"

"I will—forever. I promise."

Her forehead laid against his chest, and he was fine to stay there like that with her for as long as needed, letting her cling to him like he was her lifeboat. Because frankly, she was the only lifesaver being thrown out for him to catch, too. She gave him a sense of purpose in his life, in a way he hadn't had before, and he wasn't sure he'd be able to forgive himself for relapsing.

For using her as an excuse …

Roman made a mental note to talk to Marky as soon as he got back to New York. His best friend deserved an apology for his behavior and resistance. No matter the shit he took for it, Marky had been there reminding Roman what, and who, was important.

Over Karine's shoulder—Roman noticed a staff member from the facility walking hurriedly towards them down the path.

"Someone's always gotta shit on my parade," he said.

• • •

As it were, Marky had been attempting to reach him all morning, so he had no choice but to call the facility and ask for him directly.

Demyan warned Roman not to leave New York—his father was clear, but somethings just mattered more than an order. He hadn't told anyone where he was going except for Marky because he needed at least one trustworthy, reliable connection to home. Since he was the only one who knew the name and location of where Karine was admitted—other than Demyan—he took on the responsibility of tracking the phone number to the facility down.

He must have managed to get the right motherfucker on the phone.

"You need to get back here. There's been an incident," Marky said.

"What incident? What do you mean—I've only been gone a day and a half?"

Roman called him back after he switched on the burner phone he'd picked up as he left town. They were a dime a dozen in airports. Available at every turn. Karine still stood in the garden where he could see her in the distance, walking along the path and reaching out to feel the bushes as she passed.

Her momentary happiness calmed him. It amazed him how such simple things about her made him smile.

"Masha, she's gone."

For a second, Roman's thoughts cut off.

_{THE}MARRIAGE

And then he asked sharply, "What do you mean she's gone?"

"She's disappeared."

"From the house?"

"Nobody thought she was a flight risk. Like, what is she running from? Who is she running to? It isn't like the woman's got anybody here, Roman."

Marky had a point.

But this was just another *thing*.

Something else to handle.

Fuck.

Roman resisted the urge to kick the decoration at his foot next to the path. It might soothe his irritation for a brief time, but it also wouldn't last. Masha's recent behavior had certainly been a red flag, and while he thought he'd dealt with it, he clearly had not.

Or not well enough.

"Do we have any leads?" he asked.

"She's taken some things. One of your mother's Fabergé eggs, probably to hock, and a bag—"

"Anything else?"

Roman eyed Karine who was laughing with a staff member now. The woman had come walking up the path from the opposite direction, but Karine didn't appear to mind the conversation. Her hair fell back over her shoulders while she squinted against the sun. He couldn't help but fantasize about her on a beach somewhere. She would look beautiful against the backdrop of a roaring sea. Far away from here and the uncertainty he found looking at the future.

Was it so bad that he wanted this to end?

That he wanted time to love her?

"Marky," Roman asked again, "is there anything else?"

The man sighed, making the speakers crackle from the breath. "Some personal items of Karine's that Claire brought from the Vermont Lodge. A coat. There could be more, your parents live in a *big* fucking house, okay?"

Yeah, yeah.

"So if she's taken the time to gather things to take with her, this was a deliberate escape. It's not like someone kidnapped her," Roman added.

"No. But we're not sure where she could have gone. Is there a chance she's working with Dima?"

Roman considered that.

Had she fed information to Dima before—was that how he stumbled upon Roman the first time and caused the car accident? Nobody had thought to keep a close eye on the lodge phones; everyone had their own devices, and Masha was always *so* concerned with Karine day in and day out.

It was possible.

Anything was.

"Shit. If she is, I wouldn't have guessed it, though," Roman admitted, hating that he even uttered the words. "She seemed dedicated to Karine. She has to know what he's capable of doing to her."

What he did to her, he added silently.

Marky stayed quiet, and Roman wondered if that was the right time to apologize. Or even, say something to make up for the shit he kept putting his best friend through. Nobody had his back quite like Marky.

He didn't because his friend spoke first, reminding him what was most important at the moment.

"I think you should get back here, Roman."

"Yeah, I think I should."

The call ended abruptly, and Roman could still hear the lingering bitterness in his friend's final words. He didn't fault him for still being sour.

Roman tried to put it out of his mind for now. Separating from Karine was going to be difficult—no matter how many times he had to do it; it hit him like a punch to the gut to say goodbye.

Not that it changed anything.

Every time, he still had to go.

• • •

THEMARRIAGE

They returned to her room together holding hands, and he didn't let her wander more than an inch or two from his side the whole time. He wanted to keep Karine as close as possible for as long as he could.

"I'm sorry I just got here only to go again," he said.

Karine had taken it surprisingly well when he told her he was returning to New York. He decided to tell her the truth about Masha's disappearance, as well, refusing to keep anything more from her. He wasn't going to treat her the way she had been treated all her life—fragile, and easy overlooked.

She wasn't a sensitive flower who couldn't handle the breeze. Perhaps the way she dealt with her fears wasn't the way someone else might want her to, but she was stronger than anyone knew. She'd been doing this for years.

He couldn't forget that.

"I want to say there's a good reason for her leaving—she's probably freaking out because she doesn't know where I am. You should have told her. Maybe she thinks she can come and find me. I don't want to think she has bad intentions, Roman."

"Then, don't. I will."

"But—"

No buts.

He'd do what she couldn't.

Roman interrupted any argument from Karine by pulling her in for a kiss that left his chest aching with the need for breath. He kissed her long and hard, pinching her chin between his forefinger and thumb to keep her right where he wanted her while he licked the taste of his last breath off her lips.

She didn't shy away from him, and he adored that. Her tongue moved over his, firm and sure in what she wanted. Despite the relationships she had with the men in her life— Karine always kissed him boldly.

Like she was showing the world ... *he's mine.*

From the moment they first met, she had decided to take him. Even if he hadn't known it then. He had no choice in the matter.

This instability between them—the constant coming and going—couldn't be good for her mental health, even Sylvia said it. They didn't know how his departure would affect her progress. Was he chipping away at her?

"I'm sorry," he repeated again. "I'll let you know how long you'll be here, or at least when I'll be back, as soon as I can."

"I'll be fine."

Roman stilled. "Will you?"

"Here, yeah. I think so. I don't want you to worry about me. You should be with your family now—focus on them, and what needs to be done there. I need you to do that first so that we can do this again soon," she finished in a whisper, fisting his shirt in her balled hands, and pulling him close again.

Roman hadn't believed he would hear those words from her mouth—for Karine truly understand why he had to do what he did.

He stroked her hair and she pressed herself further into him.

"Do you forgive me?" he asked, barely above a breath.

He didn't want anyone else to hear it, anyway. This was meant for him and her alone. It was between them, and would always be.

"For what?"

"For this place. For bringing you here. For taking you to Vermont and Michelle. The therapists and doctors. The people constantly watching you. Any of it—all of it, Karine. I just ... wanted to know," he said lamely, with a shrug.

Karine licked her lips and looked away. He wished she wouldn't. "I know you're trying to help me. Sometimes I don't understand it, or it doesn't really seem fair, but I know *why*. Your actions sometimes speak louder than your intentions when I don't think they match, but I picked you, and I didn't say you had to be perfect when I did it, Roman."

"You tried to run once here."

She laughed, shaking her head and glancing back at him with a twinkle in her eye. "You can't lock someone up and think they won't crave freedom—I still forgive you. I know why you did what you did."

ᵗᴴᴱMARRIAGE

"The world is yours the second I make it safe for you."

"And you want these people," she said with a smirk, waving around them, "to tell you it's safe for me to be out there, too."

"That you can handle it, yeah."

He kissed her forehead and pressed the tip of his nose to hers. Any bad days together would be worth it just to have a few good days like this with her.

Quieter, he added, "And the world was the one that did this to you, Karine, so fuck them, anyway. I don't care about anybody but you. It's me and you first, babe, from here on out."

He kissed away the tears that spilled to her cheeks, whipping away what wetness remained with his thumbs right after. Giving him a rueful smile, she latched onto his thumb and sucked the taste of her tears away.

God, he loved this woman.

"You should go," she whispered, her fingertips tapping the underside of his jaw. "Give my love to Claire. And if you find Masha, tell her ... tell her I am okay. I'll be back soon, but right now, I'm okay. Give her at least the benefit of the doubt, Roman."

He stared hard at her, not wanting to make that promise.

"Please?" she asked.

"Karine—"

"*Please.*"

"Depends on what happens. That's the best I can promise."

"Fair enough. I love you, Roman."

He didn't want to leave her, as he kept picturing waking up the next morning without Karine in his bed. Here, in this sterile, lonely bedroom, she would wake up doing the same for him. From his pocket, he pulled out his wedding ring which he hadn't started wearing in public yet.

Karine's eyes brightened when he slipped it on with a smile.

"I'm done looking because I've already found everything," he said. "Everyone should know."

• • •

Nobody seemed happy when Roman arrived back in New York. Not that he expected them to be considering he'd done exactly what he was told not to.

His father demanded his presence the second Demyan knew Roman's feet were on home soil, and he drove over there to find Marky already waiting on the steps of the house.

He offered Roman a smoke first thing.

"We need to talk," Roman said to his friend, refusing a smoke he badly needed.

"Yeah, I know."

He grabbed him by his arm, yanking Marky towards himself. The two men stared hard at one another before Roman said, "Listen, I know I'm a fuck up and an asshole sometimes, but I appreciate—"

Marky nodded once, shrugging Roman's hand off his arm before he could even finish. "All's good, man. A sorry suffices sometimes, shit. That's all."

"I'll keep it in mind."

That seemed to be good enough for his friend, and after another quiet pause, Roman walked into the house alone.

Bulls milled about the grand staircase and outside his father's office where he found Demyan waiting for him. Two of the men slipped in, one was his father's spy who moved to the corner of Demyan's desk to look through a file he passed over to the man.

It was his father's disappointed eye turning on him that made Roman tense a bit on the spot. Standing just beyond the doorway, he noticed that with his mother absent from the room, the cigars filled the ashtrays and smoke still clung to the air.

"Do you have any idea where this woman could have gone to?" Demyan asked.

Roman bristled—he never did well with that tone his father liked to use. He'd been trying to get past the constant need to snap back at every comment Demyan made, but habits were hard to break. "Don't you think I would have dragged her ass back here already if I knew where she went?"

"Thin ice here, son, you're skating on it. Don't get smart with me, huh? How do you propose we find her? She was part of *your* package of responsibilities, so to spe—"

"Fuck off, don't call Karine that."

"Roman!"

He didn't even blink at his father's shout. "I get it, you're pissed. I didn't listen to you and jumped on a jet. You can be an asshole to me without taking it out on her."

Demyan's gaze burned. "Back to *that woman*—who knows what information she has or who she's feeding it to? We need to find her."

Roman wasn't stupid.

"I don't know, but I'll start somewhere. I just need some time to think."

"Perfect because you've given her a two-day start here, Roman. You know she's taken stuff from my drawers, too, yes?"

Roman couldn't remember if Marky mentioned that or not—he also wasn't surprised. "Like what?"

"In my desk. Random papers, a file on a shipment deal. Some contracts; an old day planner. Looks like she took whatever she could get her hands on, really," Demyan grumbled. "Quite a bit is missing, actually."

Shit.

Roman couldn't consider what that meant, asking only, "Why didn't anyone keep an eye on her?"

"You brought her into our lives!" his father roared, Roman's defensive comment throwing Demyan over the edge. "She came here because *you* decided to bring her, never once letting anyone believe she was anything but harmless. Why would I think I had to watch her every fucking move?"

"Who put me in Chicago in the first damn place?" Roman asked back, eerily calm.

"I didn't make you steal Dima's car, son."

No one in the room even blinked at the spat between father and son. Demyan dragged in a heavy breath, and grunted at the men, "Get the fuck out, yeah?"

Nobody needed to be told twice.

Roman wanted to leave, too, but he knew he couldn't. He was in too deep now, and this was his responsibility. Life was better when his father didn't concern him directly with the family's business. Back when he dedicated all his time and energy to the chop shop.

Demyan stuffed his burning cigar into a crystal ashtray, crushing it down with as much force as he could.

"Did you really think I wouldn't find out?" he asked when the room had finally cleared, and the door clicked shut behind the last man.

Roman assumed he was talking about his recent visit to Karine. "I had to see her. We're not in a position where I can leave her with unfinished business between us. I won't apologize for it."

"Not Karine—I'm so used to you ignoring rules. You got high, Roman. You're using. Again."

He didn't speak.

Demyan slammed his hand down to the desk, demanding, "Well—at least have the decency to lie about it if nothing else!"

What would be the point?

Demyan called Marky in shortly after because Roman's silence pushed him to that point. He had nothing to say for himself. Not yet, anyhow.

"For fuck's sake," Roman muttered under his breath when Marky strolled into the office with a tight smile. It was the men peeking into the office—who could probably hear every word his father shouted—that irritated Roman the worst.

"And what were you doing when my son was snorting lines of poison into his brain?" Demyan barked.

"Stop it," Roman said, stepping in before his friend could even get a word out. "I'm not a fucking kid—I'm a grown man who can make my own choices. And for what it's worth, he was there. He tried to stop me. This isn't his fault so leave him alone."

Marky's defense while his friend stood there was to light a cigarette, shove his hands in his pockets, and otherwise, say nothing.

ᴛʜᴇMARRIAGE

Marky wasn't going to talk back to the boss, but he also wouldn't throw Roman under the bus. His best option was to say nothing at all, and let whatever happened, happen.

Demyan plucked up the ashtray off table and threw it at the wall where it shattered into thousands of little shards, falling to the floor. "How much more of your shit am I supposed to keep from your mother?"

"None of it," Roman said, shrugging. "It's over. I'm not touching that shit again."

"You're damn right you're not. You're going to be under twenty-four-hour surveillance. Do you remember what went down the last time you went on one of your binges?"

Roman glared at his father, meeting his eyes with defiance. If there was ever a time to snort a line—this was it. He'd never had the balls to blatantly do it in front of his father's face, though.

"And how are you going to manage that?" he asked Demyan.

"You've been free to mind your own business for too long. You're going to be minding mine, now."

"I'm not a child," Roman repeated.

"And yet, you act like one."

Demyan turned to Marky before Roman could respond, snapping with a jerk of his hand toward the door, "Get out of here."

"What about Masha?" Marky asked.

Roman shook his head. "If she took things to sell, like maybe she needed cash, start there."

Like the designer bag and expensive, priceless jeweled egg she'd stolen from his mother. Those things were hard to come by, and hot goods were easier to find than some people might think.

"I'll start putting words in around pawnshops."

"Yeah—"

"Get the fuck out of here!" Demyan snarled. "Do your job!"

"I'll hold the fort down and see what I can find on Masha," Marky said, not blinking an eye at Demyan's rage before he stepped out of the room again. Out of the line of fire. His father's bad attitude was nothing new. Sadly, Roman's friend was used to taking the blame in his story, too.

Once he was gone, Demyan turned to his son once more. His anger was still plain to see, and as much as he hated the way his father presented it …

Roman knew some of it was justified. He tried to remind himself of that when Demyan asked, "This is the shit you pull as a married man? You didn't think your wife deserved better than that—that your family deserves more from you?"

"I messed up, I know. I thought I fucked up my marriage, that I lost Karine."

One of the men stepped into the office with a dustpan and broom to clean the mess. Marky must have mentioned it on his way out, but the presence of the bull was enough to quiet the men again. Not that it really made a difference. They'd undoubtedly heard everything.

Roman *was* living with his failures, dealing with the consequences of his bad decisions, and toxic lifestyle … his father just didn't think it was enough, maybe.

Perhaps it wasn't.

Demyan was already lighting another cigar by the time the man had swept the floor to find all the little shards. Pointing the cherry-red tip, smoking curling upward in tendrils, at Roman, he said, "What is happening in your relationship has nothing to do with staying in control—that's where you're weakest, Roman. And I don't know how to help you fix that, son. I never did."

THIRTEEN

Demyan kept good on his threat—Roman hadn't done much
since his father's outburst. In fact, the first chance he had to
leave the Avdonin property, he found himself face to face
with a handful of men. Who, in no uncertain terms, made it
clear what their orders were.

*"You've gotten a few knocks to the head this past month—how
many more before you're drinking food from a straw, Roman?"*

He had choices—and trying to make good ones.

Roman opted not to test the bull's theory out, and had
returned to the house.

Demyan also let it be known that he didn't want Roman
going anywhere alone. Staying in his own loft was out of the
question, and the city apartment was no-go as well.

For the first time in over a decade, Roman found himself
sleeping in his childhood bedroom.

Claire was surprised to find him at the breakfast table the
next morning. Apparently, Demyan hadn't filled her in on

anything, and she'd gotten home late after visiting a gallery viewing by a friend in the city.

"You're a sight for sore eyes," she told him, tightening the belt on her fluffy house robe.

"Coffee's warm in the pot. I'll be hanging around here for a while, Ma, so don't be too surprised to see me here tomorrow morning."

Claire was smiling because she suddenly and unexpectedly had her son back, but she could also sense Roman's displeasure if the lingering glance she gave him was any indication.

"Something tells me this is not by your choice."

Roman cleared his throat, muttering, "Some shit went down with dad."

"What did you do?" she asked while she worked on making a coffee.

"Why do you automatically assume I did something?"

Claire tipped her head to the side, fixing a bemused stare at her son from her position across the kitchen island. "Did you?"

Roman wasn't entirely sure of the conversations his mother and father had behind closed doors. Especially when it concerned him. His parents had always been careful in that regard, and Demyan's desire to keep Roman's problems out of Claire's sight didn't help with that, either.

"Well, did you?" his mother asked again.

Roman sighed, wrapping his hands around the lukewarm mug of coffee he'd been nursing for the better part of twenty minutes. "Maybe, but people around here seem to forget that I'm a grown man with a mind of my own. I'm prepared to face whatever consequences my actions have. I don't need him—"

"You'll always need him."

Roman quieted, passing his mother a look.

She only shrugged back, adding, "Roman, a lot of your actions have consequences on your father and me, too."

"Are you referring to Karine and my marriage to her?"

Claire brought a mug of coffee over to the table, and sat in the seat next to her son.

^{THE}MARRIAGE

The absence of Karine and being forced to stay in his family home like he was a misbehaving teenager had put him on edge again. He had to furiously tap his fingers on the kitchen counter to control the urge to go looking for something that might cure the itch in his spine; to quell the chaotic emotions he hated feeling all the damn time.

But he wouldn't.

It was an easy fix.

It didn't last.

"It's not just about Karine, and how dare you, because you know that I like her," Claire scolded, though her tone remained kind. His mother had never needed to be mean to get a point across. "I think you've done very well by choosing her as the woman to spend your life with. That is not the part I'm worried about. There are some other choices you make that I don't particularly care for."

Reaching over, she patted his cheek like she used to when he was a boy, and he pulled himself away. Claire still smiled, anyway.

"You and your father think I don't know about the demons chasing you, but I do, and I think I know why, too."

Even though his mother didn't seem unhappy or sad, he could sense how she saw right through him. It had probably taken her just a few seconds after she saw him sitting there to figure out what was really going on.

He didn't want her to worry, though.

"I am good, Ma—or I'm trying," he told her.

Claire nodded. "I hope so. I'm sure I can find something to keep you busy with while you're here, hmm?"

"I'm not on house arrest, Ma," he complained.

He'd certainly never been the type for *chores*. God knew she had enough maids to do things for her, anyhow. Roman promised his mother nothing in that regard, and she could tell his mood on that topic by the scowl settling into his face.

Claire broke into a laugh just as they heard feet shuffling and running outside the kitchen before two of the ladies who handled cleaning the bottom level of the house stumbled past the entryway.

Roman glanced up, his ear tuned to all the sounds. It seemed like some chaos had broken out in the house by the stampede of footsteps overhead.

"Did Demyan leave—"

"A good hour ago or more."

Something had the men who were designated to stay inside the house in an uproar. Roman had already stood from the table, not bothering to push the chair in as he spun on his heels.

"Stay here—don't move," he barked at his mother, making a beeline for the door.

Whatever happened, it started in the driveway. The two maids had been running away from the front entrance to the home, while the men thundering down the stairs were heading for the outside.

Roman joined the men.

• • •

It was Marky.

Roman recognized him right away even though he was lying face down in the driveway with his limbs twisted in crooked angles. He knew it by the leather jacket his friend wore every day—proud of the years and stories the piece of clothing could tell about a decade or more of his life.

There was a lot of blood, just not on the driveway. His friend's jeans were soaked in a deep red, and the matted, wet hair tinged the bit of slushy snow on the ground with a pink hue.

Roman came to a halt outside the front door, just at the top of the stairs, his breath having been knocked out of him. Time slowed, then, like the old reel of a film skipping toward the end as the strip started to run out.

He felt the cold air surrounding him, but he couldn't move.

Blood rushed in his ears.

Around him, the men who had been inside the house blew past his still form, running to where Marky laid unmoving. Someone running up the driveway shouted about how a truck had burst through the mansion's front gates, driving full speed.

Another guy said the body had been kicked out of one of the doors before the truck burned rubber strips onto the asphalt driveway as they left at the same manic speed. Someone had even taken a few shots at the truck, but it didn't do any damage.

The only thing Roman fixated on was how they had now started referring to Marky as *the body*. He was vaguely aware of the neighbors who had come to stand at the end of their gated driveway, surveying the damage and the scene in front of them. One was on their phone.

Calling the emergency services, he bet.

Fuck.

They wouldn't be able to hide this.

And it was already too late for Marky by the looks of it.

He took a few steps closer, wiping his palm across his mouth to hide the way his breaths shook in clouds around his face. The circle of Avdonin men—the half a dozen tasked with watching the house and property—stood around his broken friend. Nobody had the balls to turn him over.

Not a single one stepped forward to touch him. Marky hadn't once moved. Roman suspected he'd probably been dead before he even hit the driveway. In the peripherals of his vision, he could see the way their faces turned towards him in unison.

Roman stood over his friend for a moment, the whoosh of blood still loud in his ears, and his heart aching with racing beats while he took in the scene again. The gawking neighbors and the woman shouting she had called for help; his father's men waiting for him to say something; and his friend, broken and bloody, at his feet.

Bending down, he grabbed the ripped, blood-soaked arm of his friend's jacket and turned him over. The wind picked up as he laid eyes on his dead friend, and the stab wounds that peppered his body telling a horrifying story of a violent end.

He wasn't surprised the wounds were focused in the front—the cuts on Marky's hands, wrists and arms where his sleeves had been shredded said he fought. He wouldn't have turned his back or tried to run. In the final moments of his life, he'd been fighting.

Roman should have been out there with his friend, asking questions and making his presence known. It would have afforded Marky more protection because he shouldn't have had to hold the fort down by himself.

Everything about the scene in front of Roman was coldly calculated, and it had Dima's bloody fingerprints all over it. It screamed his kind of work.

Dima didn't appreciate being rejected by Demyan repeatedly. He wanted to be treated as the new Chicago boss as he believed he rightfully was. He wanted to exact revenge on the Avdonins for the insult. Marky was out there looking for Masha. Digging. Asking questions because he knew the right people to get answers, but it was dangerous work all the same.

He'd been alone with no backup, and close enough to the Avdonin family for his brutal killing to make an actual impact on the people who mattered the most.

A loud shrill shriek snapped Roman out of his daze. He turned to find his mother standing at the open door of her home. She stared straight down at Marky covering her mouth with trembling hands, collapsing into a puddle of tears.

The man who had accompanied her to the door was close enough to her grab her before she fell to the ground.

"Who would do that to him?" he heard her cry.

He knew who.

Wanted so badly to make them pay for it, too.

He just had other things to handle first.

"Take her inside. Someone call the boss," Roman barked, turning away from his friend's body.

The faint siren in the distance might not have been a cruiser coming for them, but it reminded him instantly that the police presence would be thick on their property soon.

This was going to be bad. Really bad.

• • •

™MARRIAGE

By the time Demyan returned to the Avdonin home, the cops were already littering the property, their cruisers, and forensic vans filling the driveway. His father wasn't pleased, and had his wife not been home, likely wouldn't have returned to the property but sent lawyers in his absence.

No crime boss wanted this mess.

Not that Demyan had to worry. The moment a pig walked across their threshold, nobody had anything to say. That was the law of the land for people like them. As much as it killed Roman, his statement was the same as everyone else's when the police and detectives cornered him earlier.

He didn't know Marky.

Didn't see what happened.

Didn't have anything to say.

They'd have to prove differently.

"Where is she?" Demyan growled at one of his men who stood at the front of the house with Roman.

The bull gestured at the house, directing him inside to Claire. There was already a clear line drawn between the police doing their job and the rest of the men—the ones that *had* to stay, anyway. A few had already taken off to avoid the police presence. The second the detectives that showed up started talking about taking people to the station, lawyers were called.

Roman stood back, watching while his friend's body was bagged up and lifted onto a stretcher heading for the coroner's van. He met the gaze of the plain-clothed detective standing next to the van for a second before turning away.

There was nothing he could do about it. Nothing anybody could do about the situation. Marky was gone, and Roman didn't have a chance to say goodbye. He didn't even have the chance to thank him like he intended to, just those few passing words.

His friend deserved more.

Leaving Demyan's men to deal with the cops, Roman went back into the house. His mind still wasn't out of the dark cloud he'd sunk into. None of it seemed real.

In the foyer of the house, his mother's cries echoed from one of the rooms deeper in the house. Demyan's encouraging whispers accompanied her sobs.

He went to them, finding his mother a mess in her sitting room. Sobbing into her hands where she sat on a chaise in the corner.

"I think we've let Dima go on for long enough, don't you?" he asked his father. "Has he done enough yet—is *here* where I should really be now, Papa?"

His parents looked over at him—Demyan from his kneeled position in front of his wife. Claire, through her fingers, wet with her tears.

"No, Roman, please. Demyan, you can't let him just get himself killed. He can't be the next *body* thrown in the driveway!"

Roman refused to look at his mother because he wouldn't be swayed. Her pain was justified, as were her fears, but that didn't change what would happen after today.

Dima would pay for what he did to Marky.

If they didn't act *now*, or soon, they were essentially giving him the go-ahead to do it again. Who would be next—*Karine*, maybe?

Demyan stood, letting go of the hold on his wife's wrist to rub his hands together.

"Do what you need to do," he said.

"Demyan!" Claire shrieked. "Roman, please, just give it a day ... let things calm down before you do something rash. I know you're angry, but—"

"He's getting too close—too bold," Roman said sharply, cutting his mother off as she winced. "I'm not going to keep playing these fucking games, Ma. His next target isn't going to be you, or Karine. It's over."

For the first time, Demyan simply stood back and said nothing, maybe blaming himself for what happened. He just wasn't the kind of man who would admit it. His last interaction with Marky wasn't a particularly friendly one, and while his father was a lot of things, he wasn't a monster. He did send him off on the job, though.

A job that got him killed.

ᴛʜᴇMARRIAGE

"He's made it clear, Ma. It's a war, now. It won't stop until the right man dies."

Dima had won the first hand, but Roman needed to win the table if he was going to keep Karine alive.

He didn't wait to hear anything else his mother had to say. Leaving his parents together in the room, he absentmindedly stroked the butt end of a cigarette with his thumb. If Marky was there, he would have handed him one without Roman asking for it.

Always waiting just outside the door, ready for his friend.

He lit the cigarette just beyond the threshold of the front door. Chaos continued to ensue outside with police lights blinking in the driveway, and vehicles crowding the front lawns. They're certainly drawn a crowd from the neighbors.

The last time their family had a police event this large at their home, his mother sold the property the second she could and bought this one. He'd been quite young when that happened.

He figured for this, she'd do the same.

Roman understood why. Already, he couldn't stand to be there. All he could see was the spot where Marky had laid. It's all he would ever see now.

FOURTEEN

Karine thought she would be fine.

When she kissed Roman goodbye and told him not to
worry, she genuinely meant that. Maybe ignorantly, but she
was hopeful enough to believe their separation wouldn't
affect her as greatly as she let it in the past.

Recovery was something she craved; starting with trusting
the people she worked with every day, and making an effort
to at least try. At anything—everything—Karine was willing
to try. Even when that meant waking up in a room that had a
locked door, cameras, and didn't feel like hers, or talking
about her most shameful secrets, memories she wished she
could forget forever. If it would make the next day better, if
she could start it new each time, she did it.

However, she wasn't prepared for it to still hurt when he
wasn't there. It was as though the more time they spent
together, the harder it became for her to be without him.
Every time she saw him, he left her a little more hooked on

him. Just like the pills she used to take, she became lost in the happier, brighter world she found when he was around.

It didn't stay when he was gone.

The morning after Roman had left—Karine woke up physically sick. She couldn't remember if she'd eaten dinner or the last time she drank any water. The staff coaxed her out of her room, into therapy sessions with Sylvia and activities around the facility, but her mood remained the same.

Bleak.

Empty.

One day melted into two, and then five in a blink. Her contact with Roman had been limited to a couple of short conversations where she gathered enough to know something had happened after he arrived home in New York. He also made it clear it wasn't something they could discuss over the phone, so she was once again in the dark.

Soon, Sylvia or someone from the staff would be knocking on her door any minute now. Even though she was hungry, she didn't want to eat any of the breakfast they'd bring her. She still would because health started with providing her body with what it needed, even if that was food that she couldn't really taste.

Not that she wanted to, but Karine was sinking into that lonely hole of abandonment and betrayal again. Though she worked hard to tell herself what she felt today might not be the same as what she woke up feeling tomorrow, it didn't seem to matter. She wished her emotions weren't so constantly broken, whipping back and forth to create a storm she couldn't escape.

A soft sigh of desperation escaped her lips, and she fell back into bed—just as there was a knock on the door, and she had been considering hiding back under the blankets.

"Go away," she called out.

Either not hearing Karine, or just not caring, the lock on her door clicked loudly swinging open to expose Mrs. Hughes, one of the women who worked closely with her. She leaned just far enough in the doorway to show a brilliant smile.

"Oh, good, you're awake, Karine. Your father is here to see you, and I just wanted to check if you're okay with that."

What?

She stared blankly at the woman, sure she'd heard her wrong. Her *father?*

"Sylvia is at a bad location today, cell service is spotty—we also can't reach your husband to clear the visitor, but your file filled out by him did check off immediate family as approved visitors. And it is noted in your file that having guests really does improve your mood and days. We're willing to accommodate the visitor for a short time, if you're interested."

It was almost as if she was saying *no harm, no foul*. We won't tell if you won't. Karine was beginning to think there was more than one thing about the Twin Rivers facility that wasn't exactly above board.

Karine just blinked.

She was sure that box had been checked by her husband either by mistake, or simply because there wasn't another option. Maybe he'd been distracted.

Alarm bells rang in her mind.

Silently, but loud all the same.

"Karine?"

"My father—you're sure?"

"Maxim Yazov. You did mention him the other day when we went on our walk, remember?"

But briefly, in passing.

She knew better than to spill the truth about her father and every sordid detail of her history.

How did Maxim find her hiding place? If he was even alive like Roman claimed. It was just a theory, and he didn't have actual proof that Maxim was alive.

What if it was Dima claiming to be her father? Or one of his men. Was he *that* cunning?

Mrs. Hughes must have finally noticed the hesitance in Karine because she stepped into the room, and closed the door slightly behind her. Leaving only a crack open. "You don't have to see him if you don't want to. I can ask security to escort him out. We certainly weren't expecting any guests for you, and you're not required to have any. I simply thought you'd like the choice either way."

Karine could feel her lungs collapsing painfully in her chest. The possibilities of danger were endless, and suspected the staff in the facility had never truly known the full scope of her situation. Otherwise, this wouldn't be happening in the first place.

However, this could be her only chance. To put an end to everything.

If it was Dima and he'd found her, she wasn't going to be safe here anyway. It was already too late. Or perhaps her father had come to collect on his dues.

Maybe this was her opportunity to put everyone out of their misery.

"Yes, you're right. I would like to see him ... but not out there with everyone else. Could I have privacy in my room, and see him here? Thank you."

• • •

Karine quickly changed out of her pajamas, splashed some cold water on her face, brushed her teeth, and tied her hair up in a tight ponytail after Mrs. Hughes had left her room. She didn't want to appear weak, even if she felt like exactly that.

She stood at the end of the bed with her hands clasped at her front. Outside the door, she could hear Mrs. Hughes' voice and footsteps, muffled but getting closer with every passing second.

The harsh knock on the door made Karine stand a little straighter—and then it opened.

She heard the exaggerated sound of air rushing into her lungs and then blowing out through her nose. Mrs. Hughes was smiling up at the taller, older man with broad shoulders. His three-piece suit was cut perfectly to his large form.

Karine wasn't listening to anything being said. The only thing she could do was stare at the face of her father.

It *was* him.

Maxim Yazov stepped into the room, peering around as if nothing he saw bothered him, and he was perfectly comfortable in the unknown surroundings. Finally, his gaze rested on her. Karine searched for words to say, her spine ramrod straight, and heart beating against her ribcage wildly. How was a daughter supposed to react to a father who had given her away? A father who had disappointed her— neglected her in every possible way?

Maxim looked at Mrs. Hughes with a charming smile, one Karine recognized from her father. It drew people in, meant for them to think they were safe in the gaze of a predator.

"Thank you for your help," he told the woman. "Really appreciate the accommodation today, yes? I'm sure her husband will also be ... thrilled you made an effort."

Karine swallowed hard, her stare darting to Mrs. Hughes who seemed entirely entranced by the handsome, older man beside her.

"Of course," she replied. "I'll let you two get at it. I'm sure you have a lot to catch up on. Just to note, should you require help, you'll have to knock on the window of the door, as staff remains in the halls, or press the red button in any room. We turn off the cameras in private rooms for the sake of confidentiality during day-time visits."

Mrs. Hughes beamed at them both, then left the room, shutting the door behind her.

It had been a very long time since Maxim and Karine were alone in a room together. They never had any need to be. Maxim didn't think he ever had anything private to say to her, and as a younger girl and in her early teens, she'd become accustomed to his roar whenever she did disrupt his peace. It always sent her running scared, intimidated by the one man who should have kept her the safest.

"Karine ..." He said her name softer than she had ever heard his voice dip before. It was almost disconcerting.

She tried stepping away, but the back of her legs hit against the end of the bed, and she sat down with a thump, losing balance. And yet, she couldn't take her eyes off him. Already, she'd lost the will to keep her strong stance in the face of what awaited her.

ᴛʜᴇMARRIAGE

Here he was.

And she didn't know what to do.

"You're really alive," she murmured.

"Unfortunate news for some," he admitted, shrugging.

"You shouldn't be here ... how did you find—"

"This was a delicate thing, yes? Tricky," Maximin interjected with a quick laugh. "The details aren't very important, of course, and while I knew this meeting with you would be inevitable, I didn't think it would have to happen so soon."

Confused, Karine continued staring. Silent.

"It's too bad I had to betray someone who didn't deserve it to get here," Maxim added under his breath, eyeing the security panel on the wall in her room that allowed her to speak to the front desk, if needed, or vice versa. "We have a lot to talk about, my daughter, and not a lot of time to do it. Forgive me for my lack of transparency."

He hardly meant that.

She could tell.

Karine rubbed the back of her hand on her nose in an effort to hold in the tears bubbling inside her chest. "I didn't think you ever had anything to say to me, Daddy."

"I know I've done things to make you feel that way, yes."

"I can remember you shouting at me when you were drunk, every time you'd see me peering around the corner, trying to get a glimpse of you because I hadn't seen you in weeks. You'd yell *so loud*, Maxim. You couldn't stand the sight of me."

"Karine—"

"Admit it. You cared about Katina more than you cared about me. You wished it was me that was killed and not her. You have spent half of my life blaming me for what happened to her."

Her voice was so shrill and low that it actually hurt her throat to speak. However, she managed to get each word out. She still did—they *needed* to be said.

Maxim breathed in deeply and shook his head. "I did not wish your death, Karine. You've got that wrong. I just didn't know how to be a father to a dead child—I was already a broken man when they took her from me, too, no? I didn't know what had been done to you or how that was going to affect the rest of your life. I was too busy drowning in my own hell. It was an easier place to be."

Karine snapped her face away from him. "Because you're a coward—you still don't know what he did to me that day."

Or every day after, for that matter.

Dima's assaults had never really stopped. They haunted her from childhood through her teenage life, and then straight into adulthood as well. She'd been a toy that he used and abused for years, her fractured brain shelving away and categorizing each incident as something for someone else in her mind to deal with.

Never, *ever* for her.

They'd always made sure he didn't hurt her, after all. It was one of the only things she was grateful for where Katina and Katee were concerned. Her brokenness had purpose—it *did* save her. In a way.

"I do know, actually," Maxim replied, inflection dipping in his tone. "Masha told me everything."

Most of the time, Karine forgot how much Masha actually knew about what happened that fateful day when her sister was killed. Mostly because they never discussed it in real depth, and Masha had come along after it happened. Too many pills, a bit too much liquor, and she spilled the secrets in slurred words that she hadn't even thought her caretaker truly heard one evening. She wanted to hide away from the world and never talk about it again. The shame that she kept close to her heart because she continued to be abused by a monster and never had the courage to say a thing about it.

Masha created the perfect safe-space for her where she could continue to live in a dulled state of mind, always at the ready to make any bad feelings disappear the only way she knew how where Karine was concerned.

Of course, she told her.

"I wish I knew about it sooner, Karine. I wish you had told me—"

"Why?"

"Because I would have done something about it. I never would have let Dima or Leonid continue with their position in our bratva. Hell, I could have buried them in the basement the same fucking night, what difference would it make?"

"You practically fed me to him."

Dima, she meant.

Maybe her father didn't realize it, but she was willing to give him a wake-up call.

"So many times you sent me away crying, just for being near you, and he'd be there waiting ... pinning me into corners, covering my mouth, so you couldn't hear me just twenty feet away, but I could still hear you angry and raging. Once he hurt me so bad, just outside the door of your study, that I passed out. You had a maid clean up the blood. You never even asked where it came from, Daddy."

"I didn't know," he said lowly.

"But you *should* have. You should have known."

"I'm sorry—you're right. I should have known, Karine."

Was he?

Did it even matter?

Karine couldn't make herself look at her father. It was too painful to acknowledge all the wasted time of her childhood, and the way he'd—unknowingly or not—facilitated her loss of innocence and constant torment.

What if she had told her father instead of Masha? Would her life have looked completely different then?

She doubted it.

Maybe he cared now, but he never did *then*—and that was the only time she'd actually needed him.

"So, you're saying this is all my fault?" she asked. "That I did this to myself?"

Maxim drew closer to her, his two steps taking away most of the space between them. Startled by his movement, she glared at him, forcing him to moved back again.

"I apologize," he muttered, "I just ... can't stand to hear you say that. None of this is your fault. I can't blame you for surviving, even if in the end that meant you—"

"Tried to kill you," she finished for him in a whisper.

Maxi sighed. "Yes. The plot … the one she made with Leonid."

Karine heard how he said *she*—the way he twisted the word a bit, his displeasure coating the pronoun like he couldn't manage to say her alter's name. Or simply didn't want to.

"Does she scare you?" Karine asked, honestly wanting to know.

He didn't answer right away. Karine waited him out; they had the time.

"I think she's scared, actually," he eventually said. "Angry and scared."

"You're not entirely wrong."

"But I never knew how to handle it—*you*, I mean. Like that."

His discomfort with her disorder wasn't new. That was the very reason he kept her locked away from the outside world. He was ashamed of what others might see as strange or shameful.

Instead of getting her the professional help she needed— Maxim did what he thought was his only option—keep her as sanitized as possible so he didn't lose face.

Karine didn't want to apologize to him for what Katina had plotted. She remembered what Roman said—Katina's actions were not hers. She never made the decision to kill her father, fear did.

Maxim searched her eyes and dabbed the back of his hand on his forehead. "It doesn't matter, no, because I deserved all of it, anyway. I deserved it. Every bit of it. I wasn't the father to you that I should have been. I neglected you terribly. You suffered because of the restrictions I imposed. Because I failed to see you."

Karine's heart hurt because she had waited so long to hear those words coming from her father. Her therapy with Michelle and Sylvia had not included the possible repercussions of her father apologizing to her. This was never a part of the plan.

And yet, it was happening.

Maxim seemed to understand.

ᴛʜᴇMARRIAGE

"It was only at the end, when I didn't know what would happen to me—that I decided I had to do something. One last act of father who cared, even if it was misguided. I sent you away with to give you a chance. It was the only option I had, and I wasn't sad when he took it from me."

One fat tear rolled down Karine's cheek. When she didn't wipe it away, the droplet fell from her chin to her lap.

"And thank you for that," she replied.

"*Da*," he agreed in Russian. "I see that worked out for you—a marriage, yes?"

"How could I say no?"

Even her father laughed.

She didn't remember hearing the sound before—it was as strange as it was interesting.

"I wished I could have told you myself—how much I wanted things to be different between us," Maxim said, his sudden emotion stunning Karine as much as his laughter. "How much I wanted to save you from Dima and Leonid, and your fate that I had personally signed. It was just too late. I'd done what I had done."

"So why didn't you? Why did you stage your own death instead—why *run?*"

"Because Leonid had grown far more powerful than I realized. Over the years, I had been so caught up with grieving and feeding my own selfish desires that I neglected the bratva. Leonid had it all planned out—I couldn't have won. He would have taken the seat right out from under me. I wasn't going to be safe in Chicago unless I went along with his plot, but I didn't even know about it until it was almost too late. Roman gave me time by telling me what he knew— not a lot, but enough, Karine. Enough time to make another choice."

Karine's heart beat faster when she heard his name. Her husband's name. A smile erupted on her face and Maxim nodded.

"Do you love him?" he asked.

Karine didn't even have to think about it. "He's not perfect, but I love him for that, too."

"Someone told me once that love doesn't have to be perfect, only yours. I believe it to be true. And now his family is facing the aftermath of what I left behind."

"Of Dima, you mean."

"I owe them everything," he said absent-mindly checking the time on his watch. "I know I do, but I need your help, Karine."

She stared at her father with her brows raised high. Never did she believe this day would come when her father stood there—asking for her help.

Karine didn't know what Maxim's plan was or what he wanted her to do, but the part of her that had been so angry all these years was slowly chipping away. Not because she thought he deserved it, or even because she loved him. But rather, because they were two souls with a purpose that she thought might be the same …

She didn't need Roman to tell her every detail to know that things were bad, and his family needed help. If the chance was handed to her to make it happen, why shouldn't she take it?

"What do you want me to do?" she asked.

"Dima is coming after what he wants. What he thinks belongs to him."

"Me," she replied, shuddering. "You can say it."

"Can and should are not the same thing. It won't make a difference to him that Roman married you. In his eyes, you were his property the moment I agreed to the wedding."

Karine could feel her lungs tightening in her chest again. "I'm not exactly in a position to do much at the moment."

"You can be. It's a matter of more details."

Right, but what kind?

"I won't force you into anything, Karine."

He hadn't even spelled out the damn plan.

She wrung her fingers, clasping and unclasping them tightly in her lap. A thin film of sweat formed on her forehead that she wiped away with the back of her long sleeve.

Karine really only wanted one thing.

"Will I be free?" she asked.

ᴛʜᴇMARRIAGE

Maxim nodded.

"In the end, you will be. Consider it my late wedding gift to you. I think you've earned it."

FIFTEEN

Roman was in his loft, knocking back his third shot of vodka, and it was barely even noon. Disregarding all pretenses that he cared about what his father demanded he do, he was more concerned with taking care of himself.

The vodka was all he could allow—and God knew he needed something to numb the hell inside his mind. Roman wasn't touching coke again, so liquor it was. Even Marky's death wasn't going to fuck him up. He had to stay clean.

If anything, that would have made Marky proud—that his death pushed Roman's resolve in that regard. Enough to keep him on his phone, scrolling Narcotics Anonymous meetings available across New York.

Not that he'd tell *anybody*.

It was a strange feeling to be alone. Especially for a man like Roman who had never allowed himself to feel like he *was* alone, and that it was a bad thing. Because he had also never acknowledged that he was vulnerable before.

ᵀᴴᴱMARRIAGE

Getting close to people tended to do that. *Caring* left him wide open to getting hurt.

When his phone rang he almost didn't pick up. Ignoring his trembling fingers shaking, he pressed it to his ear. The vodka had settled warmly in the pit of his stomach. He just had to wait a few minutes until it went to his head, numbing him for a while.

It wouldn't last very long, but it was better than walking around with the memory of seeing Marky lying dead in his father's driveway. It at least took the edge off his desire to get so high nothing mattered.

"Yeah?" he grumbled into the phone, scrubbing a palm down his face at the same time. He couldn't even be sure the person on the other end heard him.

"Mr. Avdonin." A female voice snapped him out of it. It was a voice he recognized—*shit*, he should have looked at the caller ID.

"This is Sylvia D'Souza, from the Twin Rivers facility in Nevada," she said.

It was the urgency in her tone that gained all of Roman's attention in an instant.

"Fuck," Roman muttered under his breath, running through scenarios in his mind about what spurred on the call. It could only be a few things, and given Karine's long stretch without an alter appearing, he worried that was the reason. If only because Katina had yet to show herself and not leave chaos in her wake. "What happened? Is she okay?"

The woman on the other end paused.

Just long enough to make Roman stand from the couch, unable to stop his sudden burst of nervous energy, demanding, "Well?"

"I'm sorry, Mr. Avdonin. Your wife … this morning … a few hours ago—"

"Spit it out!"

"She escaped, sir."

Roman stilled on the spot, that numbness he'd been craving came without warning, chilling him to the fucking bone. "What the fuck did you just say?"

Because *surely* ... no, she had to be wrong. He chose that facility for a reason. Their willingness to skirt the law in some cases to help families who could afford their services, for one. And the promise, by Michelle Wang, that Twin Rivers was undoubtedly the safest place to hide Karine given their location, and the security team on sight.

"Mr. Avdonin, please calm down," Sylvia said, her voice rushed but still hushed on the other end of the call. He could only imagine *why*—undoubtedly, the facility was trying to cover their asses. "I know this is stressful. We have sent out a search party to look for her."

"She ran away—what, on foot?" he spat back, not bothering to quell the growing rage. "And you haven't found her yet? I mean, how far could she have gone without anything to get her there? What the fuck are you useless pieces of shit even doing up there?"

"This happened earlier—by the time they notified me, I wasn't even on the property today, it had been more than a couple of hours. She wasn't on foot, actually, and we suspect she might be farther than we can reach because of that. Her father was here to see her today, we had a new nurse working the front desk, and wasn't entirely familiar with Karine's file or case. She went off a miscommunication in the file, and allowed the visitation when Karine agreed. They, Karine and her father, disappeared together after. Based on the footage we've been able to find, it appears he took her with him when there was a distraction in the dining hall."

Her father.

Roman ended the call before Syliva said another word. It was all he needed to hear. Everything else fell into place far too easily.

Scarily so.

Maxim had found her—did he convince her or forcibly take her away from the facility? The only thing was—Roman had no idea where he would take her. Nobody even knew where Maxim was or where he'd been hiding all this time.

In an effort to keep Karine hidden from Dima—Roman had neglected the need to keep her hidden from her father, too.

^{THE}MARRIAGE

Apparently, the man had been waiting.

Time was up.

• • •

Roman took the stairs from the loft apartment to the garage below three steps at a time. The loud, rhythmic slap of his shoes to the stairs was the only sound he heard mixed in with his screaming, racing thoughts.

He had one option—charter a jet to Vegas, and *find her*. Catching a flight last minute would be a joke.

He didn't give a fuck anymore—not about his father's orders to stay in New York, or if he was going to be followed by Dima and his men. At this point, he literally had everything to lose. Karine was his everything, after all. He didn't give a fuck about the consequences of being seen, or how visible it would make him to officials. Too much damage had been done already. Marky was dead. They had too much attention from the FBI and police, and it wouldn't be long before the two merged to see how they might be able to help one another.

These were things that were entirely out of his control. Nothing could be done to stop what had already happened.

Roman focused on what he could—Karine, and locating her. He was the one who failed to keep her safe, no excuses.

He blamed himself for leaving her there. Maybe trying to prioritize getting her help should have taken a backseat to move her as far out of the country and reach as he could. His hubris was assuming he should have relied on anybody to take care of her.

That they were *capable*.

Nobody could be trusted.

Before he even had a chance to hit the unlock button on the fob for the rental Porsche he'd been using, a van pulled into the garage. The two men driving had parked five feet from Roman and jumped out before the garage door even closed completely.

Lincoln and Kostya nodded his way, but even their smiles were grim. He hadn't expected to see the two—men Marky

175

had considered friends in Roman's crew of guys, who worked closely for him.

"We have a surprise for you," Kostya said as Lincoln rounded the back of the van with Roman.

For a moment—Roman fantasized about seeing Karine sitting in there. That somehow, in a matter of a few hours, she had found her way to him. All the way from Nevada. It was a foolish, errant thought that he knew couldn't be true when nobody but him and the people in another state knew she was missing.

Of course, it wasn't Karine.

It was Masha.

She sat crouched in the corner in the back of the van. Her shaking betrayed the fear she was in, despite the courage with which she met Roman's eyes.

He stood there in silence, staring back at her until his brain managed to comprehend the piece of the puzzle that had suddenly been laid at his feet.

"Found her hanging around Leon's gas station," Lincoln explained as he stepped back beside Roman. "Begging for change so she could make phone calls."

"The feelers came through, then?"

The man nodded. "She was trying to sell some things—it gave us a general location. The streets did the rest."

"Who was she trying to call?" Roman asked.

Kostya jumped into the van so he could drag Masha out. Perhaps if Roman cared about the woman, or had any sympathy for the predicament she found herself in, then her screech when Kostya yanked her by her hair would have bothered him.

Instead, Roman figured, at this point, she deserved what she got. Especially if she had any hand in some of their current circumstances, and he suspected she did. Had she been a man they were looking for, she would have already been beaten beyond recognition before ever being placed at *his* feet.

"You'll have to ask her because she's not talking," Lincoln replied.

THE MARRIAGE

Bound at her ankles and wrists with zip ties, she crumpled to the ground in front of him, and she dared to look up at Roman with tears streaming down her cheeks. Her lips quivered, but she didn't speak.

He couldn't afford to let himself feel anything as he stared into the frightened face of a woman who might have answers to his most important question. Masha's disappearance had made little sense, and given she wasn't familiar with New York, wouldn't have survived without help from someone else.

There was only a couple of people she might have been in contact with—Maxim, or Dima. Roman was starting to think regardless of which man he found, one prick would lead him straight to the other. Who was chasing who here?

Where was Karine?

"Get her in the basement," he ordered the men, pulling a cigarette out to light between his lips.

He'd changed his mind about going to Nevada to find Karine.

He had seen it in Masha's eyes—she was scared for a reason. She did have answers. Roman intended on prying them out of her.

• • •

The men carried Masha to the basement of the garage without removing her binds. As Roman flicked his cigarette butt to the floor and approached her, he noticed the gash on the bottom of her lip which bled a little when she grimaced.

It wasn't a *new* injury, the split through the healing scab said it had been reopened.

"Who did that?" he asked, curious if she would tell him the truth. Whatever that truth was, even if it was as simple as someone on the streets had roughed her up. Her willingness to be honest and talk was the only thing that might allow her to see the outside of this basement.

Masha wouldn't meet his eyes, then, but she also didn't bother to struggle with her ties. Likely knowing it was a pointless endeavor.

177

"Maxim," she whispered. "Because he found out I had stolen things that could be traced."

Masha constantly surprised him.

More than he should let her.

"Leave," Roman demanded to the quiet space, needing privacy for the conversation and events that might come next. The men locked the basement door behind them when they left, and he already had his sharp gaze back on Masha. "You're going to tell me everything—right fucking now."

Masha shook her head, those eyes of hers growing big and wild. "I can't—you don't understand."

"What the fuck did you do?" Roman hissed.

He had no reason to raise his voice. Masha was well aware of what men like him could do. Her whole life was a testament to it.

Still, she said nothing.

Roman gave her a second chance. "How did you find out where Karine was?"

Her admission of being near Maxim geared his questioning in that direction. He was trying to connect dots; testing the waters to see if he hit the right mark with Masha, but she gave him nothing.

Definitely, she refused to speak.

As if she had a *choice*.

When she dared to square her trembling shoulders in the face of his anger, he lunged at her, grabbing her by the jaw, and digging his thumbs into her cheeks. She gasped, letting out a broken cry while she struggled to get out of his grip, but she was powerless.

Roman drew her forcibly towards him, pulling her by the face and feeling her hot, wet tears slide over his fingers. "Let me make something very clear to you—in the grand scheme, you mean nothing. Not to me. You will tell me everything in the end, every detail of what you did, or what you know. Whether or not I have to make you tell me, Masha, is where you can make it easy, or I can make it really hard. And trust me, the only person it's going to be hard on—is you. I'll enjoy watching you bleed."

ᴛʜᴇMARRIAGE

He let go of her, shoving her away and Masha fell back with a sob, still shaking like a leaf in the wind.

Roman stood over her, telling the woman, "She thought of you as a mother. A protector. Someone she could trust, and look what you did to her. You betrayed her. You betrayed me. I swear to God if he's going to hurt her, I'll fucking kill you. I'll keep you alive until I know, and every second will be so painful for you."

Masha pulled in a shaky, loud breath before saying, "I-I didn't hurt h-her. All I ever did was keep her safe. She is the only ... the closest thing to family I have. I j-just want to keep her s-safe."

The words seemed to break the woman. Her sobs became more violent, and she couldn't contain her shuddering as she cried.

He didn't feel sorry for her. He hated her pitifulness, and that part of him believed her. Whether it was her willful ignorance, or something else, he did think she truly cared for Karine like she proclaimed to. If only that made a difference to *him*.

"How did you find out where I took her?" he asked again.

Masha tried to breathe slower. She gulped in large mouthfuls of air, exhaling in steady streams of three and four seconds long. Eventually, she'd calmed enough to mutter without stuttering, "Your father's office. I found some contact information in his desk drawers from a file I had taken. We were trying everything. It was just a number and a name on a Post-it, but when I called it—"

Roman cursed severely under his breath, stopping Masha from saying anything more. He knew it. The rage coursed through him like a leather belt whipping his back. He was mad at himself for being so careless. He never should have shared that information with his father. Yet, what was done was done.

"She's where she should be," Masha suddenly whispered.

And just like that, the anger simmering inside of him boiled over. He wouldn't have struck her so hard with his open palm had he been even a couple of steps back, with her out of reach. But instinct drove him to slap away the lie that she dared let slip out of her mouth.

Fuck her.

Karine had nothing and no one before Roman—and he was nothing and no one without her.

Masha fell with a piercing shriek, sprawling on the floor.

Roman straightened up again.

"Fucking bitch," he groaned under his breath.

He *really* didn't want to do that—hit her. It wasn't his style to hit women, and when a situation came up, he often let others do the job … if it absolutely had to be done. He always saw his mother or sister's face, and couldn't stop himself from imagining how it would feel to see a man beat them.

In their business, justified or not …

Regardless, Roman would do whatever he needed to do here to get the information he needed about Karine, and her current whereabouts. He hadn't lied, by the time they were done here—Masha *would* tell him everything.

He allowed the woman on the cement floor to gather herself before he spoke again. The slap to her face was just a demonstration of what he was willing to do to get the information he needed from her. The *only* sympathetic part of him hoped she had learned her lesson before this got way worse.

Masha managed to sit up again after a while, rubbing at her cheek with her bound hands the best she could to soothe the sting. "I had to do something—you took her away from me! I didn't know where she was."

Roman pulled a chair out of the corner—an old, foldable thing someone had thrown into the basement and forgot about it. Turning it around, he sat facing her with his arms propped up on the back of the chair.

He shook his head. "Actually, from where I sit, it looks like you wanted to find out where Karine was to supply Maxim with that information."

Masha said nothing but her wet gaze pleaded with him, begging him for some respite. It wasn't coming. This wouldn't end until he had everything he needed from her.

^{THE}MARRIAGE

Sighing shakily, she whispered, "Karine belongs with her father."

Was that what she honestly believed?

"The father who treated her like shit for all her life—who hid her away because he was ashamed of her? The one who was willing to give her to a *monster*—that father?"

"He didn't know what happened," Masha rushed to say like it was going to make a difference. "He never knew. *I* told him, and you don't know Maxim … not like I do."

He felt an ache in his body; somewhere deep that he couldn't quite shake when she said those words.

"You knew all along and did fucking nothing?" he asked, coldly calm.

Masha's gaze hardened at his accusation. "I did the only thing I knew I could do. The only thing within my power. I kept her as safe as I could when I was with her but—"

"You kept her hidden."

"You took her away," she snapped back. "You have no idea what it was like to live in that house, to be around those men. If Dima or his father thought Karine would ever talk or reveal the truth, they'd have killed her just like Katina. The only reason they let her live was because her behavior proved she would never talk. And she never did."

Masha gulped more air into her lungs, trying to regain some semblance of control, but it didn't help. Her lip bled even more from the blow Roman had dealt across her face.

"So you plied her with drugs," he said, lifting a shoulder. "You call that helping? Feeding her a concoction of medications that aren't even proven helpful for her disorder?"

In fact, he was starting to believe that shit had only made her worse.

Masha shook her head. "The drugs kept her subdued."

"The drugs kept her submissive when she was *high*. To you and her father. Or to anyone else who wanted to do what they wanted with her."

"Maxim knew nothing. He thought his daughter was … different," she tried to argue.

"He thought his daughter was unworthy of his love or attention. That she was something he could use to get what he wanted. A union with Leonid's family, to strengthen the control he thought he had over the man, and to get her off his hands. Let's not pretend different."

Roman was certainly beyond that shit.

"He never would have agreed to it if he knew what Dima had done!"

The way she said that made him think those weren't her words, but Maxim's. Just how much time had she spend with the man while she was missing?

Roman narrowed his eyes at Masha. She seemed unnaturally sympathetic to a man who had been nothing but a master to her for a good portion of her life. He never allowed her to be a free woman, but she still showed him a loyalty Roman didn't understand.

"You care about him."

"He gave me a life. Better than the one I had," she returned simply.

If only that mattered.

"I don't give a fuck what you think Maxim would have done if he knew the truth. You say he knows the truth now. So be it—where has he taken Karine?"

Her mouth hung open, and her chest collapsed roughly with a rattling breath. Her shoulders shook with the effort of trying to catch her air, her sob as wet as her tears. It was a pitiful sight.

"I swear to you—I don't know," she replied.

He could have killed Masha. Right then, right there. He had his weapon tucked into the back of his pants, and it would have taken so little effort to pull it out and shoot her in the head. She fucking deserved it.

Maybe they all did.

So many of them had failed Karine.

Over and over.

Again and again.

Even me, he thought.

⁓MARRIAGE

Masha had single-handedly fucked up his plan for keeping Karine safe. All because she thought she knew what was best for her.

The only thing that did save her in that moment was Karine. Roman didn't kill her because he wanted to leave her alive for his wife to make the final decision; her emotional attachment she had towards this woman, and the fact she had, in a way, tied her future to Karine meant that she should decide how, or if, Masha's life would end.

Roman didn't consider that he wouldn't find Karine—not for a second. He would bring her back to him, and when he did, she could decide what needed to be done to the woman who had betrayed her.

"You won't be able to keep Maxim's hiding place from me for very long. I will find Karine, and when I do, everyone who was involved in taking her from me will pay for it. Mark my fucking words, Masha."

Tears freely rolled down her cheeks as she said, "I don't know where they are. Maxim wouldn't give me that information."

Roman was sure it was true. Maxim would have used Masha to gain access to Karine—and no matter what their relationship was, he wouldn't risk being found by divulging his whereabouts to Masha. Clearly, she was as disposable to Karine's father as she was to Roman. Shame that the only one who did care for Masha was the same women she had put in danger by doing what she'd done.

Roman rubbed a hand over his face, the frustration growing as the questions bounced between one to another in his mind. Where would he even begin looking for her? Where could Maxim have taken her—back to Chicago? Were they hiding out in the Nevada deserts? Was he going to return her to Dima and make peace?

How long do I have to find her?

"You helped someone take her from where she was safe. Where she was finally getting the help she needed. Now what? She's with the same man who has used and manipulated her all her life."

Masha yelled her anger back at him. "He is her father! He deserves a chance to—"

"He deserves fucking *nothing*. I was taking care of her! You saw what she was like in Vermont. How much better she was doing. You saw that, Masha. *Why?*"

The woman said nothing, her pursed lips wet with her tears, and a hard gaze turned on the wall away from him.

That was it.

Right then, Roman was done.

"Fuck this," he muttered, standing from the chair. "You're insane. All these years, Karine was wrong in thinking you were on her side when all you did was whisper in her father's ears. How long have you been warming his bed?"

Masha shook her head violently. "I love her, too. It's not just about him."

Roman was already walking away.

She shouted at his back, "You have to believe I love her, too!"

"Yeah, but at what fucking cost."

He didn't wait for a response before he left the basement.

SIXTEEN

His mother rarely ever came to the loft to visit him, and that suited Roman just fine.

So, when he emerged from the basement to find Claire standing next to a vehicle that was in the process of being chopped down by two of the guys—who had scattered earlier when the boys arrived—Roman was more than surprised.

"Ma."

She looked away from the pieces of dismantled vehicle to find him wiping his hands on a rag one of the guys had left on a work bench. More red than usual, her cheeks and sunglasses belied the calm way she presented herself. She didn't have to say she was worried—he could see it.

Claire still fixed a warm smile on her face and walked open-armed toward her son. Tipping her head sideways at the car, she asked pointedly, "Can we talk—why don't you invite me up to your loft?"

"We can go upstairs," Roman told her, "but I don't want you cleaning up after me."

His mother was who she was. Cleaning was the way she coped, but he hadn't needed his mother picking up after him since he was a boy. She didn't need to be in his business in that way, either.

"No, don't worry, I'll leave that for Karine—if you'll even let her tidy your things. You always were particular about that."

Claire curled an arm around him so he could lead the way. Hearing Karine's name made him a little sick. He wasn't sure if his mother knew that Karine was missing from the facility. How would she?

In the loft, he found it amusing the way his mother refrained from pointing out all the little things that might make his place feel more like home. Or rather, a home to her standards. She wouldn't mean any harm, but he'd learned to like less.

"Coffee?" he asked, trying to ease her into the reason she was there.

Adrenaline raced through his veins. Masha was still in the basement, tied up and left in her own misery until he was ready to say otherwise. Claire would have undoubtedly, immediately gone to the woman's rescue if she knew— regardless of what Masha had done.

Is who she is, he repeated to himself.

He couldn't say he was the same.

Clearly.

Karine was still missing, and Roman had every intention of going out there to look for her, the very first second he could. Even if he didn't have shit to work with. He prepared the coffee while his mother surveyed the *Guns & Ammo* magazine he'd left sitting on the island.

"You and Karine will have to get a bigger place when she's out. A much nicer place. I'll start looking at some properties. Of course, we'll want the two of you to live close to us," Claire said. "It'll probably make things easier."

Her rambling told him that she was trying hard to cover her own emotional turmoil. Marky dying would have been a blow to her, too. As graceful and strong as his mother was—kindness and humanity were at her core. It's why she'd been a nurse for so many years. She formed emotional attachments easily to the people in her life. The people she liked.

"Like what things?" Roman asked as he brought a mug of coffee over to her.

She offered him a weak smile. "I didn't mean anything. With Karine, I just assum—"

"We don't know what it's always going to look like."

Claire nodded, then shook her head. "We're here to help. I know the last few days haven't been easy for you, son. Marky didn't deserve what happened to him, but Roman, you're married now. You have a woman who relies on you and loves you. You can't put yourself in danger for revenge. Blood keeps spilling."

He understood. Roman let his mother finish speaking, before he took a sip of his own coffee.

She stared at him, waiting for a response, but he really had only one thing to say.

"I'll deal with Marky's death later. Right now I have to focus on finding Karine."

"*Finding* Karine—what?"

"Maxim broke her out of the facility she was staying at."

Claire quickly found the stool to sit down at the island, and she clung to the coffee mug in her hand like she needed the warmth. Her lost stare gazed into the creamy pool of coffee for a long while before she finally asked, "How … how could this happen? They were going to keep her safe there. You made sure of it, right? Your father said—how did Maxim find her?"

"It was Masha. Some of the paperwork she stole from Dad's office had information on the facility. She's been in contact with Maxim this whole time, and I think you can figure out the rest."

Roman sat in the chair across from his mother, drumming his fingers to the island before clenching them into tight fists to stop the jitteriness racing through his veins. Helplessness was not his strong suit.

He didn't know where to go looking for Karine. He didn't know the first thing about locating Maxim. What plan did he have—what did he even fucking *want* with Karine? At this point, Roman suspected it wasn't for anything good. How long did he have before she was no longer safe with her father?

Was it already too late?

For the first time, he acknowledged that helplessness and wondered if that was how Karine felt.

All the time.

Not knowing what would happen to her next. Being in the dark about every aspect of her own life.

Claire covered her face with both hands. "Does your father know?"

"Nobody knows. I've only recently found out myself. I have to go looking for her, Ma."

"Roman," she hissed, shuddering as she glared at him with bloodshot eyes. "*You can't.* You wouldn't know where to look. Where would you go? Think about it."

She wasn't wrong.

He also wasn't rational.

"I'll start with Nevada. There has to be something for me to find. The man isn't a fucking ghost."

Claire shook her head.

"Your father will never allow it. You can't go anywhere. It's too dangerous right now, Roman. Look at what happened to Marky."

"My father doesn't need to know. At least, not until I'm already gone."

Claire stood up, then, placing the mug softly down on the table and meeting his gaze at the same time. "I suppose that means you'll have to get past me, then—will you do that?"

Goddammit.

• • •

"This feels like a trap," Demyan said. "You can't leave New York. Not now when all eyes are on us. Even the cops are trying to watch every move you make. They'll trail you wherever you go, so if you think you can rush in, guns blazing, and find Karine—it's not going to happen. You'll just end up leading everyone else to a bigger problem that nobody needs. Or worse, you'll lead Dima directly to her."

The only way Claire moved out of the way back in his loft was when Roman agreed to take her back to the house and talk to Demyan. She stayed close to him the whole time—like she thought Roman wouldn't leave if she was at his side the moment he stepped out of his place.

Really, it was a matter of respect—he wouldn't defy his mother's wishes.

At the house, even though she didn't want to leave—Demyan made Claire go up to her room and take a bath so she could relax. Before she left she made Demyan promise that he wouldn't let their son leave New York.

Roman stood there, blazing up with rage and frustration while his father made the promise to his mother of, "He's not going anywhere."

Satisfied, because her husband always kept his word when he gave it to her, Claire stepped out of the office. Finally, the two men were alone.

"What kind of a trap?" Roman asked

Demyan sucked in a deep breath, tapping his pen on the desk. "Karine going missing and word getting back to you that Maxim went off with her—it feels like a trap. Look at it as if it all feels very convenient. A ploy to lure you out of New York and alone in Nevada."

"You think Maxim is working with Dima?"

"I don't know what to think. I can't figure it out. There are a lot of holes in this story."

Obviously.

Knowing that did nothing to help, though.

"So you don't trust Maxim, either?"

"I do trust him," Demyan returned fast, adding after, "... or at least I'm foolish enough to. Our last conversation— right before the house burned down—was something else. He sounded like a different man."

Tigers didn't lose their stripes.

Roman arched a brow. "Why would he take Karine out of the place she was safest at, then?"

"Maybe he didn't look at it that way. Maybe he thought you were the one who abandoned her, and he had to step in and take care of the girl," Demyan answered.

There was very little Roman could do to control his frustration at that ridiculous answer. He gripped the back of the leather bucket chair until the blood ran out of his knuckles, and the skin turned white.

Demyan said and did nothing—allowing his son the outlet to release his rage.

Just when Roman thought he was back on track with Karine—just when he thought he would prove himself, get his act clean—he lost his best friend, and now he didn't have the first clue where his wife was. His sick wife who had, time and time again, believed in him to her own detriment.

Was he good for her?

Was Roman *any better*?

"We will find her, son," Demyan said after a long pause between the two.

"I'm not going to stop until I do. So yeah, you're damn right we'll find her. I just hope we're not too late. Unlike you, I haven't seen the good side of Maxim. I don't trust him to do right by Karine—he never did before. The past says a lot more about someone than a future they haven't even lived."

"He did right by her when he told you to take her and leave."

Roman tried not to think about that day in the car when they drove to New York. When she sat beside him, staring out of the window at a landscape she had never witnessed before, switching right before his eyes between herself and Katina as he tried to find some sense of steady ground amidst chaos. She'd found it with him—briefly.

Somehow.

She'd trusted him.

And where had that got her?

SEVENTEEN

Twenty-four hours.

Roman counted each of them.

Again and again.

Over and over.

He kept counting them. What else could he do?

Twenty-four hours of not knowing where Karine was, or how she was. Who she was with, even. And in that time, Roman had been able to do nothing other than pace around the house, waiting for something to happen.

As much as his father wanted to believe that Maxim wouldn't hurt his only living child, it was impossible for Roman to erase the memories of how he saw Karine being treated in the Yazov mansion.

Maxim had been dismissive and uninterested. Karine's very life and secrets were proof he had been neglectful and selfish, at least. Roman found it hard to believe that the man changed without an underlying motive, and he didn't want Karine to be her father's collateral.

Demyan didn't say it directly, but it was obvious he considered Roman a flight risk. The unspoken concern might have been encouraged by Claire who was in a constant state of paranoia that Roman was going to make a run for it.

And she wasn't off the mark.

So, not only was Roman back to being not allowed to return to his own loft, but he was also being constantly watched by the bulls again.

His every move was being reported back to the boss.

Roman itched.

Just *to go*.

It would be easy—yeah, it'd make a scene. But he'd made messes before. His father cleaned up more than once for his son. He was trying to do better, though. Roman wanted to be better for his parents, and Karine, too.

But barely.

He made phone calls to every contact that was relevant.

One of the many reasons Roman had picked that facility for Karine's treatment was because he didn't have a strong connection in Nevada to anyone or anything. He knew neither the Yazovs nor the Avdonins had much power or control out there, so she would be safe outside their territories where contacts were limited.

That backfired.

Roman didn't have many people to draw on as he raced to catch up with whatever footsteps Maxim and Karine might have left behind.

A lot of good it did.

He was in the same place where he started—right in the middle of fucking nowhere.

His guys at the loft were watching over Masha, and she still hadn't talk, sticking to her claim that she knew nothing. Maxim hadn't divulged that information.

Roman had come terribly close to ordering her death. The call would have been easy, and the minutes it might have taken before he got the confirmation could have been sweet, but he didn't.

His remaining conscience stopped him but still, the rage inside him festered. Poisonous as it ate away at his dying heart. It wasn't even the anger killing him—it was the unknown sucker punch to the fucking chest with every passing second that his wife wasn't beside him doing the job.

Fair was fair.

The universe gave Roman everything he felt like he deserved.

Distracted in his self-loathing, it took his cell phone three rings before he noticed it vibrating in his hands. Peering over the back property from a spare bedroom, he answered the call with a snapped, "What?"

Exhaustion was getting the better of him, but who could sleep?

"What's the fucking plan?" Lincoln asked. "For the rat problem in the basement, I mean."

Even on burner phones. One couldn't be too safe considering the circumstances. Roman immediately knew what the man meant as they were still holding down the issue at the loft with Masha.

Roman scrubbed his hand over his face to muffle the sigh. Masha needed to be kept in check and subdued until Karine was found, and then he would decide what to do with her. She was the least of his problems when she was just one more issue that was better kept contained at the moment. It was the man's short patience for watching Masha that irritated Roman the most, though.

"I have other shit to handle, man," Lincoln told Roman.

If only he cared.

"*And?* The organization has a problem. It trumps yours every time. As for the rat … leave it be, feed it occasionally. Otherwise, nothing," he growled into the phone.

He knew the guys didn't want the added responsibility of having to keep an eye on Masha. Tough shit—they really had nothing left to do after they removed the remaining stolen car from the garage. Work was out of the question with attention on them again, anyway.

Reminding himself everybody was human, he unlatched the window's lock, pushed it open, and lit a smoke. He went back to the conversation with Lincoln after the first drag of nicotine soothed his frayed nerves with a slightly better attitude.

Not by much.

"Listen, I get nobody wants to play babysitter, but it won't be for long, okay?" he asked the man.

Lincoln grumbled something too low for Roman to hear before muttering, "Whatever, man."

"Bill me for the food," Roman joked dryly. "It's the least I can do."

"Don't speak so soon. Kostya just made another run about a half hour ago. That's our fifth in—"

Beep.

Roman jerked the phone away from his ear to eye a number on the screen he didn't recognize. Call-waiting. Only a select few people had the digits to his burner phone at any given time as he replaced them often and only kept in contact with people he needed to at any given moment. Everything else could wait, and for a long time, it served him well.

Lincoln's voice buzzed in the phone, but Roman was already answering the strange number. "*Da?*"

The Russian came out smooth, and the reply was damn near as instant.

"Roman—it's Chet."

The unknown voice spoke like the two men were friends.

"Who the hell are you?"

"Not important. Listen, it's unfortunate that your man Kostya had to die, but he was kind enough to give me your phone number. Tell his friend I left the food on the dumpster. The rats might get it, though. I digress ... I have a message for you." Roman didn't even have time to process what was being said before the man named Chet added, "A message for the Devil of Little Odessa—bit dumb, that name."

A hired gun?

Maybe.

He got that impression, but who knew? Dima could be working with anyone. A lot of people would do a lot of things for the right price.

ᴛʜᴇMARRIAGE

"Who's sending the message?"

Although, he was sure he knew. Bringing up a childhood moniker that had chased him into a wild adulthood like it was a joke screamed pettiness.

And Dima.

Roman wasn't wrong.

"Dima wants to meet with you," Chet said on the phone as Roman checked the windows, scanning the property. He had moved into the room across the hall to survey the front of the house as the man added, "Your father has refused to sit with him, so he will settle for meeting you instead. For now as this is his last attempt at peace."

Peace?

Since when had Dima shown any concern for someone's peace?

At the moment, Roman was fairly certainly Dima didn't have eyes or hands on Karine. Gut instinct told him that, more than anything else. Dima might not get him closer to her, if anything, and he wasn't going to entertain the asshole if it could be helped.

Not if Karine wasn't safe ...

It was clear the guy had a sick plan for her. Roman's mind was just creative enough to torture him with possibilities. He wouldn't inadvertently walk his wife into a lion's den.

"You can tell him to go fuck himself. Nobody from the Avdonin family will ever talk to that piece of shit. He's a dead man walk—"

"Your best friend was just the start of it," Chet interrupted smoothly, seemingly unbothered by Roman's rant. "Dima wants what he wants. He has nothing to lose. You have everything, see. I hear your mother likes roses ..." Giddy laughter followed before the man said, "The choice is yours—but don't take too long to think. I'll call again with details."

The call hung up as fast as it had come in, and just like when it did, Roman was left staring at the screen.

His messenger was gone.

The only thing he was left with was a choice.

• • •

Demyan poured vodka in two shot glasses and walked over to his son with both in his hands. "Do it on his terms, then. If he's made a threat on your mother—"

"You can't be serious," Roman replied.

"It's not exactly like he can kill you in broad daylight, either. And he is looking for exactly this reaction from you and the rest of our family," Demyan added, shrugging as he fell into chair behind his desk. He'd come home from a lunch with Roman's mother the second his son called about the message from Dima.

Down the hall, he could hear his mother talking to his grandmother—Viviana. Nobody liked being moved to safe places when bad stuff went down because of their association to the mob, but that was the life they had all chosen. Sometimes, the only thing they could do was bicker amongst themselves about it.

Roman tried to ignore his mother's conversation to deal with the one at hand with his father.

Demyan hadn't missed a beat. "He doesn't like being ignored, and that's what we've been doing so far. He feels like we aren't treating him with the respect he deserves."

"He deserves to die."

"Does he?" Demyan passed his son a look. "You've only said some. I didn't want to ask for more than you were willing to tell me about her … and him."

Roman swallowed hard, refusing to meet his father's gaze and instead fixing his own on the window and the view outside. "He's mad."

"As in—"

"What does it matter?"

There were things Roman didn't want to repeat. He knew Karine wished the same, but she'd never be released from her memories.

"Exactly the reason why we need to take his threats seriously. Before he does something that lands us all in jail for a spell. We don't know where Karine is right now. We don't know what Maxim is planning, either. The only thing we can do is give in to Dima's demands. Or at least make him believe we are, and if you think about it … we do have the upper hand."

"Christ. How so?"

"We know something he doesn't realize we know."

Roman fell into the chair in the corner of his father's office with his head in his hands, trying to make sense of his current state.

If he went in for a meeting with Dima—he wasn't sure how he could walk away from there without ending the man; without making him suffer.

"Why do I feel like the key to this is understanding how much of a sad and pathetic fuck Dima truly is," Demyan said, although he didn't pose it as a question.

Which was fine.

Roman didn't really have an answer.

"When the messenger calls again with details," Demyan said, pushing up from his chair to head for the wet bar and vodka with his empty glass, "agree to the meet."

• • •

The abandoned farmhouse made of bricks on the border of the New York state line was as far from Brighton Beach as Roman could imagine. He'd suspected Dima was using a property within the state as a haven, but they hadn't been able to pinpoint exactly where. The tiny, rural communities that took them through their trip would have kept the visitor safely hidden from view as long as he came and went quietly.

They were also told to bring no more than one armed bull each—otherwise, they'd be shot on sight.

Roman tried to argue with Demyan again on the legitimacy of their plan. They would be severely outnumbered by Dima's men if they followed through with this, but his father was quick to remind him that they had no other choice. This was it.

If they refused to meet with Dima now, their bratva would be met with more violence. How hot could the water get before it boiled them to death? His family couldn't bear the pressure bearing down around them.

Roman gripped the steering wheel hard as he drove to the farmhouse in his car. He had one bull assigned to him, while his father drove his car behind him. Pavel was with him. He whispered Karine's name under his breath a million times on the drive just to keep himself focused.

She was why he was here—doing this.

Simple as that.

Dima's men guarded the front of the farmhouse. Armed and ready for an attack. They didn't speak as the Avdonin men and their bulls were directed inside.

Dima hid his surprise at seeing Demyan there—but not well, and only for a second. It was the only upper hand Roman and Demyan really had. To bring the boss that had been consistently refusing to even grace Dima with his attention.

Until he hit the right button.

Demyan's wife.

At their entrance, Dima didn't move from where he sat in a tattered, old armchair in the middle of a large room which may have been a flourishing domestic scene at some point. Now, however, the walls were all broken down with holes littering each and every one. A cracked portrait lay in pieces on a dust-covered floor.

One lightbulb flickered on the ceiling, and there was a large enough hole between the second floor and in the roof that he could look straight up and see the moon overhead. He bet the place had been a cheap, fast buy. It looked like something that someone would want to just … get off their hands. He was shocked it even had power.

Dima was a bright contrast to the mess of the room in his black, three-piece suit and shined loafers. Twisting an unlit cigar between his fingers while his gaze jumped between father and son, the rest of his men stood in a small semi-circle behind him.

A silent wall of threats.

What a greeting.

ᴛʜᴇMARRIAGE

Dima was taking extra effort to command their respect—from the unknown location that was out of the way, to the quiet men eyeing them, ready for their first move. It was laughable.

"It's been a while, Dima, and I was starting to get worried about you," Roman said jokingly.

Dima didn't seem to appreciate the dry humor. "Quit playing the fool. You should be fucking grateful I didn't kill you on that highway when I had the chance."

Roman nodded, smirking a little. "No, you just left me there to bleed or freeze to death. It was exactly the reminder I needed."

"Reminder of what?"

"That I don't like being told what to do. You're right, man, you should have killed me when you had the chance."

Dima's face molted with his rage but despite the way he glared like he might jump out of his chair at Roman, he only muttered back, "All of this can be over very soon. You have something of mine, and I want it back. Just like that—simple. It's all I'm asking."

"*It?*" Roman asked, his tone edging dangerously low.

"You know what I'm talking about. I told you, yeah? We're done playing stupid—and I refuse to indulge spoiled *sukas*. We're here to do what we have to do, no? Let's do that, pup."

Roman didn't even acknowledge the insult.

The bastard wanted it.

Dima leaned towards one of his men, sticking his cigar between his lips. The guy lit it without question, and the two were cloaked behind a cloud of smoke for a few passing seconds.

"Karine isn't an object to own," Roman stated, wanting that to be clear. He didn't care how his tone came off, or if he had plastered just enough *fuck you* in it for the other man to hear, but he figured the words did the job regardless.

Demyan made the slightest movement beside him, likely to serve as a reminder for Roman to not lose his shit. He'd already figured that was going to be a toss up. They *did* need this asshole to back off a little in New York because his

199

antics caused an already-growing pile of problems to get larger.

Roman couldn't forget that side of things, either. There were so many reasons this meeting needed to go well, and so many more that he had for it to end as bloody as possible.

Dima smiled.

It truly was a strange sight, knowing what he did about the man ... He could make his face seem *so* friendly, even if it was without sincerity, but one wouldn't necessarily know it straightaway. *Disarming*, really, that monsters looked so much like everyday people.

"Is that what you think she is—*human*?" Dima barked out with a laugh. "She's nothing but a bitch who's lost her marbles. If I had a dog, yes, he would make more sense than she fucking does."

Roman considered ending the man—he went as far as to mentally count the steps it would take to cross the room, reach him, and strangle Dima with his bare hands. Of course, the men with the weapons would have made it impossible but nonetheless ... he considered it.

It might have been worth it.

"So, what will it be? Are you going to sacrifice your bratva to keep my property hidden temporarily? Because you know I will find her," Dima continued, shrugging though his facial expressions didn't waver from his jovial, kind smile. "I will keep coming until finally I hit the mark. What then? You're the one whose home reeks of pig shit lately, old—"

"We're not friends."

It was Roman's turn to chuckle, the sound of it wiping that smirk from Dima's face as he scrubbed his palm down his own, and shot his father a quick look from the side. The man was an idiot.

"She's gone," he said with a little grin.

Dima's façade slipped—his brows dipped low.

Roman lifted a shoulder, not giving the prick a chance to respond before he added, "Yeah, man, I couldn't believe it at first, either. We can't all be perfect, though, but you made a big mistake."

ᴛʜᴇMARRIAGE

Dima started to stand from the chair, asking in a snarl, "What do you think you *know* about my mistakes, huh?"

"I know that you left someone alive, and you were trying hard to keep everyone else from finding out, too."

Demyan lifted a hand, as if silently saying *hello,* before adding quietly, "Your attempts at getting a meeting with me was for nothing after all—we don't actually have what you want. And seeing as how Chicago hasn't cleaned up its own mess, I'm sure you can understand why New York will take a step back from here. Unless you want word to travel about Maxim … I mean, how long are you going to last here in the state once word gets around that you've been lying to gain people's *favors?* Pretending to be a king … I already sent out a few messengers to specific heads of enterprises I know you've worked with since arriving. You're one big target, Dima."

Roman's father flipped an indifferent wave of his hand, letting the steaming man across the room bear the brunt of more disrespect. Like he was saying he was done in a gesture because nothing more was worth the effort.

"And the beauty of this is—even I don't know where she is," Roman told Dima, nodding, "but she's not with you, and that's all I give a damn about."

Dima finally lost his composure, shouting, "She's to be married to *me!*"

Yeah, *about that* …

"Too late—she already married me."

It took a second to register.

A glorious second.

"What did you just say?"

Dima's face mottled red.

Time to bounce, Roman thought, already spinning around to leave with his father on his heels. He could hear Dima's tantrum spilling over, but Demyan's threat was clearly a real concern for the asshole because his men let them leave.

He waved a hand high, saying, "Yeah, we got married— kept it small and private, sorry you didn't get an invite. I have a feeling you don't love weddings. Don't really seem like the type, you know?"

201

"It doesn't mean shit," Dima yelled at his back.

"It does," Roman murmured over his shoulder.

Of course, it meant something.

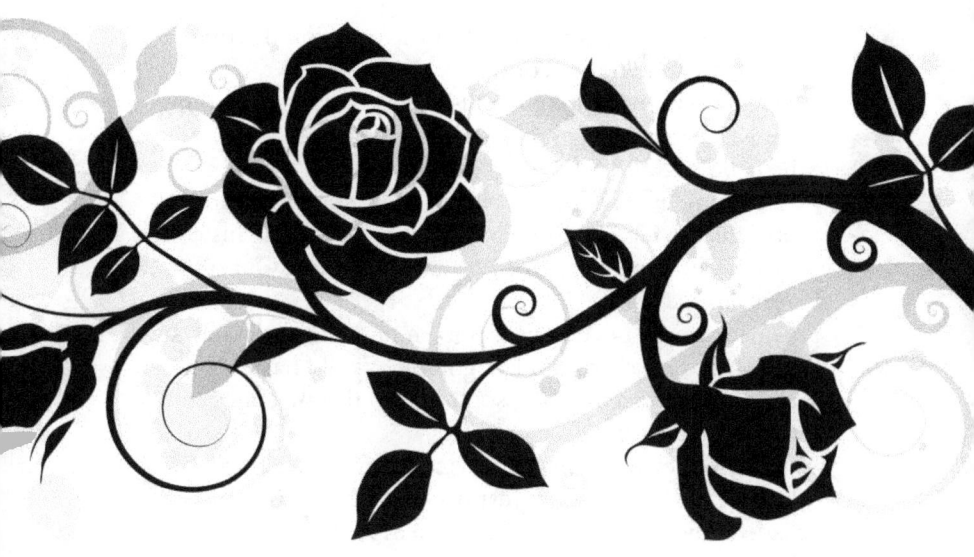

EIGHTEEN

Demyan Avdonin had never been the type to believe all was well, even when things worked to his favor. So even as the scene with Dima faded into the distance, seemingly over for a moment, the bratva boss's mind was still making sure everything was fine elsewhere.

Which was why as his man driving put more miles on the freeway, Demyan sent a message to his wife. He'd promised to, after all.

Tonight was one of the most difficult of his life.

In many ways.

He was an old friend to loss, and a long time ago, would have welcomed death just to escape the monster of that trauma. Yet, nothing quite matched up to what it felt like to stand in a secluded, dilapidated farmhouse surrounded by men who would have killed him and his son without hesitation—if it came to that.

Demyan had needed to be so sure of his hand walking in there, and he'd only been a little comfortable, to be honest.

A bad ending was never out of the question. It could have happened at any moment.

He'd done that enough in his past—rise, when nothing else was certain. Anything could have changed everything at the drop of a hat.

This time it was different because his son was there. All too often, it felt like Roman was the one running his own show. A lifetime away from his father's reach. Out of Demyan's control.

Claire would never have forgiven him had their only son not walked away from this night. She would have blamed him for encouraging their son to go to this meeting, and he would have let her do it.

Before they left, she was sent to a safe house for the duration of the meeting. Just because he and Roman had made choices in life that placed them in dangerous situations didn't mean his wife couldn't be safe while they did business.

So, he told her as much.

Claire would understand.

There was a lot more he wanted to tell her, but never would. He'd learned a long time ago she didn't enjoy watching her son step into the shoes and shadows of men who came before him.

Nonetheless, Roman had impressed him tonight. There was a lot on the line for his son, and Demyan supposed he was finally starting to show just how far he'd go for it.

Like always, Roman did things on his own time and schedule. Sometimes, he'd fit in what others around him needed, but at the end of the day, he still took what he wanted. Did what he had to do.

Like all leaders.

There was a reason they got to the top.

Claire's reply to Demyan's text, her confirmation she had arrived home before him, didn't come until he was minutes away from their gated community. By then, he'd gotten another text.

From security at the main gates.

Demyan paid a lot of money for the association of their community to look the other way and disregard his guests, along with not keeping a proper log to trace. He left nothing to chance.

"Drive faster," he demanded of Pavel in the front seat when he read the text from the guard.

A Mr. Yazov has been granted access to the community as your guest.

Demyan filled Pavel in on their new situation as he shot his message a message to Claire right after—*Get a gun.*

He only knew one *Mr.* Yazov.

What was Maxim doing now?

• • •

He found them in the kitchen, but Demyan sensed something was different the moment he'd stepped inside his house. The one thing he hadn't concerned himself with were his men—they'd known what to do the moment Pavel made a single call.

Claire would be safe until he got home.

That was *all* he cared about.

He stopped in his tracks at the kitchen door when he saw Maxim Yazov sitting at his kitchen table. He had been almost completely certain Maxim was alive, so much so that he'd been willing to send a number of messengers about such a fact, but Demyan was still taken aback to see the man just … there.

Claire was making coffee with her back turned to him, but she looked over at Demyan with a sweet smile.

Always *perfect*, she seemed entirely unconcerned by the scene, or the fact there were men posted just beyond her kitchen door. Of course, the bulls came and went often, but they weren't so formal.

Not like they currently stood, eyes averted when their boss walked in.

Demyan noted the gun his wife had set on the edge of the island, except it wasn't one he recognized. Maxim seemed to notice his stare.

"I offered her mine at the door," his old friend filled in quietly.

Demyan nodded, but said nothing else.

The kitchen was mostly dark, other than a dim light at the counter that helped Claire do her work making coffee.

It took him a moment to speak again; to find the words …

"You look well for a dead man," Demyan said.

Maxim immediately broke into a smile.

Claire brought two cups of coffee over to the table and placed it there. The second cup wasn't for herself, but for her husband. She glanced disapprovingly at Demyan, and he could read her mind with nothing more than a look into her eyes.

She was unhappy. Anger and frustration tugged her lips into a frown.

Her son and husband's lives were in danger tonight—and the man who was at the core of that was now at her kitchen table. She would be hospitable and polite, but she wasn't going to be friendly or warm.

Demyan didn't expect more.

She also retrieved the gun from the island, and placed it right in the middle of the table.

"I'll be in our room if you need me," she said before taking her leave from the kitchen. Her job was done. Maxim was Demyan's responsibility now, and he watched her go in silence.

He waited until Claire's footsteps had faded, and his men slipped out of the room before he turned back to Maxim.

"Where is your son?"

"Likely still on the freeway—we *are* trying not to draw attention, hmm?"

Maxim's brow raised high. "My apologies."

Demyan didn't really need the remorse—all the cameras were off, his house was swept daily for bugs at this point, and he had noticed the nondescript black car with tinted windows all the way around that Maxim had arrived in. Without a driver. The keys of that car sat on the table, closer to Demyan than the other man.

They had every reason to believe the agents tasked with watching their house couldn't actually get close enough to see anything worthy.

ͭͪᵉMARRIAGE

As long as Maxim left as quietly as he came, Demyan doubted anyone but the people there at that very moment would even know he'd been there to begin with.

"And I wanted to apologize to her for all the trouble I've caused," Maxim said. "If she'd let me, no?"

Well ...

"I don't think words are going to be enough to cut it," Demyan replied. "At this point, if you know what I mean."

Then he pulled up a chair and sat across from the man everyone thought was dead. The two stared at each other, seconds ticking by far too slowly, before Demyan sighed.

"What the fuck were you thinking," he muttered.

It wasn't even a question.

Flatly, Maxim replied only, "I wouldn't go out like that. By Leonid, while they curled like snakes around my legs. I deserved a better death than *that*."

Demyan sat a little straighter in the chair. "You realize the position you've put me in, and how it—"

"I'm sorry. What can I say, yeah? Who else would have cared, old friend?"

He didn't glorify that with a response, even if it was true.

Instead, Demyan asked, "How did you do it?"

"Leonid thought he was coming for me that night, but I was really there for him ... It doesn't matter, I got my answers."

"Answers?"

Maxim lifted his broad shoulders, and for the first time, Demyan noticed the man wasn't as well put together as he normally might be. His shirt wasn't perfectly pressed. His suit jacket had needed a wash a while ago, by the looks of it. And none of it appeared to bother the man at the other end of the table.

"About my daughters, and his son ... I had to know, Demyan," Maxim explained, glancing down at his clasped hands.

Demyan didn't ask details, just like he hadn't with Roman. And he wouldn't—unless they offered. It didn't feel like his business.

Why inflict more trauma?

"But in the end, I didn't really need to ask Leonid anything," Maxim added after a moment. "It didn't matter if he knew or not. All that mattered was he knew what his son was capable of, and that he wanted me dead."

"How long had he worked on this plan?" Demyan asked.

Maxim shrugged, and finally picked up his coffee to take a swig. Smacking his lips, he said, "I suspect it had always been his plan. He played a long game, Demyan. Snakes have the greatest patience."

Didn't Demyan know it?

A man was never ready ...

All the talk was nice and everything, but Demyan figured he should move on to what was most important. What he suspected his son was probably racing there to ask himself.

"Where is Karine, Maxim?"

"I heard about the wedding," the other man said flatly.

Demyan let out a hard breath, eyeing the gun between them, though he had one in a holster at his back. "He does love her."

"I know. She wasn't safe there, you see, if I could find her ... Dima would, too, eventually. Better that's on her terms, I think. If she sees him coming, maybe—."

"What do you mean?" Demyan interjected fast.

Maxim didn't answer, asking instead, "Did you tell her what I asked you to say?"

At first Demyan was confused, but then he remembered the end of that fateful conversation before the fire. When Maxim made him promise he would tell Karine that her father loved her.

"I haven't had the opportunity," Demyan admitted. "A lot has happened."

Maxim nodded and looked away.

"But it doesn't matter now, you can tell her yourself," he added. "Why didn't you?"

"*Nyet*," came the strong refusal. "I was never worthy of saying it."

That was a mindset Demyan couldn't comprehend.

He knew something about unspoken words and lost promises; he'd saw what life looked like when it didn't turn

out exactly how one planned. He remembered that clearly—
but also what it was like to feel something real for someone
again. To love his children unconditionally.

Except, Demyan suspected Maxim didn't share the same
growth. Somewhere along the lines, the man had been
stunted in his grief … did love start to feel a little dangerous?

Not quite worth the risk?

"I want you to do it for me, Demyan. I want you to
promise you'll tell her someday. Soon," Maxim pressed as he
met Demyan's gaze. "It's important … I just can't do it."

Demyan had to nod, although he didn't understand why.
Compelled by the man's insistence, he agreed.

In the shadows of the kitchen, the two were so quiet that
he could hear shuffling of feet somewhere outside the space.
The sound gained Maxim's attention, too, drawing his gaze
to the entryway.

"I'll tell her," Demyan told Maxim, wanting his stare back
on him so that maybe he could get those answers for his son,
"but I want you to know that you'll kill my son if something
happens to that girl. Where is she?"

"Exactly where she needs to be."

Maxim delivered that news with a hollow tone that left
Demyan cold right down to his bones. Disbelief washed
through him just as fast, but didn't leave him any warmer.

"What have you done?" Demyan asked.

Because nothing else made sense.

Demyan was still missing something.

Maxim dropped his gaze, saying, "You've always been too
smart for this business."

Fuck that.

He wasn't going in that circle again.

Demyan's fists hit the table hard. "This is starting to feel
like a fucking set up to me—like you're forcing me to walk
into another pile of shit I don't see. Give me some fucking
answers."

Maxim's attention fixated on the gun between the two
sitting in the middle of the table, although closer to Demyan.

"You'll have to … get rid of it," Maxim said. "And the car
outside, too."

Demyan's brow sipped low. "What?"

"Your bratva will have to claim the killing of Dima."

The killing—

"You're not making any sense."

"I am," Maxim returned just as fast, "you're just not getting all the details."

And when were they ever important?

Demyan heard what the man didn't say.

"What are you really here for, Maxim?"

"Chicago will be leaderless. It's already in ruins. They'll fear you. They already respect you. Dima's death with just—"

"You're insane," Demyan uttered.

Again, his gaze fell to the gun just an arm's length away. The fog of confusion and frustration was beginning to clear, and Demyan could see where Maxim was going with this. Even if he didn't seem to want to outright say it.

He wanted to end his story his own way.

"It's right there, Demyan," Maxim said, his voice urging Demyan to met the man's eyes. "Pick it up, finish the job here ... I've already put everything else into place. Make sure they find the body. Claim this death, too."

"I don't know that you've done anything, actually."

"This way, we both get what we want."

"*This way?*"

"Demyan—"

"You can't ask me to do this," Demyan barked.

"I haven't even properly asked yet. Would it make you feel better if it felt like I forced your hand?"

"How can you joke about this?"

Maxim only smiled. "What good is a friend if he won't kill you when there's no other choice?"

That joke fell flat, too.

Demyan was cold all over.

"It'll work," Maxim assured quietly.

He couldn't look away from the gun again.

"You said to claim Dima's death, but he's not dead, Maxim."

"But he will be."

ᴛʜᴇMARRIAGE

Demyan reached for the gun, then, the butt smooth against his palm as he felt that substantial weight of metal in his hand. "One last time—where is she?"

"She'll find you."

He didn't bother to ask what that meant.

What good would it do?

"I would rather have you do it than someone else," Maxim said when Demyan flicked off the safety and racked the gun without a word. Maybe his rambling helped soothe whatever nerves were making themselves known in those last seconds. "I can trust you to make it quick, and clean. I won't do it myself. Not the ... honorable thing."

A piece of Demyan understood that ...

"Anything else you want?" Demyan asked.

The man only really came here to die, anyway.

"Tell her what I said, look me in the eye when you do it, and don't waste time," Maxim replied. "I've wasted enough already. I'm sure everybody would just like to get on with it by now."

So be it.

Demyan stood up from the chair, and aimed his gun. He didn't take his eyes off Maxim when he pulled the trigger.

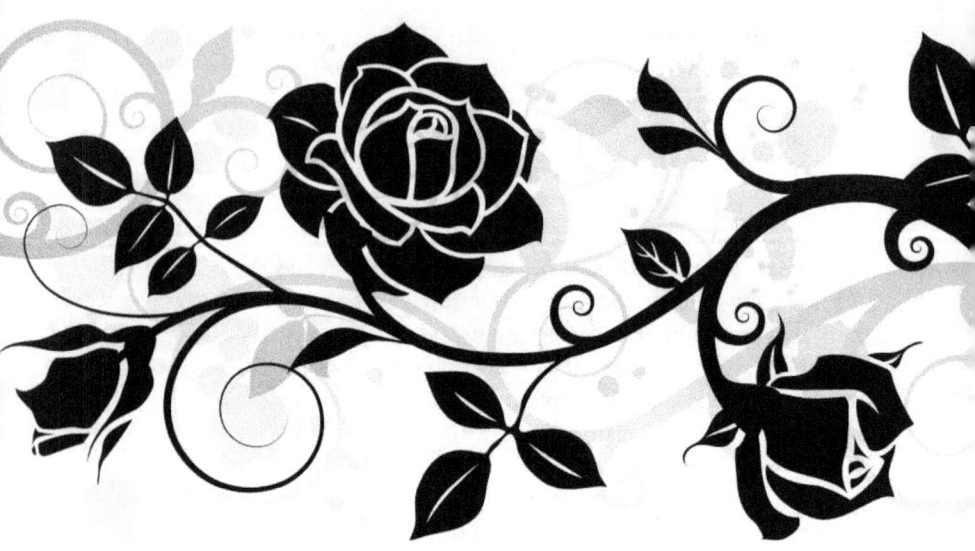

NINETEEN

"You're *still* sitting in here—shit, have you even turnt a trick?"

Karine's head snapped up at the sharp, high-pitch voice of a girl that had made more than one comment since she walked through the door three days before.

Neena, with her long, beachy waves and loud personality was just one of a few girls in the Madame's stable that kept trying to bring Karine out of her shell. You'd think there'd be more cattiness amongst women who specifically gathered for the sole purpose of selling sex, but actually, they all seemed quite friendly. Like a little crew that constantly came and went through the front doors of Madame Cherie's Chicago townhouse.

She didn't think the girls meant any harm, but she was well aware of things they would never know …

Like someday, she wouldn't be here.

They were only a means to end.

What was the point in making friends?

™MARRIAGE

"You know, I got two nights before I finally got turned out," Neena told Karine. "You've got an extra one on me. You nervous?"

Why was she still trying to make conversation? Hell, Karine had yet to figure out why she agreed to this plan of her father's ...

Or if she could see it through.

"I—"

She was saved from having to make conversation with the young woman when Cherie made her presence known in the doorway of the bedroom Karine had been allowed to use. The Madame didn't knock or even ask if she could enter before she did—and that partly answered a question Karine had about this place, and these women.

They weren't completely free here, either.

Everybody paid a due.

"I found a wig for you," Cherie said, striding over with a chunky blonde mane of unruly curls in her hand. Even at six feet tall, the woman still wore towering heels. Her height was as impressive as her cold demeanor could be when she dealt with her girls. "Although, it'll need some work. Neena—did you have something for me?"

Just like that, Neena was reminded of her place, and made her presence scarce without another word. They didn't want to make their *mom* mad, as most called Cherie. Or that's what Karine noticed. Every woman that came in and out of the house with phones constantly beeping or ringing, never left without putting money on the counter. And they were all well cared for while they did it.

As long as Cherie was happy.

Karine smiled, unable to contain her amusement, while Cherie stood behind her to help her put the wig on. First, Karine's hair had to be tied up and glued down, the woman explained, but even a good tug wouldn't bring it off by the time she was done.

"I think we should go with something white," Cherie told her. "It's exactly the look Dima would appreciate in the girls. He often asks for it, and I'm sure when he gets back tonight and makes a call for a favorite, he'll be happy to hear there's someone new to try."

Karine couldn't meet the woman's gaze in the mirror anymore.

She hadn't known when it would happen—when all of this would suddenly turn real—but now felt as good as ever.

"So, what's in it for you, April?" she asked.

Karine didn't allow herself to get pulled into the rushing current that was her thoughts. Her mind was a dangerous place, and more so, one she wasn't sure she could currently control. As long as she didn't go there—

"Are you listening to me?"

April.

Right.

Karine blurted that name when she'd arrived on the madame's doorstep. "What do you mean?"

"Why are you doing this—why are you working with Maxim Yazov?" Cherie asked. "Anyone who knows anything in this city should be all too aware that it could be risky business at the moment. From the rumors … well, he shouldn't even be alive."

Karine couldn't take her eyes off herself once her gaze landed back on the mirror. She didn't like the blonde, and didn't recognize herself with the hair let down so long.

"Why are you?"

Cherie grinned at the sudden question. On the second day of her arrival, the woman had admitted to Karine that she seemed like *just* the type.

Her words, not Karine's.

Already broken, easily manipulated, a perfect girl to make money off men who meant nothing. Karine wasn't entirely sure what that said about her. Or if it said more about Cherie, and what was really going on with her stable of women at her every beck and call.

Maybe that was why Karine wasn't entirely surprised to hear Cherie's barked laugh before she told her, "Well, he's in the way, and then there's the money—I couldn't very well say no."

ᴛʜᴇMARRIAGE

...

A good madame always knew her Johns. Cherie was no exception, and she'd been right. Dima sent a dark limousine to the townhouse to pick up his new girl before his flight had even landed. In the air, he'd made arrangements.

It screamed *control*.

Karine wondered what kind of mood the man must be in to immediately want a woman to either break or enjoy— likely both, in a twisted way—in his bed the very second he arrived back in the city after being in New York.

Not a good mood, she suspected.

Karine wasn't a liar, but it was all she could do to maintain her calm composure. She even dared to listen to the vicious, victorious whispers of Katina who only had one thing to say.

We're going to end this, Karine ... we have to end this.

Cherie came with her, riding in the backseat together to the estate he had successfully bid on and purchased the month before, according to the woman who supplied his steady stream of pussy.

Was it possible that the only reason Maxim's plan might work was because of Dima's predictability?

It's not that easy, she knew.

Karine still had to finish it.

Neither woman spoke much on the drive. Karine was lost, toeing the cruel edge of her thoughts just enough to hear what she wanted, but reject the pressing urge of her fear to take control.

What happened tonight if this did work? Would Karine *really* be free, like her father promised—what did that even mean now?

"Are you going to be able to handle this?"

Cherie's voice interrupted Karine's peace, mere minutes before they entered the gates to the suburban estate just outside city limits.

Maybe the woman had sensed Karine's fragility—she bet that was exactly why Cherie was as revered as she was feared by her girls. She knew right where it hurt, and the quickest way to find it.

The thing was … Karine already hurt everywhere. She was getting really tired of that pain being poked.

She smiled, reaching for the hat that sat between them on the car's backseat, and fixed it on her head. The floppy brim covered half her face. For too long, she'd used a mask to hide away from things she didn't want to face. For the first time, Karine was exactly where she wanted to be, doing just what she needed to do.

Even if it terrified her.

"Of course, I can handle this," Karine replied just as fast. "The question is—can you?"

• • •

The men who led them into the house said very little, while Karine didn't even bother looking around. She had no interest in assessing the lay of the land when her task there was the only thing she was interested in.

To be left completely alone with Dima.

She couldn't help but notice how Cherie and the men at the large estate moved around one another like they had done this dance before. From how they opened the limo door, to the curt nod each man passed the madame when they had walked through the front doors. The place did need some work, as the gate was broken, and the driveway had cracks in the asphalt.

The inside was about the same.

Old.

Tired.

He won't think twice about it, Cherie had told Karine on the way over about her coming along. *It's the only way I can get a girl back in a livable piece as it is with the asshole.*

Karine didn't ask for more details.

She didn't really need to, though.

Cherie remained downstairs while one of the men gestured for Karine to follow. She gave the madame one last look as she was led up a winding, metal staircase to the second floor of the quiet mansion.

ᵗʰᵉMARRIAGE

She could still hear the woman's warnings from earlier in the car.

Don't meet his gaze.

Do what he says, he won't suspect a thing.

He usually starts with a belt ...

Karine had counted every step. Across the entry, up the stairs, and even down a long corridor until they stood outside a door to a room where she could hear some muffled sound. Every fourth step, she'd taken a breath.

She needed to remind herself to do it.

And why she was here ...

For Roman.

For her sister.

God ... for herself.

She didn't bother to peer beyond the brim of the floppy hat to see the face of the man who directed her where to stand. She was too busy remembering the way her sister had begged that night, and how much Dima enjoyed it.

The man knocked hard on the door. Dima's voice came through. Commanding. Grotesque.

Dull.

She didn't expect him to sound so flat.

Like he was bored.

Goosebumps bloomed on her arms, and like she was floating in a dream, with no control over her own legs, she strolled into the room when the man opened the door. He shut it noiselessly behind her.

The bedroom was big, but not well-decorated with Dima standing at the end of the bed. A glass of vodka in his hand, and the big screen TV with a rugby game playing that he put on mute explained the muffled noise. His eyes remained glued to the screen even while she stood there, trembling at the sight of him.

She was *too close* to him.

Her heart didn't just race, it screamed.

Karine had spent every waking and sleeping moment these past months—hoping she would never have to see him again.

And there he was.

Dima held the glass up to his lips, without glancing at her once. "Take off your clothes and open the drawer next to the bed."

He usually starts with a belt ...

"You'll find what I want in there. Bring it to me on your knees."

Karine breathed in deeply—just once so she could feel all that air fill up her lungs, as dusty as it tasted on her tongue, it still settled her. She said nothing as she slipped out of the dress, but she did feel Dima's gaze following her as her back was turned. Maybe the long blonde hair did it, but as the dress dropped to the floor, he didn't seem to recognize the body he'd used and abused for years.

In fact, the TV came off mute, and when she chanced a glance over her shoulder, under the brim of the hat, she found him watching the game again.

Karine didn't bother losing the hat.

Or her bra and panties.

Not even the heels.

She did open the drawer, and there, she found the belt. As she picked it up, she found the other thing Cherie promised the girls reported that Dima kept in the drawer.

A knife.

He truly did enjoy scaring them.

He got off on the fear.

Karine picked the blade up, too.

Then, she turned for him, getting close enough to make him turn to her. His brows furrowed while his face darkened with irritation.

"Didn't you fucking hear what I just said? Get that stupid fucking hat off your head, and the rest, too," he snarled.

Karine held out the belt instead, keeping the knife hidden behind her other hand at her side. Angrily, Dima reached for it, angry his scene wasn't playing out the way he'd scripted it.

He didn't see the knife coming, and every stab she made into his throat left her with a slice of her own to pay for what she had to do.

She didn't even feel it, though.

All she saw was the blood.

^{THE}MARRIAGE

• • •

"It's very personal," Cherie had told Karine earlier. *"Stabbing someone, I mean. You'll have to make it fast, hard, right in his throat, and then don't stop until he's not moving. I don't think you realize—"*

"What other choice do I have? Can I walk in there with a gun?"

Would she have even been able to shoot it?

She understood what Cherie really wanted to ask—*do you know how to kill a man?* The sad thing was, she did. Cruelly, Dima showed her once exactly how to get the job done.

Nonetheless, the madame had been right. Karine didn't realize just how much work it would take, how close she would be when Dima took his last breath, or even the way his dark pupils would blow so wide as he mumbled his final gurgled words …

And she couldn't forget it.

It sounded so much better than the memories of Katina's death.

If there were ever a time for Karine to disassociate, tonight would have been it. Yet, she maintained control. Whether or not that was a sign things were changing for her, she didn't know.

But she dared to hope.

Karine kept a tight hold on the bloody knife that she'd used to kill Dima as she headed back downstairs. It left a trail of tiny drops the whole way.

Cherie hadn't left the entry of the large home. Karine hadn't been able to take a gun up with her, but she knew the madame had brought along two that she kept hidden inside her fur coat.

"It's done?" she asked when Karine reached the bottom steps.

"His stable is yours."

The woman smiled and looked in the direction of the room at the far end of the entry, down the hall beyond the winding staircase. "That's his office—if Dima's distracted, his boys think it's time to play. I always bring them a little something, too."

Karine raised a brow at that.

Cherie only shrugged. "I do what I've got to do. I laced the coke with fentanyl. You're a mess."

She didn't know what to make of this woman.

Or was that entirely the point?

"Do you know who I really am?" Karine asked the madame, ignoring the way her hands stung and ached from the many cuts that crisscrossed her palms and fingers.

Cherie was already heading for the office, pulling the guns from beneath her coat. "Of course I do—a long time ago, Maxim paid well, too."

Just like Cherie said, the three men in the room were already high.

And starting to nod off.

For the first time in her life—Karine wasn't afraid of walking in through a door without knowing what she would find on the other side. The men who should have been watching Dima's back barely reacted to the women slipping inside the room, and one even started to lift his head up where he'd slumped in a chair.

That was the man Cherie shot first.

Right between the eyes.

Only then did the other two move.

"*Holy fuck*—"

Karine ignored the brain matter spattered up the wall as she took the high-back chair behind the large, old desk and sat down, declaring as she did, "Chicago is being taken over by the Avdonins."

She kept her back straight in that chair and spoke in the same manner she had witnessed her father use all her life. Back when all she could do was observe him from afar because she wasn't a part of his circle.

Now she was in the center of it.

In fact, she might have always been.

"And we'll be staying right here until they arrive," she continued.

^{THE}MARRIAGE

The men had nothing to say, barely able to keep their heads up or their eyes open. How many lines had it taken before they realized it wasn't *just* coke Cherie snuck them— or did they just not care because high was high?

What did it matter?

Karine had to make a phone call.

TWENTY

"Are you going to tell her?"

Across from where his father sat on the private jet, Roman's gaze drifted away from the porthole window and the flickering lights of a city he'd hoped to never see again.

"Tell her what?" Roman asked.

Demyan shrugged as he murmured, "That it was me who killed him."

Frankly, Roman's mind had been running a million miles a minute from the moment he'd gotten word from the bull driving his car that Maxim Yazov was at his parents' home.

Blatantly.

Once upon a time, Roman might have believed *he* was a bold motherfucker, but compared to Karine's father, that just wasn't the case.

The last thing he'd had time to think about over the past handful of days was whether or not he would tell his wife, a woman he was only partly certain might still want him at all, that his father killed hers. He was still trying to piece together how a supposedly dead man had managed to make so many moves behind the scenes that he'd orchestrated an entire game no one but him really knew they were playing.

He had a lot to think about.

Demyan's bloody hands were only one of them.

"I don't know," he settled on telling his father.

And this certainly wasn't a conversation he wanted to be having on a chartered jet to Chicago because a call had come through—Karine had essentially taken over the small estate property where Dima had, for all intents and purposes, declared his headquarters to the Chicago bratva.

Demyan let out a hard grunt before reaching for the glass of vodka in the gold cup holder. He slammed the remaining alcohol back, waving the cup high for the flight attendant to see, before saying to his son, "Yeah, I don't know very much, either. I guess you don't always get to be the hero, though. Sometimes you're the villain no matter what you do—you're just a catalyst in someone else's story. You don't get to write it."

"Philosophical."

Demyan shot him a look.

Roman only shook his head, and smirked. With his gaze back on the porthole, he muttered low, "It's not always so bad being a villain. I hear they get the best women."

That earned him a laugh from his father, but Roman didn't bother to say more. The attendant refused to refill Demyan's glass if only because they were putting the bottles away to begin the descent. Here he was, a couple of hours from reuniting with Karine, and he still hadn't figured out how it all happened.

Oh, he knew the details.

He'd been sleeping off a drunk on his father's office couch when she made the phone call, because, after days of scrubbing away the evidence of her father's murder, they still couldn't find *her.*

And he didn't trust the last words of a dead man to be true.

So when he heard that trembling voice of hers on loudspeaker—her quaking *I killed him, Demyan; Chicago is yours*—Roman learned what it meant to go on autopilot.

"He wanted his body to be found publicly. He's going to be discovered on a park bench tomorrow," Demyan said suddenly. "It'll look like a *very* suspicious suicide."

Roman's brows furrowed at that. He'd only known that the body had been quickly removed from the house along with Claire's sixty-thousand-dollar rug under the table.

"He could have just done that," Roman replied. "Why'd we have to do the business."

"You know why—we're sitting here, Roman, that's *why*. And I think he hoped to give Karine a chance to say goodbye in the end, even if he didn't want to die alone."

"I don't think he ever gave a shit about Karine, let's be real."

"He did. Because he loved her. He loved her more than he could show or tell. I know what that's like, Roman, to love someone so much and have it taken away. I felt like I couldn't be loved—but for other people, for him, it felt like love was poison. He wanted her to know he loved her, still."

Roman emptied the remaining dregs of his own vodka down his throat, but as he'd opted for a plastic cup instead of glass, the attendant had left him with his drink. Crunching the cup into broken pieces, he tossed it into the cup holder, and told his father, "I don't give a fuck anymore. I just want to see Karine."

• • •

This time, unlike their meeting with Dima at the battered farmhouse—the Avdonins were prepared. They arrived at the Chicago estate ready for a battle if they had to face one. Or start it.

Dima's men had been scattered and very few in number, to begin with after the old Yazov mansion burned down. He had tried to portray strength when the truth was he had already been deserted by most of the old Yazov crew who had clearly started noticing his ineptitude. He couldn't even stay in his own city for any length of time to handle mafia business because he'd been too busy raising hell in New York for a woman.

"What are we going to find inside?" Roman murmured as their car drove in through a broken gate that had needed to be pushed open by a heavily-tattooed man. The upturned spider on his hand told Roman the guy was probably with the Yazov crew.

What other calls did Karine make?

Had word traveled that fast that she'd taken over the estate to the men of her father's organization who would find that information beneficial?

"I have no idea," Demyan murmured, "other than there are bodies that need burned, and a woman who would like to be relieved from her position while she holds it for us."

Right.

The other bit he couldn't quite wrap his head around.

Roman couldn't help but wonder if this was all a trick. If Maxim hadn't spoken to Demyan, and given him the whole story ... well, most of it—then they wouldn't even have been here.

Now they had no choice.

The responsibility of ruined Chicago bratva was on them.

"Whatever we decide to do here tonight," his father told him as their car parked in front of a three-level home that had seen better days despite its grandeur, "we'll have to do it fast."

Roman didn't care. At this point, he just wanted it to be over.

As the Avdonin crew walked into the house, the men who stood watching the front door did so with their weapons hidden from view. There was going to be no war tonight. They even nodded at the New York boss as he passed, though he didn't make eye contact.

It was over.

Roman was growing more anxious by the minute, his questions about what had happened in this house going unanswered as a woman with a black fur coat draped over her shoulders directed them to an office. The door was already open, and Roman could see who waited within.

"The famous Cherie?" he heard his father ask as Roman met his wife's gaze inside the room.

"One in the same. I took good care of her, made sure she had everything she needed. No one touched her, of course."

"Things are starting to make a bit more sense," Demyan noted.

Roman didn't hear what they said then because he'd stepped inside the room. A bloody, white dress sat draped over a chair in the corner, and on top of the ruined fabric rested a knife. The dried, brownish stains on the blade and smeared on the dress made Roman hesitate in his step.

He heard Karine's breath hitch when he stopped. He wondered if it was Cherie that had supplied Karine with the clean, black bodycon dress that showed off her curves and made her seem older—sexy, *confident*—where she sat waiting at the desk.

"What did you do?" he asked.

It would have been a violent death, and he bet the bandages on her hands and fingers told the tale of just how much. Karine fidgeted with her hands before hiding them under the desk.

She didn't hesitate to answer him. "Everything I needed to."

What could he say to that?

He knew she wasn't wrong.

To send his daughter into the eye of the storm? To face the monster she had been running away from?

Karine slowly stood up.

Roman couldn't look away from those big eyes of hers, clear like an ocean and dragging him under like waves. "I asked you to trust me."

"And I did."

"How can you say that? You didn't stay—"

"I didn't want to be there, and this was my one chance," she told him. "It was the only one I had left to make sure he was gone for good. *Me*, I did that."

But it could have killed her.

ᴛʜᴇMARRIAGE

He bet she took the risk, knowing that.

Roman found that hard to swallow.

Goddamn.

He still loved her for it, though.

"I know this has been a lot," Karine said suddenly, dropping his gaze.

Roman couldn't help it—he barked out a laugh at that. Here she was, trying to calm his overworked ass. He could get used to that, though.

Karine smiled, then, and Roman forgot about the rest. All his unanswered questions, and that bloody dress and knife. Even the house they currently stood in, the bodies that were apparently rotting somewhere, and the people watching them.

None of it mattered but her.

He moved for her, and she couldn't even be bothered to come around the desk, instead climbing over top of it to reach him faster. He pulled her off the desk, and she wrapped her legs around his waist. Her breasts pressed to his chest, her breaths heavy, as he took her mouth with his for a kiss he was sure would leave her feeling bruised.

She didn't seem to mind.

Clung to him closer.

In the background, he could hear the woman named Cherie making conversation with his father, wanting to iron out all the details of her business. Maxim had made some specific promises to her, and she expected Demyan was going to keep his end of the bargain.

Roman pulled away from his panting, grinning wife when he heard his father reply, "Let me say hello to my daughter-in-law properly first, then we'll do business. Family first."

Karine hadn't looked away from Roman's eyes.

Yeah.

Family first.

• • •

They had a mess to clean.

A *big* one.

Demyan told Roman he would handle it—gave his son the night to do what he wanted before they'd have to gather for direction. Roman didn't need to be told twice by his father.

He wasn't staying there.

Didn't bother to check on the bodies before he left, or the mingling men ready to take orders from his father the second they stepped out of the office.

Karine remained quiet, happy to disengage from the people as long as Roman was there for her to shrink into. As he led her away from the house and the things that had transpired within it, he realized Karine was still very much who she was, no matter what she did that might seem different.

Roman let her stew in her silence and thoughts as he navigated unknown roads, and the car's GPS, to get them to a hotel in the city. ID and a credit card with no limit nabbed them a decent penthouse suite for a week, and Roman didn't even concern himself with the bill.

It was only once he had his wife stripped naked, sitting on the edge of the bathtub filling with hot, bubbly water that she spoke.

"My hands hurt again."

He passed the bandages a glance. "You were alone with him?"

"I had to be. It was the easiest way to get inside the house. We only had to be *in*. He trusted Cherie; as long as he didn't hurt the girls too bad, she brought them back. He didn't even recognize me. Barely looked at me. That was the thing, I think. None of us meant anything to him. Women, I mean. We're not even human, as far as he was concerned."

Roman's gaze traveled over the beautiful, naked body of his wife who spoke without remorse about a plan he hadn't even known existed until it was too late, and already over. All the work he'd put in to protect her, and she was the one who ended up doing the dirty work for them all. He didn't seem to notice the splats of blood all over her anymore.

"I'm proud of you, Karine," he murmured.

Scared to death, too.

A little amazed.

Still trying to catch up …

And proud all the same.

She reached for him, her bandaged hands shaking just a little, but he didn't know if it was because they hurt, or something else. Her fingers skated lightly over his jaw, and then his lips before she whispered, "I wanted everyone to know what I would do—for the people I love, I wanted them to *know*, Roman."

"I'm sure everyone got that message. Loud and clear, babe."

Including him.

When she sunk under the water, even her bandaged hands, he was undressed and already sinking with her. He held her tight, made every promise he intended to keep while her skin softened from soapy hot water, and she cried.

Only a little.

Just long enough for him to know …

She'd never have to do this again.

• • •

Later, when Roman thought Karine was finally asleep in the unfamiliar hotel bed, he made a call to his father, and then decided to watch the lights of the city flicker instead of making his way to the bedroom. He needed a moment.

Just to settle his mind.

It kind of felt like those lights, blinking or too bright.

In nothing but unzipped slacks, Roman polished off three mini bottles of vodka from the wet bar, and made a note to ask for full bottles first thing the next morning. Who knew how long they were going to be here?

Instead of letting his mind wander to *that* place, he settled on the vision of fucking Karine bent over the footboard of the bed. God, she'd been so wet, hands on her ass to widen herself open for him while he nailed her into the mattress. She liked to be handled just rough enough that she toed the line of losing control, and he understood why.

She craved so many things.

Some that had been taken away.

Some she'd never known.

A lot she wanted back.

He could *still* smell her on him.

Sex clung to everything.

It also made everything so much better.

Apparently, a good hour of fucking his wife to sleep after not being able to touch her for way too long just wasn't enough to put Roman's overactive mind to rest.

Shocker.

"*Hey.*"

Roman spun on his heel to find Karine leaning in the shadows of the darkened hallway. She smiled, and he grinned back.

"Hey," he replied.

"The bed is warm, you know."

Roman nodded. "I know." Her smile faltered when he told her, "Maxim's body will be found tomorrow. He even orchestrated the way he wanted to die, by the hand of a friend, but since it'll likely be on the news in the morning, I better tell you now."

It took her a moment.

"How?"

He shifted from foot to foot. "My father."

Karine's brow knotted a little, the pain flashing in her face as he watched another chapter close in her life. They didn't always get the answers they wanted or needed.

"He told him to tell you that he did love you."

"I know he did," she replied soft and fast. "In his own way. And it must have been so lonely."

Demyan's words about Maxim's fear that his love was something like a cancer eating away at people he didn't want to hurt … well, maybe that held some weight.

"You'll be able to say goodbye, in a way."

"Yeah, I guess so." Karine dragged in a shaky breath, just the one, and then asked, "Are you going to ask me why I left with my father?"

"I suspect you had your reasons."

"But you won't ask?"

ᴛʜᴇMARRIAGE

"You've made it clear, Karine, that you can and want to make your own decisions."

And he didn't have to like them.

She wouldn't always like his, after all.

"I thought I would be free."

Roman didn't reply because mostly, he didn't know what to say to that. Of him—of *life*? What did she want to be free of? Maybe just didn't want the answer.

Roman fished the pack of cigarettes and a lighter out of his pocket, sticking a smoke between his lips as Karine said, "And I also wondered what it would be like to be free. I wasn't sure if you considered our marriage to be a real one. If Dima was dead and the war was over, I thought maybe it would mean the end of our marriage, too. I was scared to say it, but I did believe that."

Roman lit the smoke, taking in a heavy drag and blowing it out to the ceiling as he eyed her in the shadows. "I married you because I want to spend the rest of my life with you, but I understand if you want to be free. That you can see the world as endless possibilities right now, but I'm sure you only see one kind of life with me."

It pained him to say it, to even give her the chance to walk away from him now. The truth was he didn't know if she would take it. Maybe she didn't plan on staying. Maybe committing her to the facility in Nevada was the last straw.

Hell, maybe she didn't trust him anymore.

He'd deserve *that*.

Karine shook her head, her fingers curving around the edge of the wall as she leaned further out of the shadows, closer to him. "But I'll never be free of you, Roman. You are the only man I've ever loved. That's all I ever wanted."

When her hand stretched out for him to take, he crossed the room to do just that. The urge to follow her anywhere was strong, even if it was to yet another unfamiliar bed.

He took another drag from the cigarette as she pulled him into the bedroom down the short hall where the French doors were pulled wide open.

"I don't ever want to sleep in a hotel bed again," he told her.

"So buy me a house, and I'll find you a bed you'll wanna sleep in every night."

He didn't doubt her. Roman liked that idea fine.

Karine dropped the hotel robe down her shoulders, showing off bare skin he'd spent so much time loving earlier. Just like that, his tongue watered, his dick got hard, and he thought he might be ready to go again. Even if every part of this tempting woman had been a lie that could have destroyed him, he still would have happily died just to get another taste.

"What happens now?" she asked him.

For once, he could smile when she asked him that question because the truth didn't have to be scary. There were a lot of unknowns facing them, sure—he'd never deny that. The mess they had left behind just to stand here together now stretched from the city of Chicago to the bright lights of Vegas, and the gated suburbs of New York, New York.

He was still happy about it, though. Despite funerals to plan, and secrets still between them, what could be wasn't at all frightening anymore.

"Whatever you want, Karine."

She only shook her head at that, laughing like he was silly. Maybe he was; with her, who'd care?

"Don't you know?" she asked him, her grin blooming wider than ever as she came to stand on her tiptoes in front of him. Close enough to kiss as she said, "I told you—I want you."

"Will you always?"

"Forever."

"Even if I'm a prick?"

"Even then," she agreed.

"Even when Masha tells you I almost killed her and—"

"*Roman.*"

Her amused glower turned into something vicious in a blink. He had to laugh.

She didn't like that much, either.

"Stop that," she demanded, poking his chest.

"I'll have her flown in tomorrow," he promised.

"Is she okay?"

ᴛʜᴇMARRIAGE

With the cigarette still burning between his fingers, Roman used the pad of his thumb to smooth away that knot of concern between her eyebrows. "You're all she has, I think. I tried to keep that in mind for you."

Karine's eyes closed at his touch and words, whispering back, "You're all we have, Roman. Think about *that*."

ABOUT THE AUTHOR

The author of too many novels to count, Bethany-Kris is a Canadian, lover of much, and mother to four sons, a glaring of cats, and a pack of dogs. A small town in Eastern Canada where she was born and raised is where she has always called home. With her boys under her feet, a snuggling cat, barking dogs, and a spouse calling over his shoulder, she is nearly always writing something ... when she can find the time.

Find where to follow BK and stay up to date with all her books news at www.bethanykris.com.